Home for Wayward Elephants

Other novels by James Rada, Jr.

Black Fire Trilogy
- Smoldering Betrayal
- Strike the Fuse
- Frostburg Burning

Canawlers Series
- Between Rail and River
- Canawlers
- Lock Ready

Stand-Alone Novels
- October Mourning
- The Rain Man

For non-fiction books by James Rada, Jr., visit jamesrada.com.

CRITICAL ACCLAIM FOR
THE WORKS OF JAMES RADA, JR.

The Last to Fall

"Authors Jim Rada and Richard Fulton have done an outstanding job of researching and chronicling this little-known story of those Marines in 1922, marking it as a significant moment in Marine Corps history."

- GySgt. Thomas Williams
Executive Director
U.S. Marine Corps Historical Company

"Original, unique, profusely illustrated throughout, exceptionally well researched, informed, informative, and a bit iconoclastic, "The Last to Fall: The 1922 March, Battles, & Deaths of U.S. Marines at Gettysburg" will prove to be of enormous interest to military buffs and historians."

- Small Press Bookwatch

Saving Shallmar

"But Saving Shallmar's Christmas story is a tale of compassion and charity, and the will to help fellow human beings not only survive, but also be ready to spring into action when a new opportunity presents itself. Bittersweet yet heartwarming, Saving Shallmar is a wonderful Christmas season story for readers of all ages and backgrounds, highly recommended."

- Small Press Bookwatch

Battlefield Angels

"Rada describes women religious who selflessly performed life-saving work in often miserable conditions and thereby gained the admiration and respect of countless contemporaries. In so doing, Rada offers an appealing narrative and an entry point into the wealth of sources kept by the sisters."

- Catholic News Service

Between Rail and River

"The book is an enjoyable, clean family read, with characters young and old for a broad-based appeal to both teens and adults. Between Rail and River also provides a unique, regional appeal, as it teaches about a particular group of people, ordinary working 'canawlers' in a story that goes beyond the usual coverage of life during the Civil War."

- *Historical Fiction Review*

Canawlers

"A powerful, thoughtful and fascinating historical novel, Canawlers documents author James Rada, Jr. as a writer of considerable and deftly expressed storytelling talent."

- *Midwest Book Review*

"James Rada, of Cumberland, has written a historical novel for high-schoolers and adults, which relates the adventures, hardships and ultimate tragedy of a family of boaters on the C&O Canal. ... The tale moves quickly and should hold the attention of readers looking for an imaginative adventure set on the canal at a critical time in history."

- *Along the Towpath*

October Mourning

"This is a very good, and very easy to read, novel about a famous, yet unknown, bit of 20th Century American history. While reading this book, in your mind, replace all mentions of 'Spanish Flu' with 'bird flu.' Hmmm."

- *Reviewer's Bookwatch*

HOME FOR WAYWARD ELEPHANTS

by

James Rada, Jr.

LEGACY
PUBLISHING
A division of AIM Publishing Group

HOME FOR WAYWARD ELEPHANTS

Published by Legacy Publishing, a division of AIM Publishing Group.
Gettysburg, Pennsylvania.

Printed in the United States of America.
First printing: July 2024.

ISBN 978-8990325616

315 Oak Lane • Gettysburg, Pennsylvania 17325

PART I

HOME FOR ORPHANED CHILDREN

1

JANUARY 1933

Harrisburg disappeared, but not in a mass of flame and smoke like Jessie Parsons' house had done. No, Harrisburg shrank from a city to scattered houses. A few more miles and the tall brick office buildings in the heart of the city gave way to shorter buildings and homes that were just a story or two high.

Looking through the rear windshield back to where Harrisburg could once be seen, Jessie wasn't sure whether watching the city disappear from view was better or worse than what had happened to her home.

Worse.

Definitely worse. Harrisburg didn't have her family in it. Not anymore. She was alone, with no idea of what would happen to her. Not today. Not tomorrow. Not next year.

Mrs. Connelly drove her black sedan across a bridge over the Susquehanna River, and the city was gone, and they were in the country, a place where Mrs. Connelly had promised her she would be happy. Jessie saw nothing special about it. It was empty, like a giant park on a cold winter day.

She saw fields that stretched into the distance, patches of woods, and an occasional house. The sight depressed her even more, but then, it was winter. The sky was gray; the fields were covered with the stubble of long-harvested crops and the trees bare of leaves.

She pulled her feet onto the car seat and stared at the shrinking city through the back window until the road dipped over a hill and even that view slipped away.

Her family was gone. The home her family had lived in was gone, and now the city where her home had been was gone.

"Jessica, sit properly," Mrs. Connelly said as she tapped her on the shoulder. "You are a young lady."

Jessie wasn't a young lady. She was a thirteen-year-old orphan, but she turned and faced forward. Nothing to see behind her, anyway.

Jessie sniffled, but she didn't cry. She doubted that she could anymore. She had cried for days after fire, throughout the closed-casket funeral of her family, and when the police had left her in the orphanage. She had no more tears left in her, just grief.

Mrs. Connelly looked over at Jessie and smiled. The woman looked older than she was. Her white hair was tied up in a bun on the back of her head. She had mentioned to Jessie that she had had white hair since she was twenty-five years old. Mrs. Connelly's gray dress with white trim didn't make her look any younger.

Jessie sat quietly, which apparently disturbed Mrs. Connelly. She started talking about the weather, the traffic on the road, and the plans incoming President Mr. Franklin D. Roosevelt had for getting the country out of the depression it was in. Jessie's father had tried to explain the depression to her, saying that a lot of people no longer had jobs, which meant they couldn't afford food and places to live. He had told her their family was lucky because her father ran his own business making cigars, which he said were always in demand.

Some days, men had stopped at the house, knocking on the front door, offering to do work in exchange for food. They were dressed in shabby clothes worn almost through at the knees and elbows. Most of them were polite and removed their hats and smiled as they asked for work. Jessie's mother sometimes had them clean up the yard, but even if she didn't have a chore for the men, she always made sure to give them a couple sandwiches.

Jessie leaned sideways so her head rested against the window. She felt the vibrations from the car and the cold outside through the glass.

"Don't look so sad, Jessica," Mrs. Connelly said. "You'll like this place. I promise."

"My name is Jessie."

Mrs. Connelly clucked with her tongue. "That's what everyone calls you, but your name is Jessica. Jesse is a boy's name."

Jessie closed her eyes. She had had the same argument with other people over the past week. They might think they were being correct in using her legal name, but it just proved to Jessie that they didn't care about her. They were doing their jobs and nothing more. They were trying to take her name like the fire had taken her family.

Even if they cared about Jessica, which she doubted, no one cared about Jessie. She wasn't even sure she cared about herself.

The fire had taken everything from her. The only thing she had that was hers was her name. Even the plain blue dress she wore now, which was two sizes too big, was something the woman at the Children's Aid Society had pulled out of a drawer and handed to her. It had been another girl's dress before it became Jessie's. Jessie imagined she still smelled the other girl on the fabric, but it was just the soap used to wash the dress.

What had happened to that girl? Had she been adopted? Had she grown old enough to go out on her own? Why had she left the dress behind? When Jessie moved on, would she leave the dress behind for another little girl who had lost everything but her name? When would that be? She was only thirteen years old. How many years would she be stuck in an orphanage?

A sign on the road announced they were entering Abbottstown. The sedan rolled through the small town that seemed barely larger than the street Jessie had lived on in Harrisburg. Then it was more farms set off by rough-looking fences.

The car slowed and turned up a long, unpaved drive. Clouds of brown dust billowed up on either side of the car. Jessie clenched her eyes shut. It reminded her too much of smoke.

The car stopped, and Jessie opened her eyes. The dust settled, and she saw a three-story house with a wide front porch. Off to the side, she saw a barn and a smaller outbuilding. Two old tires hung on ropes from branches of a large maple tree. She also saw three bicycles and a wagon sitting between the house and the barn.

"This is an orphanage?" Jessie asked.

It was nothing like she imagined when she read about them in books. In her mind, she saw an orphanage as a prison, with too many children crammed into small rooms. Guards walked the halls looking for reasons to punish the orphans who were made to wear potato sacks for clothes. That wasn't at all what she was seeing here. This place was a farm.

"It's a group foster home. You'll feel like you're part of a big family." Mrs. Connelly smiled. Jessie believed the woman meant it to be reassuring, but it didn't look natural on her face. It made her look a little like a clown in a circus. The smile was too wide, and her lips were too red.

Mrs. Connelly climbed out of the car and walked around to Jessie's door and opened it. Jessie slid out and looked at the whitewashed house. A sign mounted on the porch overhang read: "Wilson's Home for Children." Jessie's gaze traveled up to a nearby window on the second floor. Two girls, close to her own age, looked back at her. They didn't smile or wave.

Mrs. Connelly walked over to speak briefly with a man standing on the porch. Then she came back to Jessie, gave her a hug lacking any warmth, and said, "Be a good girl, Jessica."

The white-haired woman climbed back into the car and drove off. Jessie tried to wave away the dust the car raised with no luck. She sucked on her lower lip to try to keep from crying.

"Jessie?"

Jessie stared at the middle-aged man standing on the porch. He looked friendly with bright blue eyes and wavy brown hair combed straight back.

He held his arms out wide, not to invite her to hug, but to present the farm. "Welcome. I'm Mr. Frank Wilson. You can call me Mr. Frank. My wife and I own this place. Would you like to come inside? Miss Erin—that's my wife—and I will get you settled in."

He sounded pleasant enough. He also didn't look like a dungeon master or a jail guard. Jessie had read *Oliver Twist*. She had also read *Anne of Green Gables*, but that wasn't set in an orphanage. If anything, this would be more like *Oliver Twist*, which meant this man would be like Fagin. She would have to watch herself.

Mr. Frank looked like a farmer, though. He wore blue jeans and a red flannel shirt. His cracked leather boots were coated in dirt.

He put his hands on his hips. "It doesn't look like you have a bag or suitcase."

Jessie shook her head.

Mr. Frank cocked an eyebrow and stared at her. "Well, that just doesn't seem right."

He reached over and picked up a small brown bag that sat on the porch railing and passed it to her. Jessie felt the weight of something inside.

"You can look inside if you want," Mr. Frank said.

She opened the bag and saw assorted home-made cookies. She caught a whiff of sugar and chocolate that had been trapped in the bag.

"The other children baked you their favorite cookies to welcome you," Mr. Frank explained. Then he lowered his voice and said, "If you want to eat one before we go inside, it's all right. You can't hand a child cookies and tell her not to eat them."

Jessie reached into the bag and pulled out an oatmeal raisin cookie. She nibbled on the end. It was delicious. She took a larger bite.

"Thank you," she said in a near whisper.

"It's from everyone here, but you can't tell Miss Erin I let you eat one already. She'll be mad at me for spoiling your dinner." He winked at her, and Jessie decided he was making a joke. Maybe he wasn't Fagin after all.

She nodded and took another bite. She wondered how long she could make this cookie last. The longer it did, the longer it would be before she would have to go inside.

A carved sign hung on the door read, "Home, Sweet

Home." It seemed like a contradiction to the sign above the porch. "Home, Sweet Home" was a place filled with love and family. It was a secure place, a place where you belonged and wanted to return to. A "Home for Children" was an orphanage, an institution like a school where you were one of many and lost among the crowd. It was a place you were passing through until you were adopted or too old to remain.

When Jessie went through that door, she would no longer be someone's daughter or sister. She would be an orphan. Alone.

Mr. Frank opened the wide door and waved for her to follow. Jessie entered a large living room with two sofas and two armchairs. The walls were covered with pictures of children, most of them smiling. A large floor radio sat in one corner of the room.

"Miss Erin, she's here," Mr. Frank called out over his shoulder.

A woman walked into the living room from the back of the house. She was younger than Mr. Frank, with her red hair pinned on top of her head. She dried her hands on her apron and walked over to kneel in front of Jessie.

"Hello, Jessie, I'm Miss Erin. I know right now everything is very confusing to you, but I have no doubt that you'll quickly get the hang of things and fit right in. We do have our rules of the house, but Mr. Frank and I will explain them to you as they come up. That way, you won't get overwhelmed on your first day. For the time being, just behave as I'm sure your parents taught you. Listen to me and Mr. Frank, and if you have any questions, ask us. Okay?"

Jessie looked into Miss Erin's green eyes. They were kind and looked a bit sad.

"Yes, ma'am," Jessie answered.

Miss Erin smiled and rubbed Jessie's shoulder. "Good

girl. We have twelve children here, and we keep them evenly split between boys and girls. I'll introduce you to them soon. Don't worry about learning all their names right away."

Jessie nodded. Miss Erin stared at her for a few moments and then took Jessie's hand in hers.

"I know you're sad, Jessie. You shouldn't have to be here, but that's the way things are. Right now, this is where you need to be, and I promise you, one day, you'll be happy again."

No matter how kind Miss Erin was, Jessie didn't think she could keep that promise.

Miss Erin stood up and walked over to the staircase. She picked up a teacher's school bell off a small table next to the stairs. She gave it three quick shakes while Jessie covered her ears at the loud clang.

Miss Erin looked over and smiled at Jessie. "I was a teacher before I got married. I kept my old bell. If I had to yell every time I needed to gather everyone together, I'd be hoarse all the time. So, the first thing you need to know is if you hear this bell ringing, go to it."

Children started streaming down the stairs from the second floor. From what Jessie could see, they ranged in age from around four to her age, or maybe a year or two older. The boys wore denim jeans and shirts of different colors. The girls wore simple dresses. None of them wore shoes. They were all in their socks. Jessie glanced over at the front door and saw a line of shoes of varying sizes and styles against the wall next to the door, including lace-up boots, Mary Janes, and leather shoes.

The children weren't quiet as they came down the stairs, but neither were they yelling. They talked, a few laughed, and some said nothing. One little girl with blonde pigtails waved at Jessie.

The children lined up in the living room in two rows with the older children in the back row.

"Where's Jeremy?" Miss Erin asked, looking around.

"Here I am," said a tiny voice.

The children started laughing. Miss Erin and Jessie turned around. A little boy about five years old waddled down the stairs with his pants around his ankles.

Miss Erin put her hands on her hips. "Jeremy, what are you doing?"

The little boy stopped on a step, his brown eyes wide and round. "I was on the toilet pooping when you rang the bell. I didn't have time to pull them up."

The children laughed harder, and even Mr. Frank laughed, though he tried to hide it behind his hand.

Miss Erin rolled her eyes. "Well, pull them up right now before you trip and tumble down the stairs."

The little boy sat on the wooden stairs and tugged his pants up. He wore overalls, which meant he had to pull the straps over his shoulders. He struggled with that, so Mr. Frank hurried over to him and helped.

"Thanks," Jeremy said.

Mr. Frank ruffled his hair. "You're welcome. Now go join the rest of the kids."

"Children," Miss Erin said. "This is our new friend. Her name is Jessie Parsons. She used to live in Harrisburg."

The little girl with the pigtails raised her hand.

"Yes, Laura?" Miss Erin said.

"Is she an orphan?"

The boy standing behind her lightly nudged with his hand. "Of course she is," he muttered. "That's why we're all here."

Miss Erin held up her hand. "No pushing, Jeffrey. Yes, Laura, Jessie is an orphan like all of you, but it is up to her whether she talks about her life in Harrisburg. So don't pester her with those types of questions, okay?"

"Yes, ma'am."

Miss Erin had the children introduce themselves. All of them were smiling, except for a boy named Ralph who was about Jessie's age. He looked angry; not at her necessarily, just angry at the world. It was a feeling Jessie could identify with.

Counting Jessie, an even split between the boys and girls lived in the home just like Miss Erin had said.

"Now, I want you all to remember how you felt when you first came to live here and treat Jessie like you would want to be treated," Miss Erin said.

She turned to Jessie. "You'll share the bedroom with the older girls, Leanne and Mary. We have three children in each bedroom." Miss Erin waved Leanne and Mary over.

Mary was quite pretty, with blonde hair and light blue eyes. Although she was only fourteen, she looked years older. Leanne was a year younger than Jessie. She had a bright smile and looked like she was ready to laugh at the drop of a hat. She had been the first one to laugh when Jeremy came down the stairs with his overalls down.

"Girls, why don't you take Jessie up and show her the bedroom?" Miss Erin said. "Then you can start to show her around the house. The rest of you get things ready for lunch. You know your chores, so take care of them so we can eat."

Leanne grabbed Jessie's hand and tugged her toward the stairs. "C'mon, you'll like our room. Our window faces west, so we get to see great sunsets at night, and we don't have to worry about the sun waking us up in the mornings."

"No, we have to worry about Miss Erin doing that," Mary said.

They climbed the stairs and turned left. The hallway was

covered with children's paintings. Mary pointed out the bathroom.

"We have two bathrooms," she said proudly. "Most houses only have one. Some of the houses around here still have an outhouse." Mary wrinkled her nose as if she smelled something unpleasant. "This is the girls' bathroom. Miss Erin and Mr. Frank also use this one. The boys' bathroom is upstairs." Two bathrooms? Jessie had never heard of a house with two bathrooms. Her house in Harrisburg had only had one bathroom on the second floor. Mary continued, "There's an outhouse by the barn if you need to go when you're outside. I have to use it sometimes because I started menstruating."

Jessie's brow wrinkled. "You talk about men?"

"What?" Mary said.

Leanne laughed and pointed at Mary. "You do that!"

Mary frowned and stood with her shoulders pulled back. "Not men-stating. Menstruating. I'm becoming a woman."

"Then why isn't it womanstruating?" Jessie asked. She had never heard of such a thing. It made little sense. She frowned and shook her head.

"I don't know," Mary said, frustrated. "That's the word."

"What's it mean?" Jessie asked.

"It means she bleeds once a month, and she thinks that makes her special. I think it's gross," Leanne said.

Mary blushed. "It is special. Miss Erin said so. She said it happens to every girl when she becomes a woman."

"Then it's not so special, is it? It sounds gross," Leanne said. "And it makes you act weird weirder than usual."

"Just wait until it happens to you," Mary said, waving a finger at Leanne. "Then I'll be laughing at you."

The girls led Jessie into a bedroom that was a little larger than the one she had had in her house before it had burned down. Of course, that had been her room alone. She would be sharing this room with Mary and Leanne.

The room was bright, with the walls covered in floral wallpaper. The walls also had mounted shelves for books and small toys. The room had a set of bunk beds and a single bed. It also had an armoire, a desk, and dresser.

"New girl gets the top bunk," Leanne said.

"My clothes are in the armoire," Mary said. "You and Leanne will share the closet and bureau."

Jessie looked at the floor. Even these girls, who were also orphans, had more than she did. "I don't have any clothes other than what I am wearing, and these aren't even mine."

Leanne's chipper attitude was unfazed. "That's okay. Miss Erin will take you upstairs to the clothes store."

Jessie looked up quickly. Was she going to get to go on a shopping trip like she used to do with her mother in Harrisburg?

"Clothes store?" Jessie repeated.

Leanne nodded. "That's what we call it. It's a big room upstairs where all the clothes no one is using are kept. When we outgrow something, we get new clothes from the clothes store, and our old clothes are kept up there until someone grows into them."

Jessie's smile slipped. Who had ever heard of a clothes store in a house? Whenever Jessie had needed new clothes, her mother had taken her shopping on Market Street. They would ride the trolley to Bollard's or Weinstein & Young for clothes, and then her mother would take her to F. W. Woolworth's where they would have lunch with ice cream for dessert. It was always a fun day with her mother. Sometimes, they would even stop in to see her father at his business. He made cigars at a factory on Paxton Street near the riverfront. They were sold all over the East Coast.

"So, it's not a real store where we can get new clothes?"

"We get new clothes sometimes if Miss Erin gets a bargain at a store in town."

Mary added, "Miss Erin is teaching me to sew, so I'll be able to make my own clothes."

Jessie looked at Leanne. "Not you?"

Leanne grinned sheepishly. "I stuck myself with too many needles. She said she would try again next year. She said she didn't want me to bleed to death."

Jessie giggled, and Leanne smiled.

"We also use a big closet in the hall for linens, towels, and things like soap, toilet paper, and toothbrushes. We call that the general store," Mary said.

The hand bell started ringing.

"Time for lunch," Leanne said.

She grabbed Jessie's hand, and they hurried out of the room and down the stairs. The girls were hurrying, but the boys came pounding down the stairs from the third floor, rushing toward the kitchen. They pushed past the girls, without so much as an "excuse me," to be the first downstairs.

The kitchen took up the back of the house. It had two large tables pushed together and lined with bench seats, although there was a chair set at each end of the long table. The kids found a place at a table and stood waiting.

Leanne grabbed Jessie's hand. "Sit next to me, Jessie."

They found two spots together and stood.

"What are we waiting for?" Jessie asked.

"Just wait."

Miss Erin set a large pot on the table and then called out, "Let's see your hands." The children held their hands out, and Miss Erin looked them all over to make sure they had been washed. "Nice job."

Mr. Frank walked in and stood behind one of the chairs. "Let's bless the food."

"Let's see your hands," Miss Erin said.

"I'm an adult, dear."

"You have hands, don't you?"

Mr. Frank rolled his eyes and held out his hands. Miss Erin glanced at them and pointed to the sink. The children laughed.

"Frank, you need to set a good example for the children."

"I was just getting ready to wash them," he said as a way of defense.

Miss Erin cocked an eyebrow at him. "At the table?"

He walked over and washed his hands in the sink. He dried them on a dishcloth and held them up for Miss Erin to inspect. She smiled and nodded. Jessie had the feeling that this was a scene that had played out before, probably more than once.

Mr. Frank sat down, and everyone bowed their heads. Jessie copied them, unsure why. Mr. Frank said a simple blessing on the food and thanked God for bringing Jessie to be part of their family. When he said, "Amen," everyone repeated it.

The children sat down, and hands started reaching out for the ham-and-cheese sandwiches, potato salad, and sliced apples.

Jessie realized she was hungry and happily filled her plate.

2
JANUARY 1933

Jessie enjoyed lunch with the other orphans in the kitchen of the Wilson Home. Leanne was a chatterbox, but Jessie couldn't help but like her. She was bubbly and friendly, and her laugh made Jessie think, maybe, things wouldn't be so bad here.

After lunch, Leanne stayed to wash dishes with two other girls. Everyone had assigned chores to do, and they changed from week to week. According to Miss Erin, it was her way to make sure all the children learned responsibility and would be able to care for themselves when they left the home. This happened when a child turned eighteen, if he or she wasn't adopted earlier.

Jessie was thirteen years old. Did that mean she would be here for five more years? Her parents would never come for her. Her brothers would never play with her again. She had nowhere to go.

While the girls were cleaning up after lunch, Miss Erin led Jessie up to the third floor.

"This is the boys' floor," Miss Erin told her. "But we also

have the clothes store up here."

Jessie nodded. "Leanne told me about it."

Four doors opened onto the third-floor hallway. Miss Erin led her to the door at the back of the house. She used a key to unlock it and flipped the lights on as she entered.

Shelves lined the walls of the room, and wooden dowels hung from the ceiling. Clothes filled the shelves and hung over the dowels. The room didn't look like a clothing store. It looked like a giant closet that smelled of mothballs.

"Eventually, you might buy some of your own clothes when you start earning money, but we do have clothes in all sizes. We reuse them until they are worn out. When you out-grow something, we trade it for something bigger," Miss Erin said.

She looked Jessie over and walked to a set of shelves. She pulled a dull yellow dress off the shelves and held it up next to Jessie. It hung to just above her ankles.

"That should do."

Miss Erin handed the dress to Jessie. It was a plain dress with no frills or even an interesting pattern to the fabric. Her mother had always liked interesting designs, but Jessie had no mother anymore to help choose her clothes.

Miss Erin pulled multiple sets of undergarments off the shelf and had Jessie set them on a table by the door. Jessie wondered how many other girls had worn them before her.

Miss Erin moved onto other shelves and picked out an assortment of dresses, skirts, and blouses. Each one was sized by her practiced eye. She even gave Jessie a pair of blue jeans.

"These are for when you have outdoor chores with Mr. Frank. It's hotter to wear than a dress, but it will hold up better in the dirt," Miss Erin explained.

Jessie left the room with a complete wardrobe piled in her

arms. She walked downstairs to her room to put her things away in the bureau. She had clothes to wear now.

Were they really her things, though? When Jessie outgrew the clothes, would she return them to the clothes store and trade up to larger sizes? She did not own these clothes, and if she didn't own them, they could be taken from her.

Dinner was at six o'clock, and afterward began the long process of getting ready for bed. It was a mixture of chores, showering, brushing teeth, and waiting for her turn in the bathroom. The kids who had evening chores were among the last to get time in the bathroom. Jessie quickly learned it was not a bad thing to have other girls whining outside the door for her to hurry. It meant that she was more likely than those girls to have hot water for showering. No one ever took a bath because it meant that person bathing would spend too much time in the bathroom when other people might want to use it.

The bathroom gave Jessie the only privacy she had in the house. As she slipped out of her dress to put on her night gown, Jessie stared at the burn scars on her arms. They were no longer bandaged as they had been for a week after the fire, but they still looked red and the skin was somewhat tender. They looked like flames eating at her flesh and not just the scars from that happening. Either way, it was a reminder of the worst day of her young life. She pulled her nightgown over her head and then brushed her auburn hair.

Everyone was in bed by nine o'clock. That was when Miss Erin started going from room to room, checking that the kids were dressed and in bed. She also gave each of them a kiss on the head.

It surprised Jessie at first, and she stiffened. She wondered why this woman was taking liberties with her, but after all that she had been through the past week, she found Miss

Erin's gentle touch reassuring. Jessie could smell the fresh soap on Miss Erin's skin. It was different than her mother's floral scent, but it was just as pleasing.

After a moment, Jessie relaxed.

"I'm so glad you're part of our family," Miss Erin said.

Jessie couldn't help but think about her family and home. All of that was now gone. This was what she had now. It might not be so bad.

She had been terrified during her few days in the orphanage in Harrisburg. There had been so many children, and they had been treated as if they were soldiers having to obey orders. Some of the children had been bullies, but more of them had been like Jessie, scarred over the loss of their families.

The meetings with the headmistress had been interrogation sessions. The woman hadn't worried about what Jessie was feeling. The headmistress had just peppered Jessie with question after question about possible relatives who might take Jessie in.

Before one of the meetings, Jessie has seen a man through a window of the headmistress's office. He had watched the interview, although Jessie wasn't sure how much he could hear through the glass. She didn't recognize him, but he stared at Jessie as if he knew her.

And all of that had led to this. Was it better? That was hard to say, especially after one day, but it was different.

Miss Erin turned off the bedroom light. "Goodnight, girls."

Jessie lay on her back in the dark listening to Mary and Leanne shift around, trying to get comfortable.

Jessie fell asleep and dreamed that she was back in her house. She lay in front of the fireplace reading *Alice's Adventures in Wonderland*. Her mother had just gone upstairs to put Brian and Bruce, her twin one-year-old brothers, to bed. Her father walked into the kitchen to make himself an evening snack.

A log in the fire popped, and sparks flew out of the fireplace and landed on her book. Jessie brushed them away, but one must have landed where she didn't see. It caught the book on fire. The page she was reading turned brown, then black, and then a flame appeared. Jessie yelped and tossed the book away, not wanting to be burned. It landed in the fire. Instinctively, she reached into the fireplace to grab it. When the flames burned her hand, she flicked the book away. It landed on the couch and caught it on fire.

Jessie screamed again, louder this time. Her father ran out of the kitchen. He tried to put the fire out with water, but it seemed to grow faster than the water could douse it. The bright flames grew larger, consuming more. The heat started scorching her as sparks flew in different directions. Jessie cried and screamed.

Jessie heard her brothers yelling, and she ran for the front door, which was now on fire. She tried dodging out of the way. Part of the ceiling in the living room fell. She backed away. A flaming curtain fell on her arm. The flames burned her skin. She screamed, trying to shake it off.

Jessie and her father got out of the house quickly, but then her father ran back inside when he heard his wife screaming for help with the Jessie's brothers.

"Jessie, wake up! Wake up!"

Jessie opened her eyes. She was in the bed in the Wilson Home. Leanne was shaking her shoulder.

"Are you all right?" Leanne asked, her eyes wide.

Jessie sucked in air, trying to catch her breath. "I had a bad dream."

"I'll say," Mary said. "You were screaming and thrashing around on the bed. I thought you were going to fall off."

The door to the room opened, and Miss Erin flicked the light switch. "What's going on in here?" she said sharply.

"Jessie had a bad dream," Leanne said.

Miss Erin hurried over to the bunk bed. "Are you all right, Jessie?" Jessie nodded. Miss Erin brushed Jessie's hair out of her face. "Are you afraid of the dark, Jessie?"

"No, ma'am. It was just a bad dream."

She trembled and tried her best to hide it from Miss Erin.

Miss Erin stared at her for a few seconds and then nodded. "Okay, well, you girls need to get some sleep. Tomorrow's Visiting Day."

Miss Erin tucked Jessie in and then did the same for Leanne who had climbed out of her bed to help Jessie. Mary hadn't even bothered to sit up in her bed.

Miss Erin walked to the door, turned off the overhead light, and then closed the door as she left the room.

Jessie lay in bed with her eyes wide open. She rubbed on her left forearm. She could feel the twisted flesh underneath the nightgown. Her arm seemed to throb. She doubted it she would be getting to sleep anytime soon.

And just what was Visiting Day?

3

JANUARY 1933

Sunday morning came too soon for Jessie. It seemed Miss Erin had barely closed the door and said good-night before she was opening it again to say, "Time to wake up, girls."

Jessie moaned and rolled onto her side, so she faced the wall. Leanne shook her shoulder.

"C'mon, Jessie, we need to get ready for breakfast. If you're slow, you don't get hot water."

Hot water was overrated. Jessie wanted to sleep.

Mary was already out of the room, and Leanne hurried after her. Jessie went back to sleep only to wake up when the girls came back into the room, freshly showered.

"Jessie, you need to get up. You're lucky you don't have morning chores yet," Leanne said.

Mary opened the armoire to get clean clothes out. "Let her miss breakfast because she's late. She'll learn."

Jessie sat up and swung her legs over the side of the bed. She rubbed her eyes and stretched.

"What's the hurry?" she asked.

Mary laughed as she quickly buttoned up a long, green dress.

Leanne frowned and said, "You can't just do things when you want to do them. You have to shower, brush your teeth, and be dressed before breakfast. Sometimes you even have chores to do before breakfast. If you aren't ready, you don't get breakfast."

Jessie climbed down from the top bunk. She walked down the hall to the bathroom, which was free. She stepped in the shower and shouted as she was hit with cold water from the showerhead. It woke her up as she danced around, trying to clean herself with as little water as possible touching her. Leanne hadn't been lying about running out of cold water.

When Jessie climbed out of the shower, she peeled off the wet bandages from her arm and dropped them in the wastebasket. The burns on her forearm looked pink, but the skin was slightly swollen. It looked unnatural against her darker skin.

She put her nightgown back on and brushed her teeth. When she opened the door to go back to her bedroom, Miss Erin was there.

"I was told about your arm," she said as she held up gauze and tape. "Let's put a fresh bandage on it."

Jessie looked away. So, Miss Erin knew Jessie had failed her family. Had she told everyone else? Jessie stepped back and let Miss Erin into the bathroom and closed the door behind her. Jessie rolled up her sleeve.

Miss Erin winced. "Does it still hurt?"

Jessie nodded. It was more the memory of the pain now than it was actual pain. Miss Erin spread a pale green ointment on the arm and then wrapped it firmly in gauze held in place with white tape.

"Can you please not tell any of the other kids?" Jessie asked.

Miss Erin looked at her as she brushed Jessie's hair back and tied it in a ponytail.

"I can, but don't you think they will realize you have burns on your arm? Maybe not now, but when the weather turns warm, you'll want to wear short-sleeved blouses."

Jessie shrugged. "I just don't want them to know if they don't need to. I don't want to have to answer their questions."

Miss Erin nodded. "They won't hear it from me."

Jessie went back to her bedroom and pulled out a blouse and skirt from her dresser drawer. Leanne saw her and shook her head.

"You need to wear the nice dress Miss Erin gave you," Leanne said as she brushed her hair in front of the mirror. "It's for Visiting Day."

"What is Visiting Day?"

"It's when anyone who wants to adopt a child comes to see us."

"Every Sunday?"

Leanne shook her head. "Not every Sunday. We're not that lucky, but Miss Erin told us before you got here yesterday that people would be coming by today."

Jessie shrugged. "They won't be coming to see me." Not that she cared. She didn't deserve to be adopted, not after what she had done.

"Maybe not, but everyone has to dress in their nicest clothes when it's Visiting Day. Miss Erin says we want to put our best foot forward. Even Mr. Frank dresses in his Sunday best, although he squirms like one of the boys and complains he's not the one getting adopted," Leanne told her.

The school bell rang, and the girls headed downstairs for breakfast. Jessie pulled out a frilly white dress Miss Erin had given her yesterday and hurriedly dressed. Breakfast was oatmeal and peaches and fresh milk. When Jessie sat down beside Leanne, the other children were already eating.

"Don't dawdle so much, Jessie," Miss Erin said as she set a bowl of hot oatmeal with sliced peaches resting on top in front of Jessie. "It's not such a big deal on the weekends, but during the week, you'll have to get ready for school."

"Yes, ma'am."

Jessie enjoyed the meal, but she was very careful not to spill anything on her clean dress.

After breakfast, Jessie went back upstairs to lay down in her bed and read *The Wonderful Wizard of Oz*. She had borrowed it from a bookshelf in the living room with Miss Erin's permission.

She had also seen a copy of *Alice in Wonderland* on the shelf, but had quickly passed it by even though she hadn't finished reading it. She doubted she ever would. It reminded her of the fire.

The bell rang half an hour later, and the children headed down to the living room. Miss Erin lined everyone up like they had been yesterday when Jessie came into the house, except now, Jessie was part of the back row between Leanne and an eight-year-old girl named Molly.

Miss Erin did a last-minute check to smooth down collars and brush unruly hair—usually on one of the boys— into place. Based on her nervous behavior, you would have thought Miss Erin was the one who was being considered for adoption.

"Okay, children, remember to be on your best behavior," she said.

Mr. Frank ran his finger around the inside of his collar, trying to loosen it a little. Then he opened the front door and led a couple inside. The woman wore a polka-dot dress, and the man wore a business suit like Jessie's father used to wear to work. They looked to be about the same age as Mr. Frank and Miss Erin.

"Welcome," Miss Erin said with a wide smile on her face. "These are our children, and they are all happy to meet you. I love them all."

The woman smiled broadly while her husband looked at the children. He had rosy cheeks that should have made him look very happy if he smiled, but he wasn't smiling.

"Is this all of them?" he asked.

"Yes, we are not a big home because we want the children to feel like they are in a home rather than an institution. I can tell you they are all wonderful boys and girls."

The man shook his head. "No, I mean none of these children are babies or even toddlers."

Jessie felt Leanne's shoulders sag beside her. "Figures," Leanne whispered.

"No, we don't care for children that young," Miss Erin said, some of the enthusiasm draining from her voice.

The couple walked over to stand next to a small girl who might have been five years old. She had shiny auburn hair tied in two ponytails tied with red ribbons. She was the youngest of the children at Wilson's Home for Children.

"Who's this little one?" the woman asked.

"I'm Betty," the girl said.

"You look very lovely in your dress," the woman said as she knelt down next to Betty.

The little girl curtsied. "Thank you."

The woman chuckled and whispered something into her husband's ear.

Behind the couple, Miss Erin continued smiling, but now it seemed forced. The sparkle in her eyes had dimmed.

"Betty," Miss Erin said. "Why don't you show the Ewells your bedroom and the animals in the barn?"

Betty reached out and took the woman's hand. "C'mon,

I'll show you my doll. Her name is Clara."

Betty led the couple up the stairs to the second floor. Mr. Ewell still didn't look happy, but his wife smiled and couldn't take her eyes off Betty.

Miss Erin turned to the other orphans. "I'm sorry, children. I wish I could find families for all of you because you are all wonderful. I guess Mr. Frank and I will have to do for a while longer. I have cookies in the kitchen."

She waved everyone toward the kitchen. The kids broke their formation. Most of them hurried into the kitchen. A pair of boys sat down in the living to resume a game of checkers they had been playing.

Mary started up the stairs to the bedroom. Her shoulders sagged and her head was bowed. How many Visiting Days had she seen to still be without parents at her age? Did she even get her hopes up anymore?

Molly walked over and hugged Miss Erin. "Don't be sad, Miss Erin," the young girl said.

Miss Erin patted the top of Molly's head. "I just want you all to have mommies and daddies again."

"It's all right. We have you and Mr. Frank."

Miss Erin dabbed at her eyes and led Molly into the kitchen.

Leanne looked like she might cry.

"What's wrong?" Jessie asked.

"Nothing everything."

"That doesn't make sense."

They walked into the kitchen. Leanne grabbed a chocolate chip cookie from a plate and sat down at the table. Jessie took an oatmeal raisin cookie. It was still warm and smelled of cinnamon.

"I wasn't expecting them to be interested in me, but it would have been nice if they had faked it," Leanne said.

"What are you talking about?"

"When people come looking to adopt a kid, they usually want a baby like Mr. Ewell said. Did you see how when they found out there weren't any babies here, they went right for the youngest kid?" Jessie nodded. "Well, I'm thirteen. I'm not a baby, and that means I'm not likely to get adopted. It's not even worth the older kids getting dressed up, but Miss Erin is an optimist."

Jessie thought the same, but she didn't mind it. "I like Miss Erin. She's nice."

Leanne's head bobbed quickly. "She's wonderful, and Mr. Frank is, too, but they're not our parents. If you think about it, they're raising us like show cattle to sell off. Maybe it's the farmer in them."

Since Jessie had never raised animals, she didn't know if it was an accurate comparison.

The girls finished their cookies and walked upstairs. Mary lay on her bed, staring at nothing. Her eyes were red, and Jessie thought she may have been crying.

Jessie looked out the window and saw Betty walking with the Ewells toward the barn. The little girl bounced on her toes as she pointed at the tree swing, the horse in the pasture, and even the outhouse. The Ewells smiled and followed her. Betty seemed to have won over Mr. Ewell. He was actually smiling.

Mr. Frank walked along behind the group, supervising but staying far enough away to allow them to get to know each other without his interference. He stopped and turned. He saw Jessie in the window and smiled. Then he waved. She waved back.

Jessie was just as old as Leanne. Would this be her home now until she was sixteen? She could think of worse places to be, but she wished she was back in Harrisburg in her old house with her mother and father and brothers.

4
JANUARY 1933

"Time to wake up!" Miss Erin called from the door to Jessie's room.

Jessie didn't hear her at first. She was dreaming about swimming in the Susquehanna River. When Miss Erin's voice finally penetrated her dream, Jessie opened a single eye and saw it was still dark outside.

Miss Erin shook her. "It's time to get up, Jessie."

"It's still dark outside."

"What does that matter? There are things that need to be done before you go to school."

It never took Jessie long to eat breakfast, brush her teeth, and get dressed. She didn't need to get up before the sun rose.

"Jessie, wake up," Miss Erin said.

Jessie groaned and opened her eyes.

"That's better. Leanne and Mary will show you the morning chores you'll do this week. Once you're finished, clean yourself up, and dress in your school clothes. Then you can come to breakfast."

"What time is it?"

"Five o'clock."

Jessie blinked. "In the morning?"

"Yes, so you had better get moving, or you won't have time for breakfast."

Jessie sighed and climbed down from her bunk. She got dressed in her work clothes as Leanne waited impatiently.

"Hurry up, Jessie. If we miss breakfast, we'll be hungry all through morning classes."

They hurried downstairs to the kitchen where a dozen lunch pails sat open. Mary was already making peanut butter sandwiches and wrapping them in brown paper.

"Everyone gets an apple and two cookies," Mary said.

The girls packed the pails and then lined them up on the counter. When they had finished, they went upstairs to wash up and comb their hair before they got dressed.

"How far is the walk to school?" Jessie asked.

"We don't walk. The school is on the other side of town," Leanne told her.

"Then how do we get there? We can't all fit in a car."

"You'll see."

They had eggs, bacon, and hot biscuits for breakfast. Then they had to brush their teeth before coming back to the kitchen. Miss Erin handed each of them a lunch pail and kissed them on the forehead.

"Don't worry, Leanne and some of the other children will be in your class. They will help you if you need it," Miss Erin told her.

Jessie's old school had probably started by now after the winter break, but with the fire and Jessie getting moved around from place to place, she hadn't been to school in a few weeks. She hadn't thought much about how it would be going to a new school with new people in her classes.

The children headed outside. Mr. Frank drove a large

truck with wooden sides on it around to the front of the house. He walked around to the back and pulled a box out of the truck bed and set in on the ground.

"The 7:35 to the Abbottstown School leaving on track one. Let's go!" he called.

Jessie walked around to the back of the truck. She stepped on the box, and Mr. Frank helped her step up into the truck bed. A long bench ran along both sides of the bed. She found an open seat and sat with the other children.

When everyone was seated, Mr. Frank hooked a pair of chains across the back. Then he climbed in and drove them to the school in Abbottstown. It was a plain brick building that looked like a church without a steeple. It was also smaller than any school Jessie had seen.

School actually turned out to be an easy adjustment. It was a two-room school and nearly a quarter of the students came from the Wilson Home. So even though the school year was three-quarters done, Jessie didn't have worry about fitting in because she lived with many of the students. It was especially nice that Leanne was her age, so they were in the same class.

Jessie's classroom was on the left side of the building. There were twenty-one students in the class, ages ten to thirteen. Older students, if they continued their education, went to the high school just outside of town. Mary and Harvey, one of the orphan boys from the home, went to school there. Jessie's teacher was a young woman name Miss Davidson, who wore her dark-brown hair in a tight bun.

Miss Davidson brought Jessie up to the front of the class. Jessie looked over the classroom and wanted to run out the door.

"Class, we have a new student today. Jessie, please introduce yourself," Miss Davidson said.

Jessie took a deep breath. "My name is Jessie Parsons. I am thirteen. I used to live in Harrisburg."

"Why would you want to live here, then?" a dark-haired boy asked. Abbottstown had only a few hundred people living in it. From what Jessie had seen, it was barely larger than her neighborhood in Harrisburg.

"Thomas, be quiet, or you'll stand in the corner," Miss Davidson said.

"There was a fire" Jessie rubbed her arm and sniffled. "My house my house burned down. I live in Wilson's Home for Children now." She stopped and looked at Miss Davidson, hoping she had said enough.

Miss Davidson smiled. "That's fine, Jessie. You can take a seat."

Jessie walked back to her desk. When she sat down, Leanne reached over and patted her arm where the burn scar was. She flinched as if Leanne's gentle touch had hurt her. Then she turned and smiled at the girl to let Leanne know she hadn't done anything wrong.

Things went fine after that. Miss Davidson started her lessons for the day, and Jessie didn't have to draw any more attention to herself.

That peace lasted until recess. The girls were outside jumping rope when Thomas walked over with two other boys. They watched Jessie playing jacks with Leanne and another girl from her class named Emma Lawrence. Jessie noticed the boys standing behind Emma and tried to ignore them.

"Just what we need," Thomas said to the other boys loud enough for Jessie to hear. "Another orphan."

Leanne shook her head. "Ignore him. Sometimes he can be a nogoodnik."

She tossed the ball up and grabbed three jacks in a quick swipe.

"Look at her dress. They probably pulled it out of the garbage for her to wear." Thomas laughed, apparently thinking he had made a joke.

"Be quiet, Thomas," Leanne said.

Thomas ignored her and fished a penny from his pocket. He tossed it at Jessie's feet. "Go get yourself something to eat, orphan girl."

Jessie knew he was being mean on purpose. She had known boys like him at her school in Harrisburg. Sadly, she had sometimes acted like Thomas to new kids. It seemed so stupid now, but she had thought she was impressing her friends. Maybe she had, but it had been at the expense of someone else's feelings. She hadn't understood that until she was the one being singled out.

Jessie knew she should ignore Thomas. She even felt like she deserved his ridicule because of how she had treated other kids in the past, but she couldn't keep her eyes from tearing up.

"Look at her," Thomas said. "Is she an orphan, or did her parents not want her?"

"That's enough, Thomas."

A boy wearing denim jeans and a white shirt walked between Jessie and Thomas. His hair was dark blond, and he had freckles all over his cheeks and nose.

"Go away, Nathan. This is none of your business," Thomas said.

"It is because I don't like bullies," Nathan said.

"That's too bad."

"For you."

Nathan stepped closer and shoved Thomas into the other two boys. Thomas staggered, but he didn't fall.

"What are you doing?" Miss Davidson called from door into the school.

"Nothing," the boys answered almost in unison.

"You're lucky," Thomas said to Nathan.

Nathan shrugged. "I'm ready whenever you are."

Thomas glared at him and then turned and walked away without saying anything. Nathan watched him leave and then walked back to be with his friends.

"Who is that?" Jessie asked Leanne.

"Nathan Chase. His father ran the bank in town before it closed. I'm not sure what he does now."

"Why did he help me?"

"Because he's nice."

When the children went back into the classroom, Jessie stopped next to Nathan's desk. He looked up at her with light-blue eyes and smiled.

"Thank you for what you did outside," Jessie said.

Nathan blushed as he looked at his feet. "You're welcome."

"Why did you do it?"

"My father used to be the banker in town. When the bank had to close, Thomas picked on me, acting like it was somehow my fault. I took it for a while, but then I realized, I couldn't do anything about the bank closing. The next time Thomas started sassing me, I punched him in the stomach."

Jessie smiled. "That's what I was thinking about doing."

Nathan laughed. "I wish you had. He would have really been embarrassed if a girl hit him."

Jessie wasn't sure what else to say, so she sat down at her desk.

When school ended for the day, Mr. Frank was waiting out front of the building with his truck to drive the orphans home. At the home, things fell into a routine of chores, meals, and homework with plenty of time to play. Jessie and Leanne enjoyed skipping rope and playing jacks together when they had free time.

Leanne felt like a sister, and it almost felt like Jessie had a family again.

Almost.

Whenever she started to feel comfortable with the Wilsons, Jessie reminded herself that this wasn't her home, and she was the reason she didn't have a home anymore. She didn't want to feel close to them because there was always a chance she might be adopted. Not that it seemed like a big chance. No one ever came to see her on Visiting Day, although one man did come talk to her after school on a Thursday when she had been at the home a couple of weeks.

Miss Erin brought her into the living room where an older man with thin, white hair sat on the sofa, holding a homburg in his hand. He stood up when he saw Jessie.

"Jessie, this is Mr. Powers," Miss Erin said.

The man held out his hand. "Hello, Jessica. I worked for your father."

Jessie didn't recognize him, although he looked familiar. She shook the man's hand. It was soft and cool. The three of them sat down.

"Jessica," Mr. Powers said. "I was your father's lawyer. I am in charge of settling his affairs, and the good news is that your father had insurance on his and your mother's lives. That money is yours, although you won't be able to get it until you become an adult. Also, when your father's business sells, you will get that money. Until then, I have set up an account in your name and have a consultant with Briggs and Hardison managing the money."

Jessie wasn't sure what a lot of what Mr. Powers was saying meant. She didn't know what insurance was or anything about her father's business. But Mr. Powers had said Jessie would get money when she was older. That was good.

She knew she would need it when she left here.

"Thank you," Jessie said.

Mr. Powers nodded. "The bad news is that we have been working with the state agencies to try to find a relative of yours who can take you into their home. Sadly, we haven't found anyone." He looked at the floor, unable to meet her eyes. "I am afraid you'll have to remain here."

"For how long?"

He sighed. "That's just it. I can't say how long. We have exhausted all avenues in search of your family, and honestly, I feel that anyone we find at this point would be a very distant relation and as unknown to you as anyone who might come here to visit." He paused for a long time and finally said, "I'm sorry."

Jessie didn't know what to tell him. She had realized she had lost her family the night of the fire. She massaged the burns hidden beneath her sleeves. "How do you like it here?"

Jessie shrugged. "It's fine. Mr. Frank and Miss Erin are very nice."

"Good. That was one thing I was able to do."

Jessie suddenly recognized Mr. Powers. "You were at the orphanage when the headmistress was talking to me. I saw you watching."

Mr. Powers nodded and then pushed his wireframe glasses further up on his nose. "I was checking on you. I couldn't get you out of the orphanage entirely, but I could make arrangements for you to be brought here. I heard excellent things about it."

"It's much better than where I was, but I would rather be home."

"I'm sure you would, but unfortunately, we don't always get what we want."

Jessie nodded. She knew that better than just about anyone.

5

JUNE 1933

As Jessie's days at Wilson's Home for Children stretched into weeks and then months, the Ewells adopted Betty.

Her leaving created an odd mix of emotions for everyone, including Jessie. The Wilsons and the orphans were sad to see the cheerful little girl leave. It was like they were losing a daughter and sister. It brought back fresh all the hurt Jessie had felt at losing her family, but this time, she felt a joy behind the sadness. Betty was getting a new family. It was something all the orphans hoped for for themselves, and seeing it happen to one of them renewed that hope.

Also, a young boy named Howard left the orphanage when an adult cousin tracked him down and took Howard to live with him in Scranton, and everyone went through the same see-sawing emotions once again. Both of their vacancies at the home were quickly filled with new children.

Jessie tried to push the sadness away as she watched new children arrive at the home, but it lingered. She wondered where these parentless children had come from—had they all suffered like she had when her parents died in a fire? What was it in this world that took so many people away from their families?

Jessie settled into her routine of school and chores. She and Leanne became like sisters, and she also became friends with Nathan Chase and some of the other children in her class. When summer came, she said goodbye to them, thinking she wouldn't see them until school began again in the fall. Too much was going on at the farm for the Wilsons to be driving the children into town to play with friends like Jessie's parents had done during the summers in her Harrisburg neighborhood.

Summer was not vacation time at the home. The Wilsons expected the children to do other work when school was out. They had their normal chores around the house, but the older children worked at jobs in Abbottstown that the Wilsons found for them while the younger children helped with the gardening at the farm.

The Wilsons explained that they had the children get jobs for two reasons. First, it helped them learn skills that would help them get a job when they were adults. Second, all of their earnings were deposited into bank accounts so they would have some money to start their lives with when they left the orphanage.

Miss Erin got Jessie a job in the Parker Mercantile Store in Abbottstown. Mr. Parker owned and ran a store that had been in his family for three generations. He was Mr. Frank's age, but half a head shorter and much heavier. Miss Erin was pleased because she thought the job would help Jessie learn budgeting, customer service, and other useful skills for when she became an adult. Jessie thought the job was just a lot of climbing a ladder to stock cans and boxes on the high shelves in the store and fetching items from the storeroom. Mr. Parker rarely let her be still unless a customer came into the store.

Then he played the doting mentor who was helping a young person learn business skills. He made sure everyone knew he was helping an orphan.

Jessie thought he did it hoping people would spend more money in the store. She doubted it, though. It didn't take her long to notice that most people were very careful with how they spent their money. She supposed it was because the depression had left so many people without work. Mr. Parker would tell her that she was lucky he was willing to take on any help given the state of the economy.

It only took a few weeks of working for Mr. Parker before Jessie's stomach started to knot up the closer Mr. Frank's truck got to the store to drop her off each day. The other children didn't mind their jobs, or if they did, they didn't say anything about it. Leanne worked with a seamstress and was finally learning to sew and make clothing. She loved the work, now that she wasn't sticking herself with a needle all the time.

One day while Jessie was stocking the high shelves with canned tomatoes, Nathan Chase walked into the store with his mother. She was a willowy lady who wore a dress with lots of frills that looked out of place in a country store. Mr. Parker grabbed Jessie by the back of her dress, nearly pulling her down from the ladder. He had her stand off to one side while he waited on Mrs. Chase.

"Hi, Jessie," Nathan said. "Did Mr. Parker pull you off the ladder?"

Jessie nodded. "For some reason, he doesn't like people seeing me work."

"Isn't that why you're here?"

Jessie nodded. "I thought so. How has your summer been?"

"Boring. I ride my bicycle a lot and read."

"Nathan, come over here, darling," his mother called.

Nathan waved goodbye to Jessie and walked over to stand next to his mother.

"Why don't you pick out some penny candy?" Mrs. Chase said.

Mr. Parker opened a small paper bag and added the candies that Nathan picked out from the glass jars that sat along one shelf. Most of his choices were gum drops, but he also selected a few hard candies.

"Thank you," Nathan said to his mother and Mr. Parker when Mr. Parker passed him the bag. He walked over to Jessie and held the bag out to her.

"Would you like one?" he asked her.

Jessie smiled. She reached in and took a gum drop.

"Nathan, what are you doing?" his mother asked.

"This is Jessie from my school. I was just giving her a piece of candy."

Mrs. Chase looked Jessie up and down. "This is that Jessie? I didn't realize she was a girl."

"That Jessie?" Jessie repeated to Nathan.

"I told her about you."

"Not a lot, apparently."

He shrugged. "I don't know a lot."

"You know I'm a girl."

Nathan blushed. "Yes."

"Come along, Nathan," Mrs. Chase said. "I have other places I still need to go."

They had barely gone before Mr. Parker passed Jessie a box of canned peaches and sent her up the ladder again.

One morning, Jessie woke up and felt like she had a sack of flour sitting on her chest. She could barely breathe, and she just wanted to cry. It was her job. She just couldn't bring herself to go into the mercantile store and have Mr. Parker bounce back and forth between working her like a plow horse and pretending to be her best friend.

Miss Erin opened the door to check on the girls and saw Jessie was still in bed. "Jessie, it's time to get up. You've got work to do."

"I don't feel good, Miss Erin."

"Can you describe it?" She walked over and put the back of her hand on Jessie's forehead. "You don't have a fever."

"It's my stomach," Jessie told her.

"It couldn't be something you ate. None of the other children are sick."

"Do I have to go to work this morning?"

Miss Erin frowned. "I guess not. You stay in bed. If you are still sick this evening, we'll call the doctor."

Miss Erin left the room.

"You're faking," Mary said as she put on her dress. She was helping at Cornwall's Market and said that she liked the work. Jessie wished she could say the same.

"Of course, she's not faking," Leanne said. "She wouldn't do something like that."

"Then why isn't anyone else sick?" Mary asked.

"I don't know," Jessie said.

"You're just being lazy."

"I am not!"

Miss Erin's teacher's bell rang, and Mary and Leanne headed downstairs for breakfast. Jessie rolled onto her side. She could see a tree through her window and a lot of sky. It looked like it would be a pretty summer day.

Downstairs, she could hear the commotion from the kitchen as everyone ate breakfast. She was a little bit hungry, but she was just glad she didn't have to go into the store. The knot in her stomach loosened. Of course, she couldn't stay sick. She would have to go back to work sometime. Just the thought of that made her stomach tighten up again.

When she heard Mr. Frank's truck drive up to the front of the house and idle loudly, Jessie climbed out of bed and peeked out of the window. She saw the children walk out of the house and climb into the truck bed.

Leanne looked up at the window and saw Jessie. She waved, and Jessie waved back. Then the truck pulled away, and Jessie climbed back in bed. She napped for a little while, and when she woke up, the only stomach pain she felt was from hunger.

She dressed herself and walked downstairs to the kitchen. Miss Erin was kneading dough to be baked into loaves of bread.

"May I have a sandwich?" Jessie asked.

Miss Erin paused in her work. Her arms were white up to her elbows from flour.

"How are you feeling?"

"I'm feeling better now."

Miss Erin rinsed her arms off in the sink and then toweled them dry.

"Sit down," Miss Erin said. "I will make you lunch if you tell me what's wrong. Otherwise, I'll have to dose you with castor oil."

Jessie frowned. Her mother had given her castor oil once. It was thick and slimy and tasted how she imagined a worm tasted. It was definitely not what her stomach wanted right now.

"When I started thinking about going to the store today, I felt sick," Jessie said as she sat down on a bench.

"Why?"

"I don't like it or Mr. Parker."

Miss Erin's brow furrowed. "Did he do something to you?"

Jessie shook her head. "It's not that he's mean, not really, but he keeps me stocking shelves or taking out trash or washing windows. Whenever he sees me stopped, he finds something for me to do."

"You are supposed to be working."

"He doesn't. He sits and watches me or reads the newspaper unless there's a customer. Then he lets me stop and gets all nice. Leanne and Mary like their jobs. I don't."

Miss Erin nodded. "I thought the job would teach you a lot."

"It taught me how to climb a ladder holding boxes."

Miss Erin smiled. "Well, I can ask the other children if they don't like their jobs and see if they would like to switch with you."

Leanne was working with a seamstress and Mary worked in a market. Jeffrey ran errands for Dr. Byers. Paul worked with the butcher, which was gross, but he liked it because he thought it was fun to use a cleaver to chop meat.

"From what they say, they all seem to like their jobs. I want to like mine," Jessie said. She did want to like her job, not just to have some money to spend but also to have something to do during the summer.

"What kind of work are you interested in?" Miss Erin asked.

"I don't know."

"What jobs did your parents have?"

Jessie thought about things she had seen her parents do and say.

"My mom stayed home with me and my brothers. My father owned a cigar factory. I remember his clothes used to smell like tobacco when I hugged him." He had pointed out the building to her one time when they were driving through the city, but she had never gone inside, so she had no idea how cigars were made.

"The problem we run into is that not everyone wants a child following them around while they work," Miss Erin said. "We tried having one of our children help a lawyer in town, but the boy was too antsy. He didn't like all the sitting that was involved, and the lawyer didn't want to watch him while he was in court."

"I don't think I would like sitting around a lot, either. It's hard enough to do it at school."

Miss Erin sighed. "Let's do this. I will talk to Mr. Frank. He's the one who gets the various businesses to help our children. I'll see if he has any ideas. Until we come up with something else, you can stay here and supervise the younger children in the gardens and work in the barn helping out. Does that sound fair to you?"

It sounded like Jessie would be doing a lot of extra chores, but at least she wouldn't have to go into the store. She also wouldn't be sitting around with little to do.

"Yes, ma'am."

"Okay, then go help the children weed the gardens. When you all finish, I'll have lunch ready."

Jessie smiled and ran out the back door. The home farmed 100 acres of its property. While most of it was used to grow corn, potatoes, carrots, broccoli, peas, and beans, the Wilsons also had a small apple orchard. There were also small gardens where other vegetables were grown to feed the children and reduce grocery expenses. Mr. Frank did most of the farming with help from the children.

Jessie was used to doing chores in the small gardens that provided a lot of the produce that the Wilsons used. However, Mr. Frank took her out to the larger field that had corn planted. It towered above her head like a green and yellow forest.

"Is it ready to harvest?" Jessie asked.

"Not yet, but soon."

He pulled an ear off the stalk and peeled back the husk, exposing the corn. Jessie had never seen an ear of corn still inside its husk. She reached out and touched the silky threads between the husk and corn.

"When will you know it's ready?" she asked.

Mr. Frank shrugged. "It's something you learn from experience. I look at the size of the ears and color. I also consider the time of year."

"Do we have to pick all the corn like we do with the vegetables in the garden?"

Mr. Frank chuckled. "No. I will use a tractor to grab most of these stalks. What I need you to do is walk along in the areas that I harvest and pick up anything that gets missed. Then later, we remove all the ears from the stalks."

Jessie nodded and looked around, realizing for the first time just how many stalks of corn were in this field. It was too many to count.

"What about today?"

"Today, you'll just walk through the field, weeding, and making sure animals aren't damaging the corn."

She nodded and walked out into the field. She picked a spot and started working methodically, walking row by row pulling any weeds she saw. If she saw a leaning cornstalk, she pushed more dirt around the roots to support it. She saw herself as a protector of the vegetables.

When she got hot working under the sun, she rolled up her sleeves and didn't even feel self-conscious about the burn scars on her arms. Besides, no one was around who might see them.

As she worked, she felt the tension ease out of her. She hadn't even realized she had felt that way because of having to work in Mr. Parker's store every day. The odd thing was she was still working just as hard, or even harder, than she had at the store, but it didn't leave her feeling sick to her stomach.

When Jessie tired, she would sit down and rest and enjoy the warmth of the sunlight on her face for a few minutes.

By the end of the day, her clothes were filthy, and her hands had small cuts from grabbing plants with rough edges.

Mr. Frank called her in from the field before he headed off in the truck to pick up everyone from their jobs in Abbottstown. He looked her over and nodded. "Well, it looks like you worked, if all that dirt is any indication."

"Not a weed in sight," Jessie said, smiling.

"I'm sure there's plenty of areas you didn't get to. We may start harvesting the beans this week." The farm had an acre of green beans planted on the northwest corner. "We'll take a look in the morning. Go ahead inside and get ready for dinner."

When Miss Erin saw her, she yelped and rushed Jessie into the bathroom to shower. "Did you even leave any dirt for the plants? You're as bad as the boys when they help with the farming."

It felt good to take a warm shower without worrying about using all the hot water for the person coming behind her. She had to admit that Miss Erin might not be mistaken. Jessie watched dirt wash off her. It made the water look muddy.

When she climbed out of the shower, she realized that in her rush to get in the shower, she had forgotten to bring clean clothes into the bathroom. She left her filthy clothes on the floor, wrapped a towel around her, and hurried to her bedroom. She opened the door and saw Leanne lying on her bed.

Jessie yelped when she saw her friend and put her arms behind her, but it was awkward doing that and holding the towel closed.

"What's wrong with your arms?" she asked as she sat up.

"Nothing."

"Then why are you hiding them and making yourself look like one of the armless freaks in the freak show?"

"The what?"

"The freak show. Haven't you ever been to one at the circus?"

Jessie shook her head.

"Well, show me your arms if you aren't hiding anything."

Jessie was trapped, but if she couldn't trust Leanne, who could she trust? "You can't tell anyone."

She slowly held out her arms. The pink scars stood out against Jessie's tanned skin. They were about as healed as they were going to get. She had stopped using gauze and salve after a month.

Leanne's eyes widened, her expression a mix of shock and concern. "Jessie, what happened?" she asked, her voice trembling.

"I was burned," Jessie replied quietly, a distant look in her eyes.

"Today?" Leanne asked incredulously.

"No, in the fire that that made me an orphan," Jessie explained, casting her gaze downward.

"But that was months ago. How have I not seen the burns before?"

"I hide them," Jessie admitted, her gaze flickering to the bathroom door.

"Does it hurt?" Leanne asked softly, reaching out to touch one of the small pink circles on Jessie's arm.

"Not really. They used to be tender and blistered. Now it

just feels tight from time to time. I really don't want anyone to know about them. They might stare."

Feeling a rush of empathy and understanding, Leanne stood up in front of Jessie and slowly pushed up the sleeves of her dress. To her horror, she saw dozens of small circular burns covering her friend's arms. Her mouth dropped open in disbelief.

"What what happened?" Jessie whispered.

"When my father thought I was misbehaving, he would press the end of his lit cigarettes into my arm," Leanne answered, her own voice shaking with emotion at the memory.

Jessie put a hand to her mouth in shock. "That's awful!"

Leanne nodded sadly. "That's why I always make sure to wear long sleeves. I don't want people to see."

Tears welled up in Jessie's eyes as she thought about the pain her friend had endured. "Me too," she whispered, reaching out to take Leanne's hands in hers.

Leanne gave her a reassuring smile. "So, don't worry. I won't tell anyone."

"Me too," Jessie replied, feeling grateful for the understanding and support of her friend.

6

JUNE 1933

Jessie sat in the dirt of her special spot. The ground was moist enough to hold the soil together but not wet enough that the dirt clung to her. Corn grew up tall around her, but in her small spot, barely wider than her outstretched arms, she had pulled all the cornstalks to create a clearing just for her. She had replanted the cornstalks at the edge of the field, but not all of them had survived.

Jessie had chosen a place that couldn't be found easily. If you didn't know where you were going, you could easily miss it. She had tied pieces of yarn around cornstalks near their base to mark her path from a spot at the corner of the field to her hideaway. It was far enough into the field to give her privacy, but not so far away that she wouldn't hear when Mr. Frank called her in at the end of the day.

Jessie pulled out the copy of *The Jungle Book* by Rudyard Kipling that she had found on the bookshelf downstairs in the house. She wasn't sure whether she liked it yet, but she found it interesting to read the stories from the perspective of the jungle animals. Crossing her legs, she opened the book to read about Shere Khan the tiger and Baloo the bear.

Jessie needed this space where she could be by herself. The only place in the house where she had any privacy was the bathroom, and that only lasted so long before someone was knocking or, more likely, banging on the door for her to get out.

She liked the other orphans. Almost all of them. A couple of the younger boys were annoying, and Mary was too self-centered. Jessie had learned to tolerate them, but between school and the home, she was never without someone around. That was until she had started working in the fields. Mr. Frank would give her a task, and if she knew how to do it, he would leave her to it. Pretty soon, she would find herself far out in the fields alone.

The first time she had realized it, she stopped and closed her eyes, enjoying the feel of the wind that carried a slight smell of ham from dinner cooking in the house and the moist earth. She heard insects buzzing nearby, but otherwise things were quiet.

She loved it.

She loved it enough to create her own space far enough in the field that she couldn't be seen from the upper floors of the house.

Jessie had been reading about half an hour when her hands jiggled, and she lost her place on the page. She looked up. What had caused that? Sometimes she could feel the tractor when it rumbled by, but she also heard it coming before it got too close. It was loud enough to make her ears hurt. Plus, it wasn't time for Mr. Frank to have the tractor out.

She started reading again, but she heard the stalks rustling like newspaper pages shaking as they were turned. She looked up. There was no breeze, but she heard the rustling again. She noticed a discoloration through the cornstalks. It was gray, and it moved.

Jessie froze.

What was she looking at? It wasn't a deer or even a bear. They were brown or black.

It moved forward a step. Jessie slowly put her book on the ground and gathered her legs under her, preparing to run if needed.

She wanted to creep away unnoticed, but at the same time, she was curious about what she was seeing through the corn.

She crouched on the ground as the creature seemed to sense her and took a step in her direction. Then she watched as a thick, gray serpent parted the cornstalks. No, not a snake, a trunk. It was an elephant a small elephant.

Jessie wondered if she were daydreaming herself into the story she was reading. She pinched her arm without scars and looked up. The elephant was still there.

She had seen elephants in the circus and the zoo. They were large, taller than a man. A full-grown elephant would have stood taller than the cornstalks. This one was barely as tall as her.

"Hello," she said softly, not wanting to startle it. It must be young to be so small.

The elephant snorted.

"How did you get here? You're a long way from Africa. Where's your mom?"

The young elephant shook its head. It took a step toward her, and Jessie heard a rattling sound. She looked down and saw a chain around the elephant's foot about six feet long and attached to a long stake.

It had escaped from somewhere. A circus? She hadn't heard of any circuses nearby. And where had this baby elephant been hiding? It wasn't easy for such a large animal to hide, even in a vast field of corn.

She remembered from a book she had read that a young elephant was called a calf, but this was unlike any calf she had ever seen on the farm.

Had this calf been wandering around and hiding? Why wasn't anyone looking for it? How could no one notice they were missing an elephant?

Jessie reached into her pocket and pulled out a sugar cookie she had slipped into her pocket at lunch to save for a snack.

She held it out toward the calf. Did elephants eat cookies?

"Are you hungry? Is that why you came into the field?"

The long trunk moved up and down and then stretched out toward Jessie. She held the cookie up. The end of the trunk moved closer. It hesitated.

"It's OK. Take it."

The edges of the calf's trunk curled around the top of the cookie and then lifted it from Jessie's fingers. The trunk curled back, and the cookie disappeared into the calf's mouth.

Moments later, the trunk again reached out toward Jessie. She held up her empty hands.

"I'm sorry. I don't have more. I didn't know I would have company."

The trunk grabbed her fingers. The edges of the trunk were smooth and slightly moist. It was warm, and she could feel the calf's breath. The trunk's grip was firm but not painful.

"I don't have any more," she repeated. She thought about giving the calf corn, but it wasn't ripe, and she had no way to get it off the cob.

Jessie pulled her hand free and patted the trunk. It felt rough. The skin was dry and covered in short hairs.

"I wish I knew what to do with you."

She stood slowly. The trunk jerked back, and she thought the calf might bolt. She held her hand out. The calf reached out with its trunk and touched her hand, smelling it and feeling around.

"I won't hurt you, but I wish I knew how to help you."

The calf had run away from somewhere, and Jessie should want to send it back. Was it a good place though? It was someplace where someone had staked a baby elephant to the ground, so the calf couldn't move more than a few feet in any direction. That didn't seem right. Yet, she wondered if she shouldn't stake it and fetch Mr. Frank.

The trunk nudged her side, tickling her. She laughed, and the calf snorted. Jessie looked into the elephant's gray eye, which had a slight tint of blue. It looked mischievous. Could an eye show emotion? It didn't matter. That is what she saw.

She took a step forward and held out her hand. The calf stepped through the cornstalks and pressed its head against Jessie's hand. She rubbed the elephant's leathery skin.

She stroked the elephant's big ears, and he jerked his head away. She patted the back of his head, which forced her to lift her arm over her shoulder because he was the same height as her.

"It's all right. I won't hurt you. I've just never seen ears so big."

She reached out gently and stroked the edge of his ear. It flicked as if he was trying to shake off a fly. When he did, Jessie noticed something behind his ear. She gently pulled the ear outward.

On the calf's head, hidden by his ear were scars. They were red lines, and at least one looked like it was actually scabbed over. They weren't fresh, so nothing had attacked the calf, but something had hurt him. The scars probably still hurt him.

She let the ear drop back, and she continued petting him as he chewed on his meal.

A thought occurred to her. "I guess we're both orphans. What happened to your parents? Are they still alive? Were you with them before?"

The elephant's trunk started poking into her pockets.

"I don't have anything else to eat. I'm sorry."

The elephant snuffled, and Jessie felt the warmth of his breath on her face.

"Jessie!" Mr. Frank called. "It's time to call it a day."

"I'll be in in a bit," Jessie called back.

She looked at the elephant. What was she going to do with him? She didn't want to stake him to the ground. That seemed like a mean thing to do. But she also didn't want him wandering off. What if a farmer saw him and shot him?

She didn't have a choice, though. She couldn't walk into the house with an elephant calf walking behind her. She also couldn't bring herself to stake him to the ground without food or water. She would have to leave him on his own until she could return. She would just have to hope that he stayed nearby and hidden.

"I have to go, but I'll be back in the morning, and I'll bring things for you to eat. Just don't get into trouble before then."

She started to walk away, but the elephant followed her. She turned and put a hand on his head to stop him.

"You need to go back to where you were hiding. I'll be back tomorrow. I promise."

Jessie turned, and the elephant let out a soft whine. She felt horrible leaving him. He must be scared and feel so alone, but she couldn't do anything else. She just hoped he would be here tomorrow.

She was surprised to see Leanne on the porch of the house. Her raven-haired friend waved to her.

"You look like you were rolling in the mud," Leanne said with a smile.

"And you look like something out of a magazine," Jessie said, meaning her friend looked like a model.

Leanne was wearing a new pink-checkered dress with lace fringe. Leanne saw her staring and spun around, flaring the skirt.

"Do you like it? I made it myself, and Mrs. Emerson let me keep it."

"It's lovely. You did a great job."

"She wants me to make another one. She thinks it will sell in the shop."

Jessie heard a slight wail from the field and thought it must be the calf. She saw Leanne look over her shoulder toward the sound.

"What was that?" she asked.

Jessie considered what she should do. She knew she could trust Leanne, but she wasn't sure how her friend would react to an elephant in a cornfield.

"Can you keep a secret?" Jessie asked.

Leanne rolled her eyes. "I am already keeping your secret."

"Not this one. Follow me."

"But my dress."

Jessie sucked on her lower lip. She couldn't wait too long, or she wouldn't have time to get ready for dinner.

"Fine. Change as quick as you can, and if you can grab some bread or fruit on the way out without Miss Erin asking questions, do it."

"Why?"

Jessie pushed her friend toward the door. "Just do it and hurry up."

Jessie paced the porch, hoping Mr. Frank or Miss Erin wouldn't come out and ask her to do something else.

When Leanne came back out wearing her work dress, Jessie grabbed her hand and hurried through the cornfield, making turns where the ribbons indicated.

"You are acting really weird," Leanne said.

"You'll understand in a bit."

Jessie led her friend along her route back to her private place. Of course, the calf left a trampled swath behind him, so it would be easy for someone to follow his route from the forest on the far side of the cornfield to Jessie's private spot.

"Where are we going?" Leanne asked.

"I want to show you something, but you have to see it to believe it."

Jessie could tell Leanne was getting suspicious as they got closer to the clearing. Leanne could see something moving through the cornstalks. She just wouldn't know what it was.

When the girls stepped into the clearing, Leanne jumped back and yelped. Then she composed herself.

"What are you doing with an elephant?" Leanne asked. "How did you even get one?"

"He escaped from somewhere and came here," Jessie told her.

"I think we both know he escaped from a circus, but why would he come here?"

"He just wandered in here earlier today. He's probably trying not to be found."

Leanne walked around the calf and then reached out her hand slowly to stroke the elephant on the hide.

"I petted one at the circus when it was in town," she said. "What are you going to do with it?"

Jessie shrugged. "I don't know. He can't stay here forever."

Leanne snorted. "He would be pretty obvious when Mr.

Frank harvests the corn."

Jessie hadn't even thought that far ahead. She was more worried about whether this calf would be found tomorrow.

"I don't know who to tell about him, though," Jessie said. "Once they find out there's an elephant here, they'll send him back to the circus, and look here." Jessie lifted the calf's ear to show the scrapes on the back of the flesh. Then she pointed to his foot where the collar had irritated the skin. "He hasn't been treated well. I can't send him back to that. He's so scared. I want to help him."

Leanne kept petting the elephant, almost unconsciously maintaining contact with it.

"Can you ask Mr. Frank?" she suggested. "After all, the elephant is already on his farm."

"I'm afraid to. Mr. Frank is nice, but if I tell him there's an elephant here, he might send it away."

"We can ask Dr. Stultz. He's the veterinarian in town. We don't have to say that there's an elephant here. We can say we're doing a report on elephants and ask questions about how to take care of one."

"It's summer. There's no school."

Leanne rolled her eyes. "Fine. We'll say we were reading a book about elephants and were curious if there was a place around here where they could live. We can even ask him how circuses care for them."

Jessie nodded. It was worth a try since she had no idea what to do with an elephant.

"I can save my lunch tomorrow and bring it to him," Leanne said. "I also have some money. I can stop by the market while I'm in town and buy some fruit. I saw them feeding the elephants at the circus. They eat a lot."

Jessie nodded. "I know. He has been constantly hungry, and all I had to give him was a cookie."

Leanne's eyes widened. "Oh, that reminds me." She reached in and pulled two apples from her pockets. "I only got two because I thought you meant them to be a snack for us."

Jessie took one and held it toward the calf. The calf's trunk reached out, plucked the apple from her hand, and shoved it in his mouth.

"Wow! He put the whole thing in his mouth," Leanne said. "He certainly eats like a boy." She stared at the elephant as if believing it wasn't there. "You won't be able to keep him, though."

Jessie nodded. "I know. I just don't want him to have to go back to wherever they hurt him."

Leanne nodded. "I'll come back tomorrow morning with food for him. Will he just stay here?"

Jessie shrugged. "I think so. He has been here for hours already. I think he feels safe."

They played with the elephant for a little while longer. They only left when Miss Erin started ringing her school bell to let the children know dinner was ready.

7

June 1933

Throughout dinner, Jessie kept looking out the window over the kitchen sink, expecting the smells of chipped beef, carrots, and cornbread to draw the elephant calf to the house. She could barely eat. Leanne had to nudge her under the table when she stared out the window for too long.

Jessie felt guilty that she had something to eat and the calf might not. She thought about taking some food and sneaking back into the fields, but she wasn't sure she could find the calf if he had moved, and there was a good chance she might get lost in the field in the dark even with the ribbon markers on the cornstalks.

After dinner, she went upstairs to her room and sat near the window looking out over the cornfields, hoping to spot a patch of gray amid the dark field.

Mary walked into the room and huffed when she saw Jessie. "Why are you just sitting around lollygagging?"

"I finished my chores," Jessie said. "It's my free time."

Mary snorted. "Maybe you need more chores."

Mary was fourteen years old, which made her the oldest

child in the orphanage. As such, she tended to consider herself Miss Erin's assistant. She was actually helpful to Miss Erin when she wanted to be, but when Miss Erin wasn't around, Mary became domineering over the other orphans.

Jessie ignored Mary and went back to looking outside. It was too hard to see anything with the lights in the room on, though. Not that she had seen the calf. She hoped the elephant was all right. He must be scared out in the dark all alone without his mom and dad.

She climbed into her bed and pulled the covers over her. Miss Erin came in a short time later and inspected the girls to make sure they had washed and brushed their teeth. Then she gave them all a goodnight kiss and turned the light off.

Jessie wanted to talk to Leanne about the elephant, but she couldn't with Mary in the room. Mary would probably tell Miss Erin and Mr. Frank that there was an elephant hiding in the fields, and even though Jessie knew the baby elephant couldn't keep hiding there, she wanted to enjoy the time that he was here on the farm.

Sometime during the night, Jessie thought she heard the trumpeting wail that an elephant might make. She only heard it once, though, so she may have imagined it.

The next morning she hurried through her chores. She ate breakfast and then stuffed her pockets with pears and apples and biscuits whenever no one was paying attention to her.

Then she hurried out into the fields to begin her work for the day. However, she first went to her quiet spot, hoping to find the little elephant there.

He wasn't, and she had no way of knowing where he might be.

She called out, not too loudly in case Mr. Frank was nearby. "Hello. I'm back. Can you hear me? I brought some things for you to eat."

No response. Then she heard rustling.

"Jessie?"

It was Leanne. She walked into the clearing from the corn rows.

"Leanne! You scared me. Why aren't you at your job?"

"I've still got time before Mr. Frank leaves," she said. "I wasn't sure I could find my way back. Where's the elephant?"

"I don't know. He wasn't here when I got here."

"Do you think he moved on somewhere else?"

Jessie shrugged. "If he did, I hope he's alright."

Leanne emptied her pockets of fruit and biscuits. She set them down on the ground in a small pile. "I brought him some things to eat."

"I did, too."

Mr. Frank called out to the children that it was time to go into town.

Leanne put a hand on Jessie's arm. "I've got to go. I'll check with you when I get home later."

Jessie walked through the corn to where the beans had been planted and began filling a bushel basket with them. She listened to the breeze through the plants, hoping to hear a snort or a trumpet. She heard neither. Occasionally, she paused to call out, but she never heard a response.

When Miss Erin called her in for lunch, Jessie dropped off the food she had brought out in her quiet spot before heading into the house. It was just Miss Erin, Mr. Frank, and the younger orphans who were too little to work at a job at the table. That made it harder for Jessie to sneak any more food into her pockets since there weren't as many distractions.

She did manage to hide three cookies and two rolls. If the elephant did come back, he would probably be hungry. He was four or five times her size, which meant he must eat a lot. Jessie couldn't keep feeding him from the house. Sooner or later, someone would notice. She could feed him some of the vegetables from the garden, but it couldn't be too much, or they would be missed, too.

She also wasn't sure what elephants ate. If she could talk to the veterinarian, hopefully he could tell her some useful things about caring for elephants.

Jessie stopped back at her private spot and added the cookies and rolls to what she had taken in the morning. It wasn't a big pile, but it was more than the single cookie she had had the day before.

Something touched her back, and she jumped and spun around. The trunk of the elephant calf poked through the cornstalks.

Jessie laughed and petted the trunk.

"I'm glad you came back. Are you hungry? I brought food," she said to the elephant.

She reached down and picked up a pear and held it out for the calf. He sniffed at it and then grabbed it with his trunk and put it in his mouth as he stepped into the clearing.

Jessie stepped back and pointed to the pile of food on the ground.

"This is all for you, but don't eat it too fast. I don't know how soon I can get you more."

The calf chewed on the pear while the trunk sniffed at the pile of food. The trunk came up holding a cookie, which the calf put into his mouth. He definitely had a sweet tooth, but what youngster didn't?

The trunk reached back to Jessie and patted her on the head and blew her hair around with short snorts. Jessie patted the side of the calf as it grabbed a roll and began chewing on it.

"You know, if you're going to stay near the farm, I need to give you a name. My name is Jessie. I think I'll call you Willie."

The elephant didn't protest. He just kept eating.

Jessie stroked his side and studied the texture of his skin and the thickness of his legs. It was hard to believe she was touching a real elephant.

The following day, Jessie and Leanne snuck more food out of the house for Willie, and the girls fed him some of the tomatoes and beans from the garden. Jessie also brought out a jar of salve from the house. It was the same salve that she used on her burn scars. She thought it might help Willie's ears.

He flinched when she started to apply the salve. Jessie had Leanne distract Willie by feeding him while she gently rubbed the salve on the scars. She wondered if he was eating anything else other than the food they were bringing to the secret spot.

Jessie rubbed the salve over the scars that she discovered were behind both ears. She hoped it would bring him some relief and help the marks heal.

She still wondered what had made the marks. Was it some predator that thought the young elephant would be easy prey? And why had it only grabbed Willie behind the ears? It seems like there would have been plenty of other places for to grab, scratch, or bite.

Next, Jessie undid the collar that was holding the chain and stake around Willie's leg. The leg was red beneath the band because it had been so tight around his leg. She rubbed salve into that, too. At least he wouldn't continue to have to drag the chain and stake around. If it had caught on something, he might have been trapped.

After Leanne went to work, Jessie did some work weeding the fields in case Mr. Frank checked on her, but she stayed close enough to Willie to check on him from time to time.

She heard Miss Erin calling for her, which was a surprise.

It was after lunch and too early for dinner. She walked back to the house.

"Climb in the truck, Jessie, we're going to get the children from their jobs," Miss Erin said. She looked slightly worried, even though she smiled.

"Why isn't Mr. Frank going? He's the one who drops them off and picks them up," Jessie asked.

Miss Erin shook her head. "Mr. Frank has things to do right now. He can't go."

Jessie climbed into the back of the truck. She saw that the younger orphans were already in the truck bed, excited to have a break from their regular routine. Why were they all going into town? In the afternoon, Mr. Frank went into town with an empty truck and came home with the bed full of children.

They spent about an hour driving around the town picking up the other children from their various jobs. Miss Erin even stopped at the general store in town and bought each of the children a chocolate bar.

After Leanne got into the truck, she whispered to Jessie, "How's Willie?"

"He's fine. He's probably hungry again."

It felt like a grand adventure, but Jessie would have preferred spending the time with Willie.

When they finally arrived home, Miss Erin brought all the children inside to help her finish making dinner. Jessie had no chance to sneak out and see Willie.

Dinner was roasted chicken with mashed potatoes and fresh green beans. The children were excited to have been able to eat chocolate before dinner.

Mr. Frank came inside late for dinner. He washed up and sat down to eat with everyone else. When he sat down to eat, Miss Erin glanced at her husband, and he nodded.

"Children, I wanted to tell you something that happened

here today," Mr. Frank said casually. "The sheriff and some men from the circus came by today looking for an escaped elephant."

The children stopped eating and were suddenly peppering Mr. Frank with questions. Pauline and Douglas, the two newest orphans in the home, jumped from the table and looked out the window. Jessie felt a knot form in her stomach.

"Children, sit down," Miss Erin said.

Pauline and Douglas reluctantly returned to the bench and sat down.

"You won't see the elephant," Mr. Frank said. "The men found it and took it back to the circus."

Jessie glanced at Leanne and then quickly looked at her plate.

"Why didn't we see him?" Ralph asked. "Elephants are big."

Mr. Frank glanced at Jessie. She felt her cheeks flush and concentrated on her food.

"This one was a baby," Mr. Frank said. "She wasn't even taller than the corn."

"She?" Jessie asked.

Mr. Frank nodded. "She was apparently hiding in the woods and cornfields."

"How did they know she was here?" Mary asked.

"They were apparently asking around and looking for signs of an animal stealing food and asking people if they had seen anything."

"Even a baby elephant would be hard to miss," Douglas said.

"I'm glad they caught the beast," Miss Erin said. "It could have hurt one of the children."

"I doubt it. Elephants aren't generally dangerous if left alone," Mr. Frank said. "This one was so young she was probably scared and avoiding contact with people. She was a wild animal, though, so you can't be too certain, no matter how friendly they look. Elephants have killed people both accidentally and on purpose."

"Did you see her?" Jessie asked.

Mr. Frank nodded and smirked. "She was quite a sight to see. I never thought I would ever see an elephant in my fields." Some of the children laughed. "This young girl must be pretty smart, too. She had a band on her leg that had a chain and stake attached to it. She managed to pull the stake out to get away from the circus, but apparently when she got here, she figured out how to undo the band around her leg. They found it in the field, which is how they knew the elephant was here or had been here."

Jessie silently scolded herself, but who knew people would be searching the fields for the elephant?

"What will happen to her?" Leanne asked.

"She'll go back to the circus and her mother."

Jessie sighed. Willie, or rather the girl calf, wasn't an orphan after all. She had a mother, and her mother had probably been very worried about her.

"That's good. At least she won't be an orphan," Jessie said.

Miss Erin reached out and patted Jessie's arm.

"The circus men also found something interesting. They said it looked like someone had treated some minor wounds on the elephant," Mr. Frank said.

Jessie felt her face grow hot. She looked down and concentrated on her meal and hoped no one asked her about her red face.

"Really?" Miss Erin asked. "That elephant is lucky someone didn't shoot it."

"Yes, that elephant was lucky and so was the person who helped it."

8

JULY 1933

The next morning, Mr. Frank walked with Jessie into the barn after breakfast. The Wilson farm had a horse, chickens, and a milk cow. It also had a couple pigs and steers. They provided eggs, milk, and labor for the home. Mr. Frank showed Jessie how to feed each one. He also went over how to check them and make sure they were doing well. She needed to look for sores and check the animals' feet and make sure they were healthy. She was also responsible for shoveling out the stalls and feeding and watering the animals.

It wasn't hard work, and Jessie thought she would like spending time with the animals. She needed to check in on them the first thing in the morning, and it would be the last thing she did before going in to wash up before dinner each evening.

"This will be your main chore once school starts. By then, the crops will have been harvested. You can help Miss Erin with canning the fruits and vegetables, but the animals still need to be fed and cared for. They depend on you," Mr. Frank explained. "Without your care, they might starve or get sick."

Jessie nodded slowly, her enthusiasm fading. She wasn't sure she should be trusted to take care of the animals. "Mr. Frank, do you really want me to do this?"

He stared at her for a few moments, considering how to respond. "It's not that difficult, Jessie. Farm children do these chores on their farms daily."

"But what if I do something wrong or forget something? I could hurt or kill one of the animals." She paused and took a deep breath. "I did that once, and my family died."

Mr. Frank sighed and knelt down beside her. "I know about that, Jessie, and I know what happened. That's why I know you can do this. You know more than any of the other children why we can't be neglectful around the animals."

Jessie sniffled and wiped tears from her eyes. "But I killed them, Mr. Frank. They died because of me."

Mr. Frank reached out and held her hands in his rough, calloused hands. "What happened to your family was a terrible accident, Jessie, but it was an accident. Sometimes horrible things happen when nobody does anything wrong. Look at me, Jessie." She looked up and met his brown eyes. "You are not to blame. You did nothing wrong."

"Yes, sir," she replied.

He smiled and patted her on the shoulder. Then he went out to start working on digging up potatoes and carrots, leaving her alone in the barn.

Jessie missed the elephant calf, but she enjoyed working with the different animals, although it took her some time to get used to the smell of manure, wet straw, and urine. While the horses, pigs, cows, and chickens might not be as unique as an elephant calf, Jessie didn't have to worry about someone seeing her with them. She could also ask Mr. Frank if she had any questions about how to care for them.

It didn't take her long before she was spending more time

than she needed with the animals. It wasn't as quiet as being in the cornfield in her special space, but it was almost like the animals were speaking with her. She tried to learn their language or at least what they intended with their sounds and actions.

She found herself talking to them as if they were friends. She even named them, at least the ones who hadn't been named. The chickens were Larry, Moe, and Curly. They weren't female names, but the trio of chickens were usually running around so crazy that they reminded her of the Three Stooges.

Leanne would come out to talk with her when she got home from her job. One time, she showed Jessie a book she found in the library about animals from Africa. She enjoyed staring the pictures of elephants at because they reminded her of the calf.

As close as they were, Leanne couldn't understand why Jessie preferred staying on the farm all day and not working at a job in town where she could see people and do something different.

"I like the animals," Jessie tried to explain. "They are like people. Curly struts around like she's so important, a lot like Mary. When General Lee isn't working, he just likes to stand and rest in the barn like he's worried if he's seen outside, someone might put him work. And Melvin, he wants attention. He wants to be petted and talked to." General Lee was the horse and the one animal she hadn't named. Melvin was one of the steers.

"But they can't talk to you," Leanne said.

"They don't have to, and I like it that way."

One day, a truck pulled up in front of the barn. Mr. Frank came in from the field and spoke with the driver. Then he came into the barn to get Melvin the steer. He led him out of the barn and onto the truck. Melvin walked along calmly behind him, and once he was on the truck, Mr. Frank and the driver lifted the ramp and closed the back of the truck.

Jessie noticed the name on the side of the truck. Haskell Meats and Butcher. A knot formed in her stomach.

"What's going to happen to Melvin, Mr. Frank?" she asked.

"Melvin?" Jessie pointed to the steer. "He's being sent to the butcher," Mr. Frank told her.

Butcher? It suddenly dawned on Jessie what would happen to Melvin once at the butcher's. She grabbed Mr. Frank's hand.

"No, Mr. Frank, you can't do that to him," she pleaded.

"That's why we have him, Jessie. Where do you think meat comes from? We need some beef to carry us through the winter."

"Not Melvin, though."

"This is a farm, Jessie. We sell our excess, but most of it we use ourselves to support all of us here."

The truck started to drive away. Jessie took a few steps toward it until Mr. Frank took hold of her arm. She turned and buried her head in his chest as she started crying.

That evening, she didn't eat the meatloaf that Miss Erin served. She couldn't bring herself to do it. She kept seeing Melvin's face on her plate. It made her sad and sick at the same time. She didn't think she would ever eat meat again.

"Aren't you hungry, Jessie? Usually, you're famished after working all day," Miss Erin asked.

"No, ma'am."

Mr. Frank looked at her with sadness in his eyes, but he didn't say anything.

"Well, you need to eat something. I thought you liked my meatloaf," Miss Erin said.

Jessie glanced at her plate and saw Melvin snorting as he tried getting her attention so she would give him more oats. Then she looked at Mr. Frank who had gone back to eating his meatloaf. How could he?

"May I be excused?" Jessie asked.

Miss Erin started to say no, but Mr. Frank put his hand on her arm. She stared at him as he nodded slightly.

Miss Erin sighed and said, "Fine. Go upstairs and get showered."

Jessie didn't reply. She walked into the living room and out the front door. Then she ran across the yard and into the barn. She found Melvin's empty stall with its clean hay. She dropped down into straw and cried. The sounds from the other animals in the barn rose around her. She didn't know what they meant. Did they know they would stay here only as long as they were useful? How long before Porky became sausage and Larry, Moe, and Curly became a dinner with corn and stuffing? What about General Lee? What became of a horse when it was no longer useful?

"Jessie."

She looked up and saw Mr. Frank standing in the open doorway.

"You can't react like this if you're going to be around animals, especially farm animals," he said.

She sniffled. "It's not fair."

Mr. Frank stepped inside and leaned against the side of the stall. "It's how life works. When one of the cats catches and eats a mouse, do you get upset?"

"I don't see it happen."

"You don't see what happens to the animals at the butcher."

"I know what happens, though."

"You know what happens with the cats and mice, too. It's why we have cats. You and the other children might like petting them, but they are hunters, and they hunt mice."

Jessie sniffled, but didn't say anything.

Mr. Frank squatted down beside her. He took a deep breath and quietly said, "I know you helped the elephant."

Jessie froze. She stared at the ground. "I know I should have told you, but she was so afraid. She was this big creature, but she was a baby."

"That baby weighed more than you and me together. She could have hurt you."

Jessie shrugged. "Maybe, but she didn't. I could tell she was scared."

At least Jessie thought the calf had been scared, but then, she hadn't even realized Willie was a girl.

They were quiet for a minute or so, then Mr. Frank said, "I guess I should have let you keep working in the fields and not had you work with the animals."

"I like the animals."

"And that's why I brought you out here to do it, but you are too close to them. They are here to feed us or help us with our work."

"Why do we have to eat them?"

"For nourishment. Meat is part of our diet. We are carnivores like many of the animals themselves. We raise them like corn or beans."

But they weren't corn or beans. They were animals. They trusted her.

Jessie shook her head. "I don't like it."

"Well, maybe being a farmer is not for you, then, but we need meat like we need eggs, milk, and vegetables to live."

Jessie nodded. "I just couldn't eat the meatloaf because I kept seeing Melvin. I felt like it was him."

Mr. Frank rubbed his chin. "What if I got you work with Dr. Stultz?"

"The veterinarian? Would I be a nurse?"

Mr. Frank shook his head. "No. The farmers call him when one of their animals is sick. He takes care of them. He might need an assistant."

She liked the idea. She could be around the animals, take care of and help them, but she wouldn't have to watch them be taken away to be killed.

"I think I would like that."

Dr. Stultz was an older man with long gray beard and wild matching hair. Jessie thought he looked a bit like a lion, if lions had gray manes. He seemed to know everything about animals and even talked to them like Jessie did.

He traveled around the county in his truck visiting the animals on their farms. He took care of hoof problems, pains, broken legs, and anything a farmer couldn't do on his own. Most of the time, he worked with farm animals, but sometimes people from town would bring a beloved dog or cat to the office for care. Once, someone even brought in a hawk with a broken wing that had been hit with a car.

Jessie usually worked at Dr. Stultz's office in the barn next to his house. She cleaned out the stalls and kennels where the animals were kept. She fed and watered the animals and gave them medicine if they needed it.

It felt good to be helping the animals. Some of them looked to be in such pain when they came to the office. Watching them leave healthy again made Jessie feel like she was making a difference.

When she had been working with the doctor for a couple months, he began taking her with him when he visited farms. He talked to her about what he was doing and why. Jessie learned veterinary care was like trying to solve a puzzle. The animals couldn't tell you what was wrong with them so the veterinarian had to figure it out from the clues. How the animals looked. How they reacted to probing. What any tests showed.

She asked to borrow a book about veterinary care. Dr. Stultz looked over his bookshelf and picked out a textbook and handed it to her.

"It might be over your head, but it the best one I have for you to start with," he explained.

She looked at the title. *Introduction of the Veterinary Care*. She took it home and started reading it before she went to bed. The first few pages were understandable enough, but it quickly got more complicated. She didn't understand some of the words, although she could usually make out what those passages meant in context to everything else. However, it didn't necessarily mean she understood those passages.

"Why are you trying to read that manual when you can't understand it?" Leanne asked her one night when she saw Jessie flipping back and forth between pages, comparing what a passage said to what an illustration showed.

"Sometimes I figure it out."

"It would drive me crazy."

"It does me, but once in a while, things fall into place, and it makes sense to me. Other times, I get Dr. Stultz to explain things to me or show me. I like learning about the animals. I look at them differently when I know what's going on inside of them. I really like when Dr. Stultz lets me guess at what's wrong with an animal, and I get it right."

Jessie continued to work her way through the book each night. She even started making notes to ask Dr. Stultz. He explained some things and showed her others. It helped her understand a lot, but it often raised even more questions.

She didn't stop, though. She was learning the secrets of animals.

As school grew closer to starting, Jessie begged Miss

Erin and Mr. Frank to allow her to continue working with Dr. Stultz. She promised she would keep up with her studies, and she even got Dr. Stultz to agree to pick her up after school to take her to work with the animals.

Miss Erin was hesitant, but Mr. Frank knew how much helping animals meant to Jessie. He persuaded Miss Erin, and Jessie thought she had found what she wanted to do when she grew up.

9

JUNE 1934

Jessie had been working Dr. Stultz for about a year before she saw him get angry for the first time. He usually
smiled and was friendly and joking. When he examined
animals, his face took on a serious look as he concentrated on
his patient. He always called the animals patients, not animals. Jessie had even seen him sad when an animal died or
was in great pain.

But she had never seen him angry. She had begun to
think he didn't get angry.

Then one day, a man dressed in a brown pinstripe lounge
suit with a matching flat cap drove up to the barn. Jessie was
washing a lame cow name Buelah. Dr. Stultz had shaved a
rear hoof to remove a nail the cow had stepped on and driven
into the hoof.

She watched the man get out of his beige Phaeton. Instead of an ailing animal, though, he was holding a handbill.
He walked over to Dr. Stultz and started talking.

At first, Jessie couldn't make out their voices, but then
Dr. Stultz started getting loud. The man held up the handbill.

Dr. Stultz pointed at the man's car. The man shrugged and turned and left. Dr. Stultz watched him go, shaking his head. Jessie had never seen him look more like a lion that at that moment.

"Are you all right?" Jessie asked, walking out of the barn.

He glanced at the retreating car, and then smiled at her. "I'm fine."

"I've never seen you upset before."

He sighed and ran a hand through his hair, trying to push it down. "I do my best not to be. My patients don't like it."

Jessie didn't really like it either. "What happened?"

Dr. Stultz shook his head. "Oh, nothing really. The man was a front man for the circus and wanted to put up a hand-bill here advertising it."

"Is that bad?"

"Have you ever been to a circus, Jessie?"

"Once. Years ago, when I lived in Harrisburg."

"Did you like it?"

She smiled. "It was wonderful. The trapeze artists were like birds. The women looked so beautiful dressed in their fancy outfits. All the animals. The only thing I didn't like so much were the clowns. They looked scary with their odd-shaped heads, big eyes, and mouths."

Dr. Stultz nodded. "Did you notice the lions?"

Jessie wondered for a moment if he knew she often thought of him as a lion.

"Yes. They were scary, too. I'm glad they were in cages," she said.

"Do you remember the lion tamer?"

"Yes, he went into the cage with the lions."

"And how did he keep from being hurt by the lions?"

She tried to recall her visit to the circus and watching the lion tamer. Then she heard the crack of a whip in her memory. "He had a whip."

Dr. Stultz nodded. "Yes. He used that whip to hurt and scare the lions so they wouldn't attack him. He didn't have to do that. He chose to walk into that cage with them. Lions, tigers, bears, elephants… They're wild animals. They are meant to roam jungles and plains, not be in cages. And they aren't even in big cages. The most room they get is when they are in the circus ring. That kind of confinement can break an animal or make it mean." Dr. Stultz frowned and shook his head. "I don't like circuses. They are like animal jails, and they don't care for their animals well."

Jessie remembered the elephant calf and the wounds she had seen behind her ears. Someone had hurt that elephant. Had it been someone like a lion tamer with a whip?

"I was asked to treat some sick animals at a circus years ago. Their veterinarian had quit, and they hadn't hired a new one yet. The lion tamer had fed the lions bad meat. I don't think he meant to, but he should have paid more attention to the state of the food. I was shocked to see lions' condition even beyond the sickness I was called in to treat. All the animals were mal-nourished, not just the lions. They were sickly and underweight. Some were scarred from whips and bullhooks."

"Bullhooks?"

"They are staffs with hooks on the end. It is how the elephant trainers get the elephants to do what they want. Usually they will use it to prod or tap an elephant, but if the elephant doesn't cooperate, the trainer can jab it. It would be like someone sticking you with a nail under the chin or in some other soft area of your body." He poked her in the shoulder with a finger to demonstrate his point. Jessie flinched and jumped back.

She thought about what Dr. Stultz had said all day and finally decided that a bullhook must have caused the scars behind the calf's ears.

Who could have been that cruel to a baby elephant? Of course, a baby wouldn't be cooperative, but you don't hurt it to make it obey.

Late in the spring, after school ended for the year, Jessie got home after working and found all the children were excited. They were jabbering in small clusters and looking at pictures in books. Leanne grabbed Jessie on her way up to the bathroom to wash her hands.

"Did you hear?" Leanne asked.

"Hear what?"

"We're going to the circus Saturday!"

Excitement flared in Jessie, but then it was tamped down when she remembered what Dr. Stultz had said.

"Are all of us going?" Jessie asked.

"Yes, this circus lets orphans come see the show for free wherever they go!"

"Wow!"

"It's going to be so fun."

Jessie couldn't help but feel some of the same excitement. Even if she went and felt sorry for the animals, she could still marvel at the trapeze artists, tight rope walkers, and other acts.

"And the best part is," Leanne was saying, "that there is a party for all the orphans after the show. I wish I had a camera so I could take pictures."

She went walking down the hallway to the bedroom, and Jessie went into the bathroom to wash the smell of animals off her.

The circus trip was just about all the orphans could talk about the next day. They were the envy of the other children in town, many of whose parents couldn't afford the admission price for the circus. Too many people were out of work and struggling to make ends meet.

Miss Erin made sure everyone was dressed nicely on Saturday morning. They weren't in their best outfits, but they wore clean school clothes, not the clothes they wore to work on the farm. Jessie wore a light green dress that had puffy sleeves, ankle-high white socks, and Mary Jane shoes that were getting too tight for her to wear.

They ate breakfast and then Miss Erin said it was okay to leave the dishes until they got home. They needed to drive into York if they wanted to the see the parade. Everyone was loaded into the back of the truck and Mr. Frank drove through Abbottstown to get on the Lincoln Highway and drive into York.

The area near the fairgrounds was crowded with people who were already lined up to watch the parade, but Mr. Frank found a place to park in a field with other cars, and they walked over to Highland Avenue. The big top had already been set up at the fairgrounds and was awaiting the crowd for the first performance.

Mr. Frank told the children that a long train had arrived near the fairgrounds very early in the morning and the circus folk had raised the big top in the dark, so when people woke up in the morning, it was like it had suddenly appeared like something out of a dream.

It looked like the big top was large enough to cover half a dozen farmhouses. Roustabouts were still walking around, inspected the spikes and making sure all the ropes were tied tight. It didn't ripple at all in the breeze like most tents would have.

Jessie heard the calliope music playing before she saw anything. Then she heard the shouts of people as they caught sight of the approaching parade. Dancing women were at the front of the parade, followed by trucks pulling the caged animals, musicians, clowns, and performers. Everyone waved and cheered.

At the very end of the parade were people from town who followed the circus performers into the fairgrounds.

The people couldn't follow the parade past the ticket booths until they purchased a ticket. Mr. Frank presented the ticket taker with a voucher for all the children and the ticket taker waved him past.

They walked toward the big top along the midway, passing smaller tents promoting fortunetellers and freaks. Booths with games like ball tosses and rifle shooting beckoned to people passing by. Jessie smelled hot dogs, cotton candy, and popcorn.

People of all ages filtered in from York and the surrounding towns. They meandered around the midway or headed toward the big top to take in the show.

Inside the green-and-white-striped big top, two large rings dominated the center area. Wires, ropes, and bars seemingly crisscrossed each other over their heads. Bleacher seating was separated from the rings by a wide lane that ran around the performing area.

Jessie was swept up in the grandeur of it all. Both she and Leanne fell in love with the young blonde trapeze artist as he swung and somersaulted through the air with such grace.

However, her thrill at watching the lion tamer was dulled by her conversation with Dr. Stultz. It gave her a different view of who was actually the predator in the cage. She did laugh and clap loudly at the trained dogs, though. It was hard not to. She was even able to enjoy the clowns from afar.

After the performance ended, Mr. Frank told everyone to stay in their seats. Most of the people exited to enjoy the midway games or tour the menagerie. She saw a few other groups of children who were also seated and figured they must have been children from other orphanages. She counted nearly fifty of them. What had happened to all these children's parents?

Once most of the crowd had left, circus workers carried out long tables and benches into the middle of the rings and set them up. Then they set plates, forks, and cups at each spot.

The ringmaster walked out, still dressed in his red-and-white suit and tall hat.

"Good afternoon, children. Welcome to the Conroy and Pepperidge Circus. I invite you all to come down and have a seat at the table for lunch."

The children made their way down excitedly from the bleachers and rushed out to find a place at the tables while the adults tried to slow them down.

Once everyone was seated, more circus workers brought out trays piled high with hot dogs, bowls of cole slaw, and pitchers of lemonade. The adults helped serve the children so it wasn't a mad grab for the food.

As the children settled down to eat, the ringmaster stood at the edge of the ring. He tipped his top hat to the small audience.

"Thank you for joining my circus today. My name is Jeremy Conroy. I am the owner of this circus. Did you enjoy the show this afternoon?" The children clapped and cheered. The circus owner smiled. "Wonderful. I also thought with all the extra room at the tables, I might invite some additional guests."

He waved his hand, and circus performers started walking into the big top. The children squealed and waved as showgirls, trapeze artists, lion tamers, and more took their seats among the children and started talking with them. Other performers passed around the bowls and plates of food and filled cups with lemonade. It was a child's dream come true.

They felt like they were part of the circus.

Jessie looked around anxiously for the handsome trapeze artist she had watched with such interest during the show, but he wasn't among the group of performers joining the children for lunch. Instead, a black-haired woman who had spun around while hanging from a rope while only holding onto it with her teeth sat next to her.

"Hello, my name is Maria," the woman said.

She had dark hair and wide green eyes. Jessie tried to get a good look at the woman's teeth to see if there was anything special about them.

"I'm Jessie." Then before she could stop herself, she said, "I bet your jaw is so strong you could crack open a walnut."

Maria laughed. "Not quite, Jessie, but I do visit the dentist regularly to make sure I don't loosen my teeth."

"You do have a nice smile."

Maria patted her on the head. "Thank you."

As they ate lunch, Mr. Conroy walked around. Up close, he looked older. His brown hair was graying at the temples. He made sure to stop and speak with each one of the orphans.

When he stopped next to Jessie, he said, "Hello, and who might you be?"

"Jessie Parsons."

"And how old are you, Jessie?"

"Thirteen."

Mr. Conroy smiled. "You are quite the young lady then. Tell me, Jessie, do you remember your real parents?"

Jessie frowned as she remembered the fire and the screams of her mother. "Yes, sir."

He patted her hand. "That's good. I hope they are good memories. Well, you enjoy your lunch and your day here at the circus."

He patted her on the arm and then walked to the next

child, and Jessie heard him ask her the same questions. It surprised her that even though he asked about her parents, he didn't ask anything about them. He just seemed to lose interest and move on.

After lunch was finished, Mr. Conroy gave each child five tickets that would allow them to play games on the midway. Miss Erin took the girls with her while Mr. Frank took the boys around to spend their tickets.

The midway began at the entrance to the big top and ran most of the way to the fairground gates. Game wagons and closed tents lined both sides. Behind, on the other side of those wagons and tents, she could see places where you could buy food and drinks.

Jessie tried knocking over milk bottles to win a prize, but they stubbornly resisted falling when she hit one.

Beside the big top, she noticed some animals being led into another large tent. She realized it was the menagerie and pleaded with Miss Erin to let her walk through the rows of animals.

"I don't think you're allowed back there, Jessie," Miss Erin told her.

"At least let me check," Jessie said. "If they say, I can't go in, I'll come right back. I promise."

Miss Erin sighed. "Fine. If they do let you go through, look for us on the midway when you're finished."

Jessie bounced up and down on her toes. "Yes, yes, I promise."

Jessie ran over to Leanne and shoved her remaining tickets into Leanne's hand.

"Are you sure you don't want to use them?" Leanne asked.

Jessie shook her head. "Seeing the animals up close is enough for me."

Jessie smiled and then ran off to the entrance to the menagerie. It was an area set off from the midway and behind the big top, and it was filled with all the animals that performed in the circus. The dangerous ones, the lions, tigers and bears, were kept in cages while the horses were tethered to posts.

Dr. Stultz would have hated the place. He didn't even like keeping horses in a stall, but when he did, they had more room to move around than these animals did. The tent was surprisingly quiet. The animals didn't make a lot of noise. The loudest things she heard was the sound of one of the big cats bumping into its cage door and rattling it and a horse neighing. The smell, though, was overpowering. She was used to the smell of a barn, but the animal musk smell was stronger here, either because of the type of animals that were here or that there were so many of them. It was also mixed with the smell of urine and feces, which made her eyes water a bit.

Jessie spotted the elephants near the end of the row. There were a half dozen of them. They all had collars around an ankle with a chain attached to a large spike driven into the ground. It was just like the one the elephant calf had worn.

Jessie stopped to watch two young men washing the elephants. They scrubbed their sides with soapy water and rinsed them by throwing buckets of clean water on them. Meanwhile, the elephants ate apples and grain from troughs. Other than being restrained by the leg collars, they didn't seem mistreated.

Was one of these her baby elephant? She would be a year older now and presumably much larger.

"What is your job called?" Jessie asked one of the young men. He didn't look much older than Jessie. She doubted he was twenty.

"We're animal handlers," the young man said.

"Do you only work with the elephants?"

"No, we help care for all the animals." He paused and added, "You're not supposed to be back here."

"I'm sorry. I didn't touch anything. I just wanted to see the animals."

The man shrugged as he went back to scrubbed the elephant's side. "Well, don't get too close to them, especially the lions. They'll claw you."

Something wrapped around Jessie's arm. She looked over to see an elephant trunk. It tugged at her, and she saw a medium-sized gray elephant. Jessie stared at the elephant and then reached up to stroke her forehead.

She looked into the elephant's right eye. It looked familiar, and she was sure this had to be the same elephant she had met in the cornfield.

"Myrna likes you," the handler said.

"Myrna?"

"That's her name. She used to be a bit of a rebel, but she grew up and calmed down. Now she's a wonderful performer and the friendliest elephant here."

"A rebel?"

"When she was a calf, she used to pull at her chain all the time and cry a lot. Some of the other handlers thought she was too wild and couldn't be trained. I think she was just lonely and scared. We bought her from another circus a couple seasons ago, so we took her from her mom."

"So she's an orphan."

The young man shrugged. "I guess you can look at it that way, although the other elephants took her in. They're like that. Myrna did manage to run away for a week last year. It was while we were here, in fact."

The other handler laughed. "It's hard for an elephant to

hide, but she wandered on her own for almost a week. Myrna's no dummy."

Jessie felt her heart race. Myrna had run away while she was here in York? This had to be Jessie's elephant.

Jessie leaned closer and whispered, "Do you remember me, Myrna? From the cornfield?"

The elephant lifted her trunk and ran it around Jessie's head.

"I'm sorry they caught you. I didn't tell them where you were." She felt it was important that Myrna know Jessie hadn't betrayed her. Even if Myrna didn't understand what Jessie was saying, she hoped the elephant could feel what Jessie meant.

"Just push her trunk away if it bothers you," the handler said.

Jessie smiled. "It doesn't."

Jessie stayed a while longer, stroking Myrna's head and talking to her softly. When Jessie finally had to leave, Myrna huffed and then trumpeted, not loudly but loud enough that Jessie felt like she was abandoning the elephant.

While the other children talked excitedly about their adventures at the circus on the drive home, Jessie was quiet. She kept thinking about Myrna. The handlers seemed to like her. Myrna didn't look like she had new wounds, but Jessie hadn't looked behind her ears. She seemed to have plenty to eat and didn't look sickly. She was still being kept confined, though. Her life was moving between the big top and the menagerie. It wasn't natural for an elephant.

Leanne showed Jessie a small doll she had won by tossing three balls into milk bottles.

"It was hard. I used all my tickets to win her, including the ones you gave me. I'm going to call her Maria," Leanne said.

"After the lady who ate lunch with us?"

Leanne nodded. "Yes, that way I'll always remember where I got her."

"That's great."

"Are you all right, Jessie? You're very quiet. Didn't you have fun?"

"I did, but I kinda feel bad that I did. I saw the elephant calf."

"The one—" Leanne glanced around and then leaned in close to whisper, "from the cornfield?"

Jessie nodded. "Her name is Myrna."

"Like Myrna Loy in the movies?" Jessie shrugged. "How did she look?"

"She looks good. She's bigger now."

Leanne frowned. "I should have gone with you. I would have liked to have seen her."

"I think she recognized me."

"Really?"

"She was hugging me with her trunk, and trumpeted when I had to leave."

"Wow. Does she seem happy now?"

Jessie shrugged. "I couldn't tell. She didn't seem mistreated. At least there's that."

"Most of the animals seemed pretty happy in the show. They were excited, at least," Leanne said.

"But do the animals like what they're doing? The people do, or they wouldn't do it. But the animals don't have a choice."

"Neither do the animals at the farm, but you don't worry about them," Leanne countered.

Jessie nodded. That was true. They had cows, horses, chickens, and pigs at the farm. They were all kept confined and some of them were even eaten. She didn't feel bad for them.

Then she remembered Melvin being led off to the butcher. She felt terrible about that, but it didn't bother her that the animals were kept in stalls and pens. She did feel bad for the circus animals like Myrna, though.

By the time they arrived home, she realized why that was. None of the other animals had come to Jessie for help. Myrna had, and Jessie had failed her.

10

July 1936

By the time Jessie had lived three years at Wilson's Home for Children, she had come to accept that no one would adopt her. She was too old. Who would want a child who would be around for just a few years before venturing off on her own in the world?

Besides, she had come to love the Wilsons as if they were her parents. They were kind and caring and loved every child who came to stay with them. They treated the orphans as if they were their own children, so much so that Miss Erin was depressed for days after any of them were adopted.

Jessie considered all of the orphans her brothers and sisters, especially Leanne. That's why it hurt so much when Leanne was adopted. No one expected it, least of all Leanne. She said the Scarboroughs were an older couple who didn't have the energy to chase after a younger child, but they still wanted to help raise a child because Mr. Scarborough had been an orphan. He wanted to make a child's future brighter like his had been made better when he had been adopted.

When Leanne told Jessie the Scarboroughs were planning

on adopting her, something inside Jessie broke. She knew she should be happy for her friend. Things like this didn't happen to older orphans. It was a miracle, but Jessie couldn't be happy. She tried to smile, but it was a struggle. It was forced, and she couldn't hold it for long. This must be how Miss Erin when felt when one of the children left.

Nathan Chase, who had become her best friend outside of the orphanage, came to visit one afternoon and found Jessie in her private place in the cornfield. He tried to talk to her, but she just cried into his shoulder. He let her cry herself out. Then he let her talk about Leanne.

Jessie knew she was being selfish with both Leanne and Nathan. She should be happy for Leanne gaining a family. She should have asked Nathan about how things were going for him and his family. His father was having trouble finding work since the bank had let him go, and Nathan was working part-time to help earn money for his family. All she could do, though, was talk about how much she would miss Leanne who was as much a sister as a friend.

That evening when Leanne started talking to Miss Erin about her upcoming adoption, Jessie went upstairs and cried into her pillow. She fell asleep like that. When she woke, it was dark out. The bedside clock said it was four in the morning. Miss Erin must have decided to just let her sleep through dinner.

Jessie lay in bed, staring at the ceiling and wondered what it would be like next week when Leanne left. She watched the sun rise as it slowly grew lighter in the room. That's when she noticed Maria, the composite doll Leanne had won at the circus, propped against Jessie's headboard. Jessie picked it up and smoothed down the doll's light-blue dress as tears rolled down her cheeks. She and clutched the doll to her chest until it was time get up.

Everyone gathered in the living room to say goodbye to Leanne as they did for every orphan who was adopted. The younger children were excited, but Miss Erin, Leanne, and Jessie cried. Leanne and Jessie hugged each other until it was time to walk Leanne outside when the Scarboroughs pulled up in their car.

"I'll write," Leanne promised. "Take good care of Maria."

"But she's your doll," Jessie said.

Leanne hugged Jessie and kissed the doll on the head. "She's really our doll. Remember I won her at the circus using your tickets. Besides, I have a new family now. You keep Maria and remember me. I will always be your friend."

Jessie started crying and hugged the doll. "I will."

Mr. Frank left the house first with Leanne to give her and the Scarboroughs a few moments alone. When she was in the car, he opened the front door. Everyone streamed out onto the front porch and waved to Leanne as the car drove away.

Then they drifted back into the house in ones and twos. Jessie was the last one to leave. She watched the car disappear down the road until it was lost in a cloud of dust. She wondered where it was going and how far away Leanne would be living with her new family.

Jessie finally came inside and walked up to her room. Mary lay on her bed, reading a magazine. Leanne's bed had been stripped of its linens.

"I guess you have the bottom bunk now," Mary said.

Jessie stared at the empty bed and walked over to sit down on the mattress. She could almost feel Leanne's presence. Leanne had been her sister, more so than anyone else. And now that she was gone, it felt like Jessie had been orphaned again.

The Wilson Home never felt the same after Leanne left. It

didn't help that a new girl arrived one day when Jessie was out working with Dr. Stultz. Jessie came home and found Miss Erin showing the new orphan, Hazel, around the home. Jessie wondered if whoever had named Hazel did it because they first saw her hazel-colored eyes.

She was nice enough, but Jessie was reluctant to get too friendly with her. Hazel would never be Leanne, and besides, Jessie had other plans. She was alone again even though she lived in a house of orphans.

It had taken Jessie so long to call the place home, and now that her friend who had seemed more like her sister was gone, it felt like the first day she had come to the home, over and over.

She wished she could just leave and be alone with whatever her future held. She wasn't old enough yet. Even Mary wasn't old enough, but she was getting close. She vacillated between being excited about the prospect and worried over leaving the place she had known as her home for six years.

Almost unconsciously, Jessie began saving more of her earnings as Dr. Stultz's assistant. She told herself that if she wanted to go to veterinary school, she would need a way to pay for it. It was more than that, though. The more money she had, the more secure she would be. She had seen how people in town like Nathan's father struggled to make ends meet as the depression raged. Whatever the reason, she knew that the more money she could save, the better off she would be.

Each week, Dr. Stultz counted out her pay. It was just a couple dollars that she placed in an envelope under her mattress. Those few dollars added up week after week. The envelope grew thicker. Every few months, Jessie asked Mr. Frank to take her to the bank. He thought she was depositing her money, but she was actually trading smaller bills for larger ones so the envelope wouldn't be so thick. Although she had a savings account in the bank because the Wilsons had set up accounts for all their orphans, Jessie, like many other people, was leery of banks because so many of them had closed at the start of the depression and people had lost their money.

Then one Friday evening Jessie reached under her mattress for her money envelope and found it empty. The envelope was there, but it was empty.

She was still searching and re-searching every nook of the bedroom, looking for her money when Mary walked in.

"What are you doing?" Mary asked as she dropped down onto her bed.

Jessie was under the bed, searching for the money she had worked months to save. It should have been where she left it. She couldn't imagine it falling out from under the mattress.

"I had an envelope of money I saved from my job," Jessie said. "I kept it under the mattress, and now it's gone."

Mary lay back on the bed and stretched out. "Well, you should have kept it in a bank."

"Did you see it?"

Mary shook her head quickly. "No, of course not."

Jessie went downstairs and asked Miss Erin if she had seen the money when she was cleaning the room. Miss Erin assured her she hadn't, but she also told Jessie the money should have been in the bank.

Why did everyone think a bank was safer than under her mattress? Nathan told stories of how scared his father had been when people came to withdraw their money and there hadn't been enough money in the bank to cover all the withdrawals. The bank had had to shut down for days until more money could be borrowed from calling loans, and Nathan's father's bank hadn't been the only bank that didn't have enough money to pay people who wanted their money.

Jessie announced her money was missing at dinner, but

no one had even known she was saving money, let alone hiding it under her bed.

All her work was wasted! Jessie had been so careful, saving what she earned and only using her savings when she needed something important. Unlike the boys, she didn't buy herself toys. Everything she could manage to save went into the envelope. It was her future.

With no other choice, Jessie started saving her money again, but she was forced to open up a bank account and make deposits there each week.

Something told Jessie that Mary had taken the money. Jessie couldn't prove anything, but Mary started wearing some nicer clothes in the weeks after Jessie's money disappeared. Jessie asked her about it once, and Mary said she was using money she had saved up from her job.

That was a lie. The only money Mary saved was the money the Wilsons made them save. It was money they were supposed to get when they left the orphanage to help them get settled. Jessie still had that savings, but it wasn't nearly enough for her to get started on her own in a couple years.

Knowing Mary had probably stolen her money and was wasting it, just made Jessie want to leave even more. Why couldn't it have been Mary who was adopted, leaving Leanne and Jessie to be happy? Jessie knew it was a mean thought, but she couldn't help it. She missed Leanne.

Jessie saved even more for the next few months. She stashed the money in an envelope, but buried it in a corner of the barn where she knew Mary wouldn't find it.

When Mr. Frank took her to the bank one day to deposit a portion of her pay, instead of depositing money in her bank account, Jessie withdrew everything she had accumulated in the account.

Back at the Wilson Home, she packed a grain sack with a

change of clothes, some food she had managed to save, and Leanne's doll, Maria. Then she hid it under her bed.

That night, when Miss Erin came in to kiss the girls goodnight, Jessie said, "You know I love you, don't you?"

"That's an odd question, but, yes, I do know, and I love you, too."

Jessie hugged Miss Erin for a long time. When she finally let go, Miss Erin said, "What's gotten into you?"

"I was thinking about my family and how much I miss them," Jessie lied.

Miss Erin smiled. "Well, even when you're older and have a family of your own, you'll always have me and Mr. Frank."

Miss Erin stroked her cheek and then got up from the bed. She walked to the door and turned the light off.

"Goodnight, girls."

Jessie listened as the house quieted down. Floorboards stopped creaking, and she stopped hearing the murmur of voices from other rooms. Mary's breath got deeper as she fell asleep.

Even after Jessie was sure everyone had fallen asleep, she hesitated. She was scared, but she was also unhappy. Things had changed, and this place no longer felt like home.

She pushed back her blanket and slid out of bed. She reached under her bed and pulled out the grain sack, careful not to wake Mary, who would be all too happy to raise the alarm. Jessie had to be particularly careful creeping down the stairs because they tended to creak.

She took a pair of shoes from the line near the front door and eased open the door. On the front porch, she sat down to put on the shoes and pulled off her nightgown. She had remained dressed underneath it. She shoved the nightgown into the grain sack because she might need it.

Then she started off down the driveway to the main road at

a fast walk. Her plan was to walk to East Berlin, the town north of Abbottstown, where no one knew her. She would buy a bus ticket to York and then purchase a train ticket to Florida.

It was time for her to find a new home.

PART II

HOME FOR CIRCUS PERFORMERS

11
December 1936

Jessie stepped off the bus onto the side of the road. It rolled away, leaving her alone on the road, coughing from the exhaust fumes billowing out of the tailpipe. She was in the middle of a flat expanse. She could see a town in the distance. She wasn't sure which town, but she wouldn't want to have to walk there to find out.

She could see the red-and-white big top in the distance, looking like a giant peppermint candy. Green and yellow flags waved from poles above the tent about a 100 yards away.

Not for the first time on this trip Jessie wished Leanne was with her. Leanne had taken her own journey, though, and Jessie hadn't been able to go with her. In the end, they had both had to leave the Wilson home by themselves.

Jessie hefted the grain sack that served as her suitcase over her shoulder and started walking. Her destination was finally in sight.

Even though the circus winter quarters was along a rail siding, the train from York had only taken Jessie as far as

Winter Garden, Florida. From there, she had had to find a bus that was going past the circus property.

The Conroy and Pepperidge Circus sat in the middle of nowhere. It was an open, flat field near a lake, but there weren't even any trees around to provide shade from sun. It surprised her how warm it was in Florida, especially since it was the middle of December. In Pennsylvania, snow might be coating the ground now. Here, she could still have gone swimming.

The circus in winter was different than the circus on the road. She saw no ticket booths or midway games. The menagerie tent was much larger than the one she had seen in York, and it also had fenced in pastures around it. She noticed more tents set up than had been in York, and the performers were all over, relaxing, walking, practicing.

She found it surprising that she drew attention as she walked toward the big top. In this area where clowns wore full makeup, men juggled Indian clubs, and a woman who must have weighed 400 pounds walked and talked with a woman who seemed to have tattoos all over her body, a sixteen-year-old girl carrying a grain sack was an oddity. She was the one who attracted attention.

The grand big top was set up inside, its deep red and gold fabric stretched tautly over the sturdy poles. The canvas seemed almost translucent, letting in some light through the seams and the fabric. It was darker inside than out, but not as dark as she expected.

The usual rows of seating were missing, allowing for more space for performers to practice and perfect their acts. Above the bustling ground acts of dancers, clowns, knife throwers, and dog trainers, trapeze artists swung gracefully through the air and high-wire performers balanced precariously on thin ropes.

Winter was not a time for relaxation in the circus world. It was a time for hard work and dedication as performers honed new routines and mastered difficult stunts.

Jessie's eyes darted around the bustling tent, taking in the spectacle of acrobats and trained animals bouncing and twirling in harmony. She scanned the groups of people gathered, searching for Mr. Conroy, the owner of the circus. As an orphan herself, Jessie knew she was just one face among hundreds—maybe even thousands—that Mr. Conroy met every year during his travels with the circus. But he was her only point of contact in this strange world, and she hoped he would remember her.

Finally spotting him off to the side, Jessie made her way through the crowd toward Mr. Conroy. He stood tall in tan pants and a crisp white shirt with rolled-up sleeves, puffing on a cigarette as he watched the performers with a discerning eye. Occasionally, he would scribble something in his small notebook before calling out commands to the performers. Despite his outward appearance as a laborer, it was clear that Mr. Conroy was anything but ordinary—especially to those who were part of his beloved circus family.

Jessie took a deep breath and walked over to him.

"Mr. Conroy," she said as she set her grain sack beside her.

He barely glanced at her and then over at the Jack Russell terrier that was being uncooperative with the dog trainers and barking in a high-pitched yap.

"Quiet your mutt, Cecile! I've got a headache," he called out as he took a cigarette out and lit it.

"And Mary's bark is what's giving you a headache in all this confusion?" Cecile snapped.

"Well, it certainly isn't helping."

"Mr. Conroy," Jessie said timidly.

He looked over at her, longer this time. Then he noticed the grain sack at her feet. He frowned. "What do you want?"

Jessie straightened her shoulders and said firmly, "I came here to work for the circus." It was how the Wilsons had taught her to present herself for a job interview.

Mr. Conroy blew out a stream of cigarette smoke that curled around his head before disappearing toward the top of the big top. "What makes you think you can work for a circus? These performers have been training for years to do what they do."

Jessie shook her head. "I don't want to be a performer. I just want a job. I am a hard worker, and I can learn to do whatever job you need."

That gave him pause. She guessed most people had dreams of being a headline act.

"You don't want to be a showgirl or work the high wire?" He sounded like he didn't believe her.

Jessie shook her head. "No, sir."

"Why'd you come here then?"

"This was the circus I used to see as a child."

He gave her a quick glance up and down. "You're still a child."

"I'm sixteen."

"Like I said… Matt! Get the net down from ring one and set up the lion enclosure."

Jessie looked over her shoulder and saw a worker start to undo a rope that was holding up the corner of the trapeze net. It dropped slowly to the ground.

"I came every Orphans Day when you were in York," Jessie said.

Mr. Conroy stopped and stared at her. "You're an orphan?" Jessie nodded. "Did I ever talk to you?"

"Every year. You talked to all of the orphans, and you

asked a lot of us the same questions every year."

Mr. Conroy nodded and rolled his eyes. "Yes, I guess I did talk to you." Although he obviously didn't remember her.

"Why did you always ask the same questions?" Jessie asked.

He dropped his cigarette on the ground and crushed it with the toe of his shoe. "I never got the answer I wanted."

"What answer?"

"That's my business." He stared at her, his dark eyes taking her in. "So you think you can be of help here?"

Jessie perked up, sensing an opportunity for success. "I know I can. I'm willing to do anything to help. I can do odd jobs. I can sew. I can care for animals."

"Did you grow up on a farm?"

Jessie nodded, perhaps a bit too enthusiastically. "Yes, but I learned about caring for animals from helping a veterinarian."

Mr. Conroy raised an eyebrow. "Really? What type of animals did you work with?"

"Farm animals, mainly."

"Horses? Bulls? Dogs?" Jessie nodded after animal was named.

Mr. Conroy rubbed his chin. "Fine. We can always use good help taking care of the animals. I will give you a trial run. You can clean the animal stalls and feed them. When we have shows, if you're still around for the season, you can sell candy and popcorn."

Jessie clapped her hands together. "Thank you, Mr. Conroy."

Her first thought was that Miss Erin, Mr. Frank, and Dr. Stultz would be so proud of her. Then she remembered how she had left them without even a note, and it dampened her enthusiasm.

Mr. Conroy shook his head. "I've never seen anyone so

excited about shoveling..., well, cleaning animal stalls. Carl!" He started waving his hand for Carl to come over.

Carl was a midget who was about a head shorter than Jessie. He wore jeans and white shirt that were either specially made for him or a child's size. He hurried over, looked at Jessie, and then at Mr. Conroy.

"Carl, I just hired Jessie here. She'll be helping care for the animals and doing concession sales when we're on the road. Find her a place to stay."

"Sure thing, Jeremy." Jessie remembered that Jeremy was Mr. Conroy's first name.

Carl and Jessie walked out of the tent toward the rail siding. A long train sat on the line. The front of the train was made up of sleeper cars while the rear was box cars. The large, black engine at the front was massive, which it probably needed to be to pull such a long train.

"You look young," Carl said. "How old are you?"

"Sixteen. How old are you?"

Carl snorted and smiled. "Why do you want to know?"

Jessie shrugged. "It's only fair. You asked me first."

"I'm thirty-one." He walked a few more steps and said, "You'll be the youngest single girl around here. We have some younger girls, but they are part of family acts. They have rooms with their families. You'll be staying in a room with another single girl, but she'll be older."

"That's all right. I'm used to sharing rooms."

Carl chuckled. "It's generous calling the general rooms on the train 'rooms.'"

It was very warm out, and Jessie was starting to perspire from having to carry the grain sack.

They approached the train, and Carl pointed out the cars. "This one is for single women. Men aren't allowed. If they catch you with a man in your room, you can lose your job.

Since you're a first of May, you probably would."

"First of May?"

"It means that you're new to the circus and likely not last."

"That's presumptuous."

"It's experience. I've seen lots of people show up looking for jobs with the circus while we're in winter quarters, and almost none of them are still with us when we get back here."

"I'll be."

Carl chuckled to himself. "We'll see, but for what it's worth, I wish you luck."

They climbed aboard the sleeper car. It looked older than the train car she had ridden to Florida in. Although the outside of the car was clean, the inside looked shabby and smelled of metal. She saw roaches on the floor. Thankfully, they were all dead.

Carl saw where she was looking and said, "You don't want to go barefoot around here, even in your room." He knocked on the wall of the train car. "This is Carl. I've got a new girl who needs a room."

A woman walked down the hallway on one side of the train. Her red hair was in curlers, and she wore white slacks and light yellow blouse that seemed to shimmer.

"Who do we have here, Carl?" the woman asked.

"Frances Buchanan, this is Jessie. Jeremy hired her to help take care of the animals."

"She should be with the roustabouts and groundsmen. We don't have any other girl to room her with."

Carl gave her a look, as if to say, *Do I look stupid*? "If she were a boy, yes, I would take her there, but would you want to leave this young girl alone with them in their rail car?"

Frances nodded, and her curlers jiggled on top of her

head. "I see your point. Fine, I'll bunk her with one of the seamstresses."

Carl turned to Jessie and shook her hand. "Good luck, Jessie. I'll see you around."

"Thanks, Carl," Jessie told him.

Frances led her to the far end of the car. She knocked on the door. When no one answered, she fished a key from her pocket, unlocked the door, and opened it. The room was about eight feet square. Two fold-down bunks were on one wall. The other wall had a closet. The room also had a small table, a dresser, and a single window. It was smaller than Jessie had expected.

"You'll be rooming with Gail Westinghouse. She's nice and a talented seamstress."

When Jessie didn't say anything, Frances asked, "Are you all right?"

Jessie nodded. "Yes, it's just very small."

"We're on a train, dearie. It can't be too big. You won't spend much time in here. Most of the time, you'll be out with the animals or one of the common areas around the grounds. Most of us just sleep and change in our rooms. Sometimes not even that. There are shared bathrooms at either end of the car. The closest one for you is right next door."

"I'll get used to it," Jessie said.

Frances shrugged. "If you don't, you won't last long." She looked at the grain sack at Jessie's feet and then opened one side of the closet. It was empty. "This will be your side of the closet. You'll have to figure out the sleeping arrangements with Gail. She'll probably want to keep sleeping on the bottom bunk."

The room smelled like metal, which shouldn't have been surprising. What was surprising was that when she looked inside the closet, she saw a dozen or so roaches running on the floor. It made her jump.

"Didn't expect the glamorous circus life to be this glamorous, did you?" Frances asked.

"I'm not sure what I expected, but it wasn't roaches. I saw them in the hallway, too, but at least those were dead."

Frances chuckled. "Probably best to step on them if you see them, even though there don't seem to be any less of them no matter how many times you squash the buggers. You'll probably see worse before the season is over." She paused. "You can't shower on the train, so we set up shower rooms for men and women wherever we stop and sometimes additional bathrooms, too."

"Dinner?"

"Yeah, they may not pay a lot, but the circus feeds and houses us. Meals are in the cookhouse. Just ask someone where it's at, and they can direct you. They start serving at four p.m. Look for the blue flag over the tent."

Jessie nodded again, feeling overwhelmed.

"Did Carl have you sign papers yet?" Frances asked as she lit a cigarette.

"No."

Frances rolled her eyes. "Figures. He probably wanted to palm you off on me, so he could get back to work."

"I'm sorry."

Frances shook her head. "Don't be. Part of my job here is to watch over the single women."

"What else do you do?"

"I manage the midway games when we are on the road." She waved Jessie toward the door to the room. "Come on, I'll take you over to the paymaster's wagon and pawn you off on someone else."

"Don't you need to change first?"

Frances shrugged. "Not between seasons. It's only us circus

folk, and they have seen weirder outfits that what I'm wearing."

They walked toward the caboose. The rail car had bars on all the windows. Frances knocked on the closed door. A small window slid open. Jessie could see part of a man's face in the small opening.

"What, Frances?" the man inside asked.

"I've got a first of May for you, R. J."

"Why are you bringing her?"

"Carl left her with me. Jeremy hired her. She's going to care for the animals and work concessions. She needs to get on the payroll."

"Fine." Jessie heard the lock release and the door opened.

"The bars are to protect the money, not because he's dangerous," Frances said when she noticed Jessie hesitate going inside.

Jessie stepped into the brightly lit room. R. J., the man who let her inside, was tall and broad-shouldered, and he wore a pistol under his arm. She guessed he was a guard of some sort because he certainly looked like one.

The caboose smelled of cigarette smoke and was cloudy with it. She coughed. Behind her, the guard shut the door and engaged the lock. Another man sat at the desk tallying numbers. This man was closer to Jessie's size. He wore thick glasses and was almost sickly thin.

The man she thought was a guard said, "I'm Bennie McNabb, the paymaster. You'll get paid every Monday by either me or Pete here." Bennie pointed to the man at the desk. Pete looked up when he heard his name, waved briefly, and then went back to his figures. "You'll come here to get paid. You'll probably see a line. If you don't, knock on the door."

"Yes, sir."

Bennie laughed. "Sir. I haven't been called that in ever.

I'm just Bennie. What's your name?"

"Jessie Parsons."

Bennie grabbed a box up off the desk. He flipped the top open. It was a file of index cards. He pulled one from the back of the box and handed it to Jessie.

"Fill this out. You can write, can't you?"

Jessie nodded.

Bennie handed her a pencil and pointed to a chair at a desk. "Have a seat and fill out the information.

Jessie took a seat and began answering the questions on the card. Most of the information was basic: name, age, the job she would be doing. The only tricky question was the one that asked for the name and address of her closest living relative. Jessie wanted to write Miss Erin and Mr. Frank's names on the line. They had been like parents to her, but she was afraid someone might actually contact them and let them know she had joined the circus. Instead, she simply wrote, "None."

Bennie looked up what she would be paid for her duties. He had her write her job title and pay on the card. Finally, she signed the card. He took it from her and filed it in the index file.

Then he said, "Welcome to the circus, kid."

12
DECEMBER 1936

Frances and Jessie were talking when the door to Jessie's room opened and a red-haired woman walked in. She wore horn-rimmed glasses that made her brown eyes look larger than they were. The woman jumped when she saw Frances and Jessie.

"What's going on?" the woman asked.

"Gail Westinghouse, this is Jessie Parsons," Frances said. "Jessie is going to be your roommate for now. Since I've got work to do, I'll leave you two alone to get acquainted." With that, Frances strolled out of the room.

People just pawning her off on someone else. Mr. Conroy to Carl to Frances and now Gail. Was she that big a burden?

Gail looked Jessie up and down. "You look pretty young."

"I'm sixteen."

"What do they have you doing?"

"I'm going to take care of the animals."

Gail raised her eyebrows. "Really? That's unusual for a girl."

"I grew up on a farm and worked part-time for the town veterinarian," Jessie said.

Gail nodded. "Oh, that makes sense."

"Which bed should I sleep on?"

Gail didn't even hesitate. "The top. My bones are too old to be climbing up and down that ladder every morning and night."

Frances had been right about which one Gail would choose. Frances had said Gail was old enough to be her mother. That was doubtful. Jessie guessed Gail was no more than ten years older than her, but she played up the old lady act when it helped her get what she wanted.

Other than that, she was nice. That was a good thing, seeing as how the room could get very crowded when the two women were trying to dress in the morning. They tended to bump into each other a lot, so both of them needed to be tolerant and forgiving of the other.

Sleeping in the top bunk reminded Jessie of her bed in the Wilson home. Of course, Leanne wasn't sleeping below her, so Jessie couldn't whisper to her. She felt as alone as she had felt the first night with the Wilsons.

Another girl was probably sleeping in the top bunk at the home by now. Did the Wilsons even miss her? She hoped they did because Jessie missed them.

Mornings at the circus started at six o'clock, at least for Jessie. Although the sun wasn't up yet, she could still feel humidity in the air. However, the morning air was cool and pleasant, and she and Gail usually opened the window to let in fresh air before it became too humid.

They had to be at work by nine o'clock, which meant they tended to follow a routine to minimize their time spent in lines waiting to use the bathroom or shower or getting breakfast at the cookhouse. Jessie usually hurried to the shower house as soon as she was up to avoid the lines waiting to use the bathroom on the rail car. Then, by the time she came back to the rail car, one of the bathrooms was usually free.

By the time Jessie was with the circus a week, she realized it was like her school had been. Lots of people with different personalities had been thrown together in one classroom, or in this case, one big top. Some, like the performers, were considered better than others. Jessie hadn't met a friend like Nathan or Leanne. She missed playing in the yard with other orphans at the home. They had had such fun swinging on the tire swing or jumping in hay piles.

The circus was so different from the farm or even school. The different cliques didn't mix much. They even had different areas where they sat in the cookhouse. Jessie had thought she was joining the adult world and the glamour of the circus. Instead, it felt like she was back in school.

Jessie floated between two groups. She fit in with the animal handlers, but she also fit in with the seamstresses and concession workers since she roomed with Gail. However, both were somewhere in the middle of the pecking order, above the roustabouts but below the performers. She was an oddity among oddities.

Surprisingly, the animals were at the top of the order. They were what brought people into the circus. Townies wanted to see animals that they had only seen in movies and zoos. Zoo animals could be boring, though. They paced their small enclosures, slept, or hid away from visitors. The animals at the circus performed tricks, which was something every child wanted to see. Not only that, but exotic animals were a large investment, so owners wanted to keep them healthy to get a return on that investment. Jessie couldn't reconcile this with what Dr. Stultz had told her about how trainers treated the animals.

Jessie was happy to see the animals treated well. She was especially happy that she got to spend time with Myrna. The young elephant had actually trumpeted when she first saw Jessie enter the menagerie.

While Jessie had plenty of work to keep her busy, she made time to visit the elephants. Myrna reminded her she had at least one friend with the circus.

On her way to menagerie one morning, Jessie stopped to watch Miquel Torres climb the rope ladder to the trapeze. He wore a tight leotard that made her imagination race. He was a handsome man with powerful shoulders and arms.

"You're asking for trouble, Jessie."

She looked down and saw Carl standing next to her. He had seen her fawning expression. She blushed.

"Why? I'm not a bad person," Jessie asked.

Carl nodded. "No, you're great, kid, but you aren't part of his group. Miquel will treat you nice. He's a good kid, too, but he's a performer. You'll learn there are unwritten rules around a circus, and one is that performers don't associate with the workers."

"It's a stupid rule."

Carl shrugged, but he didn't argue with her.

"It's no different than out in the world," Carl said. "You don't see rich and poor eating together or taking walks together. You've seen how it is in the cookhouse."

"I don't want to date him." Carl raised an eyebrow. "Really. I met him once when I went to the circus a couple years ago. He was nice."

Carl snorted. "Of course he was. You were a paying customer."

"Not paying. I was an orphan there on Orphans Day."

Carl shrugged. "You were still a customer as far as he was concerned."

"You are callous, Carl."

He held his hands out to his sides as if showing off. "At my height, you learn about a lot of hard realities quick in life."

Jessie patted him on the shoulder. "You fit in here, though."

Carl nodded. "This is the place for people who don't fit in anywhere else. So do you not want to walk over to the pay car together?"

"Pay car?"

Carl's eyebrows shot up. "What? Are you working for free?"

"Of course not."

"Well, today's Monday. It's payday."

She had forgotten that this was a paying job, and she had been here a week already. She hadn't realized it was Monday until Carl said something. It had gone by quickly with her trying to learn everything she needed to know for her job.

"At my other jobs, the boss handed me my pay on payday," Jessie said.

Carl scoffed. "Do you know how many people work for this circus?" Jessie didn't, but she knew it had to be hundreds. "If Jeremy tried to take everyone their pay, he wouldn't finish until next pay day."

They walked to the pay car where Jessie had filled out paperwork to sign up for the circus. A line of people stood outside the car. They slowly made their way onto the car's platform where she recognized R. J. the guard standing. He allowed a single person at a time to enter the pay car.

When it was Jessie's turn, she went inside the paymaster's car and saw Bennie McNabb.

"Name?" he said without looking up.

"Jessie Parsons."

He rifled through his file box and found her card and looked at it. Then he opened a cash box and counted out her pay.

"I see you made it through your first week," he said. "Congratulations."

"Thank you, sir."

"I'm just Bennie," he reminded her.

Outside, Carl saw her with her money still in hand, he said, "Put that away."

"What am I supposed to do with it?"

"Spend it, of course."

"I don't really need to spend it on anything. The circus gives me a place to live and food to eat."

"Well, then, find a safe place where you can hide it in your room, but don't make it someplace obvious like under your mattress or in the clothes in your drawers."

Jessie remembered how Mary had stolen her hard-earned savings. She would definitely find a safe place.

"What about a bank?"

"Banks aren't safe. Look how many failed when the market crashed."

"What market?"

Carl rolled his eyes. "The stock market. When it crashed, it caused a lot of banks to eventually fail, but there are still some decent banks in town where you can deposit your money if you want."

Jessie remembered how Nathan Chase's family had nearly been ruined when his father's bank failed.

"The problem is that it's hard to access that money while we're on the road if it is in a bank."

She thought about it. "Since I don't need too much now, I

think I'll save what I make in winter quarters in the bank and hide the rest on the road."

"Not a bad plan. Want me to take you into town to the bank?"

"Sure that would be fun. We can have lunch and see what's in town."

They had to take the bus into Winter Garden. Even if they had had a car, Carl was too short to drive and Jessie didn't have a driver's license. They walked from the bus stop to the bank where Mr. Conroy had the circus accounts. People stared at Carl, and some pointed at him as they walked. He didn't seem to notice, but when people made a comment, Jessie noticed his jaw clench tightly.

"I appreciate you helping me with this," Jessie said. "Lunch is on me."

The people in the bank knew Carl and were more than helpful to Jessie as she opened a savings account. Afterward, Jessie and Carl had hamburgers and French fries in a diner. Carl patiently answered her questions about circus life and told her funny stories about the performers.

Jessie thanked Carl again when they got back to the circus and excused herself because she had to feed the animals. It was the main part of her work with the animals. She fed the chimpanzees, lions, horses, elephants, and other animals. She also cleaned the animal cages and stalls in the menagerie along with half a dozen other animal handlers.

It hadn't taken her long to be the primary caregiver for the elephants. The other handlers were more than willing to take over caring for the elephants exclusively because they took a lot of time to feed, water, and wash. Because of their size, they ate around 350 pounds of food daily. Their days were spent practicing, performing, sleeping, and eating a lot of eating. Their diet in the circus consisted primarily of hay, but also fruit, roots, and even tree bark sometimes. It depended on what was available and what the circus could afford.

Jessie didn't mind the extra effort because it gave her a reason to spend more time with Myrna. Jessie would talk to Myrna and the other elephants while she worked. She didn't feel so lonely then.

Filling the water trough and the food troughs was a workout, and Jessie found her body aching from the exercise during her first week of the circus.

She needed to wash the elephants before they ate so she wouldn't soak their food or get soap on it. She filled a large bucket with soap and water and walked over to Myrna first. She was Jessie's favorite. Jessie held up the burbling hose. Myrna nodded and reached out to stick her trunk in the arcing water.

"Bath time," Jessie said.

The other elephants stirred at the sound of her voice. In her short time with them, they had gotten used to her, or maybe Myrna had let the others know Jessie was a friend. Either way, they accepted her, often stroking her with their trunks, which made Jessie laugh.

She sprayed the elephants with water, and they jockeyed for a position to get under the stream of water. Patti flapped her ears in delight. Jo-Jo laid down in the forming mud puddle. Daisy turned in slow circle. Flo walked away from the water—at least as far as the chains around her legs would let her. Myrna waited patiently, knowing Jessie would give her a healthy dose of water.

Each elephant had her own personality, but none of them seemed dangerous. However, Samuel Atwell, the elephant trainer, had warned her almost daily to never forget they were wild animals.

"Think of them as prisoners," he said. "We are kind jailers, but we are jailers just the same. They may like us, but what prisoner, given the opportunity, wouldn't make a break for freedom?"

He had also told her the story of Mary, an elephant that had been with the Sparks World Famous Shows in 1916. She had been a trained elephant, but her unqualified handler had jabbed her with a bullhook at the wrong moment. Mary went into a rage, grabbed the handler, flung him into a drink stand, and stepped on his head, killing him.

The public outcry was so furious that the circus owner had to kill the elephant in order to keep the backlash from ruining the circus. And like a condemned prisoner, Mary was hanged by the neck from a rail car-mounted derrick until she died. It was later determined that Mary had an infected tooth, which happened to be where the handler hit her with the bullhook.

Jessie knew Samuel was trying to show her that even a trained elephant could turn on a person while also highlighting his comparison of circus animals to prisoners. What Jessie took from the story was that she needed to do everything she could to keep the elephants healthy and never forget they were wild animals.

Once the elephants were drenched, Jessie turned off the water. She stuck a long-handled brush in the bucket and got it soapy. Then she began scrubbing Myrna's side. Myrna stuck her trunk in the trough filled with drinking water and sprayed herself off.

Jessie laughed. "At least let me finish washing you."

Myrna sprayed her lightly.

Jessie washed the six elephants, singing to them as she did. She sang songs Miss Erin had sung to the orphans at the home. Jessie had tried to remember some of the songs her mother had sung to her before the fire, but she was surprised to find that she couldn't remember any of them.

Once Jessie was finished washing the elephants, she checked their feet and teeth to ensure they were healthy. She also looked at their legs and behind their ears to make sure they weren't being abused. They all carried old scars from bullhooks. Jessie had seen a bullhook, but she had never seen it used in a way that would injure an elephant, but then, these were trained elephants who didn't often, if ever, need a bullhook to get them to do something.

Their feet needed to be checked daily just to make sure they were healthy. Elephant toenails grew a quarter- to a half-inch a month. She had started filing each elephant's toenails monthly to keep them manageable. In the wild, elephants dig their nails into the ground as they grazed. This action kept their nail length reasonable. They couldn't dig in captivity, which is why Jessie filed their nails. If their nails got cracked in captivity, it was likely they would get infected, because along with eating 350 pounds of food each day, an elephant had to get rid of it in the form of about fifteen gallons of urine and 300 pounds of feces. Jessie cleaned their enclosure three times a day to do her best to keep their feet from getting infected.

They were all in good shape, so she fed them hay and oranges.

"You handle them very well."

Jessie turned and saw Samuel Atwell watching her. He was in his late thirties and was almost as thin as the dark mustache he wore. He was not how Jessie imagined an elephant trainer looked, but he was very good at his job.

"I don't have to do much. Plus, they know I'm not going to hurt them," Jessie said.

"They came to trust you quickly. That's unusual. It's not natural for them to listen to someone a lot smaller than them, especially if you're not prodding them with a bullhook."

Jessie's eyes widened. "I would never do that!"

Samuel held up his hands. "I'm not saying you did, but sometimes they need to be disciplined when they act like a children throwing a tantrum."

Jessie didn't like how that sounded because she knew how children were often disciplined. Even Miss Erin had smacked her bottom on occasion, and it hadn't been a pleasant experience. She had only done it when Jessie did something truly bad, like punch one of boys and give him a black eye.

Samuel saw the frown on her face. "You think there is a better way?"

"I couldn't say. I just know I don't like to see animals hurt."

Samuel nodded. "I don't either, but I also don't want to be hurt by one of the animals."

She wondered if she was going to get another lecture about elephants being prisoners. She hoped not. The first time she had heard Mary's story, she had nightmares for three nights.

Samuel walked over and patted Myrna's side. He pulled an apple from a bag at his side and pushed it into her mouth. She grabbed it and started chewing.

"I don't usually give them snacks for no reason, but when training is a mix of the stick and carrot, if you don't want to use the stick, you need to use more carrot."

Now that was something Jessie could agree with and not have nightmares over.

"I noticed you checking behind their ears and ankles," Samuel said. "Did you notice anything?"

"No fresh scars." She said it with a bit more relief than she had intended.

Samuel nodded. "That's because I don't hurt them if I

can avoid it. I only use my bullhook as a guide, not a poker. I treat my animals well, and I won't allow anyone else to mistreat them. If I find that happening, I stop it. Unfortunately, some of these animals have had trainers who weren't as gentle. Different trainers have different techniques. I'm surprised you know what to look for."

"I used to work for a veterinarian. He told me about bullhooks. I've also seen scars on a circus elephant before." She didn't want to name Myrna and have Samuel wonder how she had seen the scars.

Samuel sighed. "That's unfortunate, but it is the norm."

"If you don't like bullhooks, why use one then?"

"For the same reason prison guards are armed. For protection and to quell any problems. It is an extreme measure, but sometimes, that kind of extreme force is needed." He looked like he was thinking of perhaps a time when it had been needed. Jessie hoped he wouldn't tell her. She didn't need more nightmares.

Samuel watched her finish up working with the elephants. He left without Jessie noticing. When she finished, she headed over to the cookhouse. She passed a roustabout sitting in a chair in the shade and reading a copy of *As I Lay Dying* by William Faulkner.

"Is that a good book?" She was always looking for something to read during her free time because she didn't like drinking and gambling. They seemed to be the favorite pastimes of people with the circus.

He looked up from behind the book. He was not an unhandsome with gray eyes, but for some reason, he projected a sense of feeblemindedness, even though he was reading Faulkner.

"I haven't decided yet." He closed the book and set it in his lap. "It has many different narrators. It can be confusing, but it is interesting. It's about a woman who died and her poor family all have different reasons for wanting to honor her request to be buried in her hometown."

"It sounds sad."

He shrugged. "It's not as interesting to read as *Gone With the Wind*. I quite enjoyed that." He paused. "My name is Mick."

"I'm Jessie. I work with the elephants."

"I guess that's safer than lions or bears."

Jessie shook her head as she remembered Mary's story. "They may take longer to anger, but you don't want an elephant angry with you."

Mick smiled. "I'll keep that in mind."

He stared at her until she started to feel uncomfortable.

"I guess I'd better be going," Jessie said finally. "I need to eat before I head to menagerie. I'll see you around."

She gave a short wave and walked away. When she turned to go around the costume tent, she saw Mick was still watching her from his chair.

13

DECEMBER 1936

After two weeks with the circus, Jessie still felt like a fish out of water. People were friendly enough, but she hadn't found anyone she would call a friend. Gail was her roommate and slept in the lower bunk like Leanne had done, but they weren't close like Jessie and Leanne had been. Gail was like an older sister, looking out for her younger sibling. Some nights she wished Leanne was there with her, but she was probably happy with her adopted family.

Frances and Samuel were a cross between parental figures and bosses. While they were in charge of certain aspects of her life, they also watched out for her, trying to ease her transition to circus life. It reminded her of how Miss Erin and Mr. Frank had helped Jessie adjust to being an orphan. Jessie didn't miss them as much with Frances and Samuel helping her.

Jessie also didn't fit in with the other animal handlers. They were young men who talked about drinking and women. Then there was the social system that was part of the circus. It limited who she was expected to associate with.

She even had to be careful around the animals. At least most of them. She didn't want to walk behind a horse at the wrong time and be kicked in the head or have an elephant step on her foot.

At least she had Myrna. What did it say about Jessie that her closest friends with the circus were the elephants?

She walked to the menagerie for her morning routine of watering and feeding the animals and changing the hay. It was a lovely morning with temperatures in the lower seventies, and the sun was shining. In Pennsylvania, this would have been a pleasant spring day. In Florida, it was a winter day.

As she passed between the tent where the clowns changed and the big top, she watched a clown dressed in a baggy bright red suit and yellow shirt run down the alley. His overly large floppy red shoes smacked on the ground. His fuzzy orange hair bounced around as if the locks of hair were springs.

He suddenly tripped and somersaulted forward, landing on his back.

Jessie gasped. She rushed over to help him to his feet. As she got nearer, his back arched, and he flipped forward, landing on his feet. Then he saw her and took a bow.

Jessie clapped. "That was part of the act, wasn't it?"

"Yes. Did you like it?"

"I was scared for you. I thought you tripped over your shoes."

The clown straightened out his suit. "Maybe I need to make it more flamboyant, so it is obvious that it's planned."

Jessie nodded. "Maybe."

"What if I drop something or bend over to tie my shoes and then wind up falling over?"

Jessie tried picturing a funny fall in her mind. "That

could be funny. It depends on what you drop."

The clown nodded. "I'll think about it and talk it over with the other clowns."

Jessie started to walk past him.

"Sorry I scared you," the clown said. "My name is Bradley Starr. I'm a clown."

Jessie looked him up and down. "I think I could have guessed that."

Bradley held out his hand, and Jessie shook it.

"Is Starr your performing name?" Jessie asked.

He chuckled. "No, it's my real name. Starr with two Rs."

"Well, I'm Jessie Parsons. I help take care of the animals."

"I always thought taking care of the animals would be a great job. I love watching them perform. I'm always tempted to pet the lions because they look like cuddly cats."

"You haven't tried that, have you?"

Bradley laughed. "I'm still alive, aren't I? I leave the big cats alone, but I like to help Cecile walk her dogs sometimes."

The dogs weren't part of the menagerie, so Jessie didn't care for them. Cecile felt strongly that she needed to care for her own animals. They were definitely a lot safer to pet than the lions.

"I have thought about trying to work a dog into my performance," Bradley said.

"Kids like dogs. I think they'd like it."

Bradley nodded. "Yes, that's what I think, but I've got to get my skits for this season perfected before I start thinking about expanding."

"Well, I'll let you get back to work. I've got to get to the menagerie and feed the animals."

"Would you mind if I tagged along? It's been a while since I've stopped by the menagerie. I really do miss the animals."

Jessie shrugged. Bradley was pleasant company, and she needed to get moving.

A wave of urine and musk hit her as she entered the tent. It burned the hairs in her nose. She looked over at Bradley, but he seemed unaffected. Maybe the ball on the end of his nose kept him from smelling it.

While she wanted to clean the enclosures first, it would be easier to do after the animals had eaten. They would be calmer then as they digested their meals.

"I'll fill the water troughs while you feed them," Bradley said.

"You don't have to do that."

"I know, but I don't mind." He saw one of the other animal handlers filling a bin with oats and waved. "Dave, hi!"

Dave McIntyre waved back. "Bradley, what brings you here, especially in costume?"

"It's been a while, and when Jessie said she was on her way over, it sounded like a good idea."

"Maybe after we've cleaned out the stalls."

Bradley waved a hand as if it was nothing. "You should smell the bathroom after my dad uses it. If he could control his farts, he would be able to rocket himself across the big top like the Human Cannonball. Of course, if he did, everyone would pass out."

Dave laughed. "Good to see you, Bradley."

Well, Jessie knew Bradley hadn't been lying when he said he used to visit here. He not only knew the handlers, but he knew where everything was located.

While he filled the elephant trough with fresh water, Daisy played with his flared coat, making it bounce up and down with bursts of air.

"You like my costume, girl?" he asked.

Daisy wrapped her trunk around him like she was giving

him a hug. He stroked her forehead and whispered to her.

Then Jessie saw him reach into his pocket and pull out an apple. He slipped it into Daisy's mouth. She let go of him while she munched on the apple.

"You shouldn't do that," Jessie warned him.

"Why not?"

"Samuel says a treat should only be used to reward the elephants after they perform a trick right. Otherwise, they can get stubborn and expect them all the time."

"Samuel's the one I saw doing it. Besides, you're feeding them their meal. She'll think it's part of the meal."

Samuel had been the one who scolded her for giving the elephants treats. Now, she was being told he did it? It didn't make sense.

"I like to give extra attention to the lions and tigers," Bradley said. "I feel bad that they are always in some sort of cage. Even when they perform, the handlers set up fencing around them. You have to be careful around them, though. Even Sergei doesn't go into the cage with them without being armed." Sergei Valencio was the big cat trainer.

"I prefer the elephants."

"I can see that. Why are they your favorites?"

Jessie looked around. She felt comfortable with Bradley and decided to tell him the truth. Besides, it shouldn't make much of a difference now.

"Myrna ran away from the circus years ago."

How long had he been with the circus? He looked her age. Would he remember an incident from three years ago?

"I remember that. Samuel was so upset. We'd only had her a month or so. Mr. Conroy was angry because she cost so much."

"Well, I found her in the cornfield where I lived. I took care of her for a couple days and really came to love her.

Then they found her and took her back to the circus."

"You know you couldn't have taken care of her yourself. She's not a pet. You probably would have exhausted yourself getting enough food for her each day, especially when she started growing."

Jessie sighed. "I know it now, but I was only thirteen at the time, and she was less than a year old."

"So those couple of nice days with her sparked your interest."

Jessie nodded.

"So why did you want to become a clown?" she asked.

Bradley hesitated, then said, "It was kind of opposite of you. My family has performed with circuses for four generations. We are aerialists."

Jessie held up a hand. "Wait a minute. The aerialists are the Terrific Torres."

Bradley nodded. "That is my family. Torres is their performing name, so they can sound foreign. Townies think it's more exciting to see an act from another country than one from Nashville, Tennessee."

"So Miquel is…"

"My older brother, although his real name is Michael."

"Oh." She was surprised that knowing his name did change how she looked at him. Michael Starr, in her mind, was a regular-looking, ordinary man, not an exotic foreigner who could fly through the air.

"Let me guess. You think he's handsome and would love for him to ask you out."

Jessie blushed. "I didn't say that."

"You didn't have to. Half the women with the circus feel that way, including some who are old enough to be our mother."

"You sound jealous."

Bradley shook his head. "I'm not, at least not about that. I'm obviously not one of the Terrific Torres. My parents are disappointed I am not performing with them. Michael did, so he's their favorite."

Jessie's family had died before she had had to compete with her brothers for her parents' attention. She wondered if she would have been jealous of them instead of feeling guilty.

"But you're doing something you like," she told Bradley.

"I am. I want to make people laugh and be happy."

"There's nothing wrong with that."

"Maybe, but a clown is not a headliner like my family's act is at times."

He sounded sad, but with the broad smile painted on his face, it was hard to tell if he was.

"Have your parents gotten over the fact that you aren't an aerialist?"

"Oh, they still love me. I know that. And they are happy that I am with the same circus. I could have left to join a different one, and we would have only seen each other when the circuses were in winter quarters. They are just disappointed I'm not part of the family work."

They continued talking until the animals were all fed. Then Bradley said he needed to get back to the clown tent to work on his act.

"Oh, so when it's time for dirty work, you leave?" Jessie joked.

"When you can paint yourself as a clown and do prat falls, then I will clean the enclosures."

Jessie shrugged. "Fair enough."

Bradley looked surprised even under his makeup. "You mean you are going to learn to be a clown?"

Jessie threw some hay at him with a pitchfork. "No, I

mean your deal was fair, but I'm going to stick with the animals." She paused, then added, "Thanks for the help feeding the animals."

"My pleasure. I'll see you around." He waved and then walked out of the menagerie.

Later that evening while she was standing in line for dinner, she heard a voice behind her say, "Hi, Jessie."

She turned and saw a young man she didn't recognize. He had unruly blonde hair and a bright smile that reached his blue eyes. He looked her age, maybe a year or two older. She could swear she hadn't seen him among the people with the circus, let alone know his name.

"I'm sorry. Have we met?" Jessie asked.

He grinned. "You mean you don't remember me and the wonderful afternoon we spent together?"

Jessie's eyes widened. This young man knew her name, but she had never met him and certainly never spent the afternoon with him.

Then he started laughing, and she realized who it was.

"Bradley!"

She slapped him lightly on the arm.

"You should have seen your expression when you thought you had forgotten a day," he said.

"A clown is supposed to make other people laugh, not himself."

Bradley shrugged and grinned. "I'm multi-talented. I can do both."

She looked at him and thought he was just a couple years older than her. For some reason, she had thought he was older. It must have been his outfit and makeup that confused her.

"Aren't you young to be a clown?"

He shrugged. "Who can tell under the makeup?"

"Do you want to eat with me?"

He smiled. "I would love to, but we'll have to do it somewhere other than the cookhouse." Jessie had learned about the performers and workers not being able to eat together in the cookhouse, and she didn't like it. "The rule is we can't eat together in here. Performers and workers go out to town all the time. I'm sure some of them eat together. I know they drink together. So, if they can do that, I guess we can eat together in the clown tent."

Jessie drew back a bit. "Wow. You missed your calling. You should have been a lawyer with that kind of logic."

"Well, no one would eat with a lawyer."

They took their meals on trays and walked to clown alley where the clowns practiced, changed, and put on their makeup. Although the tents were large, two were still needed to house all the clowns and their equipment. One tent was set up for changing into all the outfits they wore. The outfits hung on hangers from a bar. Wigs sat on stands in a row. Oversized shoes were lined up on low shelves. Props were stored in a row of trunks along one wall of the tent.

The other tent had lighted mirrors over tables. The clowns sat on stools in front of the mirrors and applied their makeup.

Jessie and Bradley set their trays on a table and sat down next to each other. The meal this evening was meatloaf and mashed potatoes.

After taking a bite, Bradley said, "This is pretty good tonight. Sometimes you can't tell the potatoes from the meatloaf."

Jessie chuckled. "The food here isn't bad, but it's nothing like Miss Erin used to cook."

"Miss Erin?"

Jessie nodded. "She and Mr. Frank ran the orphan's home where I used to live. It was a farm. Miss Erin did all the cooking, and she was a wonderful cook."

"You're an orphan?"

Jessie nodded.

"What happened to your parents?"

Jessie hesitated, surprised to find that she hadn't thought about her family in weeks. Was she forgetting them? She rubbed her forearm through her shirt.

"They were killed in a fire," she said after a moment.

"How old were you?"

"Thirteen."

Bradley's brow furrowed as he thought about something. "So that was the same year you met Myna?"

Jessie nodded. "It was the summer after the fire. I had been with the Wilsons for a few months."

"That's tough. I can't imagine having grown up without my family, even though they weren't happy with my choice about being a clown."

"How is that? Growing up in a circus?"

Bradley shrugged. "Just the same as it is now. The family has a larger space on one of the rail cars, but it is still small for six people. It is like living in a town that is always moving, and everyone knows your parents. I couldn't get away with anything. Now, that I'm a clown, I'm starting to create my own life where I'm not with my family all the time."

"I wouldn't mind that." She wasn't with her family at all.

Bradley realized what he had said, and said, "Sorry, I didn't mean to bring up bad memories."

"Only some of them are bad."

Bradley buttered a roll and took a bite. "How do you like the circus?"

"I like it, but it's different than I expected."

"Most people say that. It will be even more different once the season starts."

"Are all circuses like this one?"

Bradley nodded. "I can remember being with three circuses. They were all pretty much the same. The big difference is the size of the circuses. Ringling is the big one with three rings. We're somewhere in the middle. Heck, even some of the people with the circuses I've been with are the same. The circus attracts a lot of people, but those who stay are different."

"It's a place for people who have no place."

Bradley thought about that. "It's more than that. It's a place for people who have unique talents and desires. One of my uncles tried to leave the circus life for a townie girl he met. He quit working as an aerialist and got a job in an office. Sitting at a desk everyday wore him down and nearly destroyed him."

"How sad!" Jessie said.

"He finally quit after less than a year. He came back to the circus, but he wasn't the same. His confidence was gone. He couldn't perform. He knew what to do, but he just couldn't do it anymore."

"Did he have to leave again?"

Bradley shook his head. "No, like you said, the circus is a place for people who have no place. Mr. Conroy had him work the concessions and games. That wound up breaking him even more. He had been a performer, a star. Seeing the family perform without him was a constant reminder of what he had given up."

"What happened to him?"

"He died two years ago. He wasn't sick or injured. He just didn't wake up one morning. My mother says he died from sadness."

Jessie laid her hand on his arm. "I'm so sorry."

"It is one reason my family didn't want me to be a clown. They thought I would be constantly reminded that I wasn't an aerialist, and it would destroy me. It doesn't, though."

"They don't understand that being a clown is what makes you happy. If you had been an aerialist, then you would have been sad."

Bradley slapped a hand on the table. "Exactly! You understand."

Jessie did. She might not be a performer, but she wasn't sad. She was working with the animals, animals that she had only ever seen in a circus or zoo. Even Dr. Stultz would have been challenged caring for them all.

This was her dream.

14

JANUARY 1937

The Conroy and Pepperidge Circus rang in 1937 with lots of drinking and dancing. The circus folk could be as loud as they wanted because no one was around to disturb. Winter quarters was a giant field outside of Winter Gardens, Florida. The closest home was more than a mile away. They were the only ones in the world, and they wanted to celebrate. Frances Buchanan even let Jessie have a beer and later a shot of whiskey even though Jessie was still too young to drink. Jessie hated the taste of both of them and failed to see the attraction. Then Frances let her take a few puffs of a cigarette.

Jessie ran as far away from the crowd partying in the big top as she could, fell to her knees, and vomited onto the ground. The smell wafted up from the green mess and caused her stomach to heave again.

She felt her hair lifted off her neck. She looked behind her between heaves and saw Frances holding her hair back.

"Believe me, sweetheart, you don't want what's in your stomach on your hair," Frances said.

Jessie clutched her stomach. "I don't think there could be anything more in my stomach."

Frances grinned. "You'd be surprised."

"Why'd you let me do that?"

Jessie's stomach still felt like it might have a heave or two left in it, so she sat on the ground to wait for it to pass. Besides, she wasn't too sure she could trust her legs right now.

"You were going to try them eventually. Better you try them with someone like me around."

Someone like her? Was Jessie supposed to be grateful to Frances for letting her get sick? How did that help Jessie?

Jessie tried to lay on her back, but that seemed to make her stomach feel like it was full of dirty water sloshing around. So she stayed in a seated position.

"Why doesn't everyone get sick?" Jessie asked.

"A lot of them probably did the first time they tried booze or cigarettes."

"Then why keep doing it?"

Frances shrugged. "You can get used to it, especially the booze. That's why I let you try it tonight with me watching. You won't feel good tomorrow morning. You might even feel worse, but at least you'll wake up in your own bed and not with one of those big top Romeos beside you."

Jessie's head was starting to hurt already, but she understood what Frances was saying. She had seen enough animals having sex to know that they weren't the only ones doing it in a circus. For some of the men and women in the circus, it was a game like the coochie show. They wanted to see how many partners they could have. Jessie wasn't sure she knew what to do or if she was even ready for that yet.

"Thank you," Jessie said.

"It's part of my job." Jessie doubted that, but she appreciated that Frances was looking out for her, even if it made her sick to her stomach right now.

Frances reached out a hand and helped Jessie to her feet. The world spun round, and she could feel each inch of movement. She felt she would fall over. Frances steadied her.

"Let's get you back to your bunk. I think you'll have to sleep with the straps up tonight."

Each bunk had straps that connected on the open side of the bunk to keep sleepers from being thrown out of bed if the train was traveling at night. The trains traveled as freight trains, so their journeys were long and tended to have lots of stops and starts as passenger trains were given higher priority. All those stops and starts could roll someone right off their bunk if they weren't careful.

By the same token, the stops and starts could also throw someone against the bunk wall, and there was no protection from that.

As they staggered toward the rail car, Frances laughed and said, "Happy New Year, Jessie!"

As promised, Jessie felt miserable the next morning. She lay in bed moaning slightly because her head throbbed painfully. It hurt to open her eyes.

"Too much fun last night, huh?" Gail said.

Jessie groaned. "I wouldn't call it that. My head feels like it's a boulder ready to roll off my shoulders."

Gail gave Jessie a glass of water and some aspirin to help her with her hangover.

"You can't stay in bed, Jessie. Your animals will be hungry, and I'm sure you don't want them to snack on you."

Jessie just groaned. Gail was right. Jessie had forgotten the animals.

How could drinking like that ever become enjoyable? Jessie could barely remember anything after her whiskey.

What she did remember wasn't pleasant, though.

Luckily, the performers had the day off for the holiday, except for Jessie and some of the other workers like the cooks. The animals didn't know it was a holiday and would be hungry, so she and the other handlers needed to work.

She walked slowly from the train and stepped softly so she wouldn't rattle her head. The smell of urine and feces from the animals in the menagerie turned her stomach. She was glad she hadn't eaten breakfast, or it might have wound up on the ground.

Jessie struggled to move a bale of hay over to the elephant enclosure when Mick the roustabout walked into the menagerie. She had never seen him here before. He took the bale from her and walked it over to the nearest elephant.

"I can manage it," she said. She didn't want Mick to think she couldn't do the work. She had been doing it every day for weeks. Of course, she hadn't been hungover before.

"I'm sure you can, but I'm here, and I can make it easier," Mick said.

"Thank you."

Jessie felt like she might topple over every time she bent over.

They walked the few yards to the enclosure, and the roustabout dropped the bale. Jessie cut the twine binding the bale with a pair of shears she carried and created hay piles for the elephants.

"You don't see a lot of girls caring for the animals," he said.

Jessie shrugged. "I like it."

Myrna wandered over and patted Jessie on the head with her trunk and sniffed her. The contact rattled her head. Jessie smiled and hugged the leathery trunk. Myrna didn't know any better.

"She likes you," Mick said.

"I like her, too. She's my favorite."

Mick stood there watching her until Jessie started feeling uncomfortable. The hairs on her arms were starting to rise.

"I'd love to talk more, Mick, but I have to get back to work."

He nodded. "Sure, sure. I'll see you at chow."

He left and Jessie got back to feeding the elephants. There were currently six in the circus. Myrna was the smallest because she was the youngest. She was about seven feet tall at the top of her back.

After the hay, Jessie brought out a bushel of pears and laid them in small groups around the enclosure so the elephants wouldn't have to compete for the fruit.

The elephants snorted and growled as they moved around to find an empty spot where they could eat. Jo-Jo and Flo got into a wrestling match with their trunks as each one tried to steal the other's pears. Some people might have been intimidated being the smallest thing in the enclosure, worried that they might get stepped on. However, both Jessie and the elephants were careful.

She noticed Myrna limping a bit and walked over to where the young elephant stood eating.

"Is something wrong with your foot, Myrna?"

The elephant flapped her ears.

"Let me see your foot, Myrna."

Jessie patted the elephant behind the knee until Myrna raised her foot.

"Good. Hold it."

Jessie ran her hand along the underside of the foot and bent over so she could see the wrinkled surface. Her head throbbed so much that she thought she might fall over, but she managed to keep her balance. It was hard at times to distinguish between Myrna's foot and something else, but she found a sharp-sided rock pressed into the underside of the foot. Every time Myrna took a step, it pressed the rock into her foot so that it couldn't fall off. Jessie was happy to see there was no infection.

She reached underneath and pulled the rock free as gently as she could. Then she checked to see if there was any bleeding. There wasn't. The rock was slightly smaller than her thumb. Myrna's ears flapped, but she gave no other indication that she felt what Jessie was doing, probably because with her foot in the air, her weight was off the rock. Jessie tossed it outside of the enclosure.

She patted the front of the elephant's knee.

"You can lower your foot, Myrna. It should feel better."

Myrna put her foot back on the ground as Jessie stroked her side. The elephant slowly rested her weight on her foot. She chuffed and then wrapped her trunk around Jessie.

"You handled her like a pro."

Jessie turned around and saw Samuel Atwell standing at the entrance to the enclosure.

"Thank you. She worked with me. I'm guessing she's happy to be rid of the stone," Jessie said.

"Yes, she did work with you, but that takes trust. I doubt she would have done that for just anyone."

Jessie rubbed Myrna behind the ear. "Well, she's my favorite."

Samuel smirked. "And you hers. Have you ever trained animals before?"

"No, but I learned to care for them with Dr. Stultz. He was the veterinarian in my town."

"Caring is not training. You got Myrna to lift her foot, though."

"She was hurting. It made her feel better to raise it."

Samuel nodded. "Yes, but the pain should have made her want to protect her foot."

"She trusts me."

"Like I said." He paused. "So what is your diagnosis for our young star?"

Jessie blushed, feeling like the trainer was making fun of her, but she answered honestly. "She'll be fine. I didn't feel any blood on her foot or see any on the stone, so it didn't puncture the skin, or it wasn't there long enough to create an abscess. I'll check it again when I file her nails."

Samuel suddenly grinned, and Jessie thought for a moment he looked like a gray-haired lion baring its teeth. "I'm surprised you made it out here this morning to feed them. That's why I came out."

So Samuel had seen her drunk, sick, throwing up or all of the above.

"I didn't want to, but I knew they would be hungry," Jessie told him.

Samuel nodded. "Very good. We must always care for them. They are the stars of the show. Most people have never seen anything as large as an elephant. How would you like to help me with the animals?"

Jessie shook her head. "I do that now."

"More than that. How would you like to learn to train the elephants? I believe I see the talent for it in you."

Jessie felt her heartbeat quicken. She could work only with the elephants? "Really?"

"Yes, I can talk to Jeremy and have him okay it. You'll even make more money, although not what a star performer makes. You'll be considered a performer, though. It will give you some more privileges."

Jessie grinned and shouted, "Yes! I'd love to."

"Good. Given how you seem to be a natural at this, I can

probably have you competent as a trainer by the time we go on the road this season. You'll be a seasoned pro by the time we return here at the end of the season."

"Thank you."

"Don't thank me. You'll earn it. We'll start tomorrow morning after you feed the elephants. From now on, they'll be the only animals you'll be working with and caring for."

The cookhouse was a tent far off the midway so it wouldn't be confused as an attraction. Not that it mattered in winter quarters, but the circus layout stayed as consistent as possible so workers and performers would have no trouble remembering what tent was where.

Either a blue or yellow flag flapped atop the cookhouse tent. A blue flag meant the cookhouse was open and serving meals while a yellow flag let everyone know the chow line was closed. The closer Jessie came to the tent, the more she smelled hot oil, beef, and baking bread.

The inside of the tent was separated in two sides with a canvas curtain. On one side, the tables were covered in cloth tablecloths; bottles of ketchup, mustard, and mayonnaise sat on the tables with the salt and pepper shakers. On the other side of the curtain, the tables were bare and covered in scratches and stains.

She walked over to the food line where men in white aprons stood waiting to dish out lunch.

After Jessie filled her tray with meatloaf and green beans, she hesitated and walked to the side of the tent with the tablecloths. She sat down at a table by herself. Bradley walked over and sat down across from her.

"You know you're not supposed to be on this side, Jessie," he said. "Some of the others won't like it."

Jessie grinned and laid a hand on his arm. "I'm a performer now. Samuel said he was going to start working with me. I'll perform with the elephants and probably even ride them in the parade."

Bradley's smile widened, and his eyes brightened. He was nearly as excited as her.

"That's great, Jessie. Congratulations."

"Samuel saw how well I work with Myrna and offered to train me."

"I could have told him that. I saw you had a connection with them from day one."

Mick walked up to the table and stared at them.

When Jessie noticed him, she smiled and said, "Hi, Mick. This is my friend, Bradley."

Mick stared at Bradley and frowned. "I thought we were going to be eating together. You're on the wrong side of the tent."

"I was promoted this morning. I'm an elephant trainer now. Well… an elephant trainer trainee." Mick looked at the ground. "I'm sorry. When I said that I'd see you here, I just meant, well, that I'd see you here and say hi."

Mick turned and walked away without saying anything else. Bradley watched him go and shook his head.

"I didn't mean to upset him," Jessie said.

"How do you know him?" Bradley asked.

"I met him when I saw him reading a book one day. We talked a bit about it. He saw me this morning and helped me carry a bale of hay to the elephants. We talked for a little bit at the menagerie."

Bradley looked over to where Mick had disappeared around the curtain that separated the two sides of the cookhouse.

"You need to be careful around him, Jessie."

"Why? He seems nice enough." She felt a twinge of doubt.

"Maybe, but I've heard stories about him. The women stay away from him."

"Why?"

"Nothing definite, but some of the women with the circus have quit suddenly. The ones who did were seen talking and meeting with Mick a lot."

"That doesn't mean anything."

Bradley took a bite from a piece of fried chicken on his plate. "No, but since the women left so quickly, they weren't around to ask about it. I wouldn't let my sister be alone with him even if she wanted to. Better safe than sorry."

Most of the people in the circus were good, hard-working people. The workers and performers treated each other like family, but like any family, sometimes there were problem children. The circus had more than its fair share. In a circus, it might be someone who was a drunk or cantankerous, if you were lucky. The circus protected its own, but that didn't mean the problem children got away with behaving poorly.

Jessie would have to ask the other women on the train about Mick. Not that she didn't believe Bradley, but the women would know what the problem was. However, since she was moving up in the circus caste system, she shouldn't have to worry about him too much. The other members of the circus would discourage it.

Even though Bradley had been willing to be friends with her, it was his choice to associate with someone "below" him. If it had been her choice, the circus folk would have frowned on it. It didn't make a lot of sense to her, but the circus was world of its own with its own customs and unwritten rules she would have to learn.

For now, she was just happy to celebrate.

15

JANUARY 1937

The next morning Jessie fed the elephants before getting her own breakfast. She felt a little guilty about not taking care of the other animals, but they still had the other handlers to look after them. Samuel had told her she was only responsible for the elephants now. She was an elephant trainer.

She wolfed down a biscuit and honey and a glass of milk, much to Bradley's amusement, and then nearly ran over to the menagerie. She arrived before Samuel did. She needed to make sure the elephants were fed and watered and ready to practice when he arrived. She didn't want to disappoint him and be sent back to being just an animal handler on her first day as an elephant trainer.

When Samuel arrived, Jessie was brushing the dirt off of Jo-Jo with a stiff-bristled brush. Jo-Jo, especially, liked to roll in the dirt. The elephant tended to clear a spot at night, pawing straw away from the ground to create her own spot in the elephant enclosure.

"It's good to see that you started with caring for the elephants first. That allows both of you to get to know each other. You can learn their personalities and develop a trust."

Jessie nodded. She knew for instance that Jo-Jo was very slow to respond in the mornings. It took her a while to get active. Daisy, on the other hand, was nearly always excited and ready to play or perform. Patti could be a bully, but she really just wanted attention. Elsa loved spraying people and other animals with water. Flo was the largest of the six elephants, but she was also the gentlest. Myrna was the adventurous one. She loved to explore and investigate anything new. It had probably contributed to her adventure meeting Jessie.

"All of our elephants are broken, so they aren't likely to wander off, although Myrna escaped for a few days when she was a calf." Jessie hoped Samuel didn't notice her blushing. "They are used to us, and they trust us. We can't abuse that trust."

"By hurting them."

Samuel nodded. "That's one way. Another is not feeding them enough or not giving them proper medical care. We have to act as their parents and raise them to be great circus performers. Sometimes, we may even have to argue on their behalf with Jeremy."

"Really?"

"The animals are expensive, and he wants to protect them, but he also has to look at the needs of the entire circus. Sometimes, it might conflict with the elephants' needs."

Jessie had never considered things from Mr. Conroy's point of view. She had to care for six elephants. He was responsible for hundreds of animals and people.

It was hard to think of herself as the parent of a ten-foot-tall baby like Daisy or even Myrna for that matter. Jessie thought of Myrna as a friend, although she always remembered the elephants were wild animals. If she ever forgot, Samuel would be sure to remind her with a story about an elephant who had injured someone.

"I have designed the elephant act for this season, and Jeremy approved it." He handed her a sheaf of papers. "You can read through them tonight. It is mostly moves that the elephants already know. You will need to learn the commands to get them to the moves, and how to encourage them if they are reluctant. I also try to incorporate something new in each season. Sometimes it works. Sometimes it doesn't, but winter quarters lets us practice and find out how good both we and the elephants are."

Jessie flipped through the papers in her hand. Samuel had written the order of moves in the act and when the act would go on. He also listed the opening and closing parades and the order the elephants would enter the big top. He even listed headpieces and blankets the elephants would need to wear.

"Those are yours," he said, pointing at the papers. "I copied them from my notes."

"Thank you."

They led the elephants from the enclosure and brought them to a field outside the menagerie. The low barriers that were usually in the big top marking one of the circus's three rings were set up in the field.

"Stake all but Jo-Jo," Samuel said.

"Do we have to?"

"Yes, we can't have them wandering off. It also helps the other elephants to hear the commands and watch what Jo-Jo does, or whichever elephant is being trained.

Jessie nodded and hammered the leg stakes into ground, giving the elephants room to move around as comfortably as they could within the confines of the six-foot chain.

Samuel led Jo-Jo into the center of the field where a circular steel tub sat.

The elephant trainer lifted his cane in the air. "Jo-Jo, stand."

Jo-Jo lifted her trunk high in the air like a serpent rising to a snake charmer's song. Then she shifted her weight back and lifted her front legs off the ground so that she was standing on her back legs. Jessie grinned and clapped.

Samuel lowered his cane. "Jo-Jo, down."

Jo-Jo slowly lowered her legs back to the ground. Samuel walked over and stroked her trunk. Then he reached into his pocket, pulled out something, and passed it to her to eat.

"What did you give her?" Jessie asked.

"Some nuts. I keep a bag of them to reward the elephants for doing a good job."

Just like Bradley had told her.

"You told me not to feed them snacks," Jessie said.

"That's when you're a handler," Samuel told her. "You're a trainer now."

"And I see you don't use a bullhook."

Samuel frowned and shook his head. "Not if I don't have to. I usually just carry my walking stick during performances. These girls are trained well enough that I don't need to hurt them, and I hope I never have to. I don't want them to fear me."

Jessie grinned. "I like that." Dr. Stultz would have, too.

"I do, too. I learned under a trainer who used the bullhook too readily. An angry elephant nearly killed him once. I took that as a lesson for what not to do."

Jessie shuddered slightly at the thought. There were so many ways that a beast that weighed ten times her weight could hurt her. Even accidentally. A swinging trunk or a misplaced foot could all cause injury to her if she wasn't careful. But an angry elephant! An angry elephant could trample or throw a person.

Samuel continued, "He let his fear get the better of him after that, and he took it out on the elephants." The elephant trainer sighed. "The sound of an elephant crying will break your heart if you ever hear it. I almost quit when I heard Pokie crying. I have to use a bullhook on occasion when I am training an elephant, but if I make an elephant cry, I also wind up crying."

He sounded like Miss Erin when she explained how she felt when she disciplined one of the orphans. It hurt her as much as it hurt the orphan, but in a different way.

"So, each morning after we take the elephants out to exercise, we will run them through the individual moves and try to train them on the new move," Samuel said.

"What's that going to be?"

"Since I have you as an assistant, I want them to pick you up. Maybe I will have them pass you between them."

Jessie's eyes widened at the thought. She pictured herself being tossed back and forth between two elephants.

"What do you want me to do?" Jessie asked.

Samuel waved for her to approach him. "Come over here. I know you are used to the elephants and they you, so I am going to start to train you."

"Me? Are you going to use the walking stick?" Jessie said, half joking.

Samuel grinned. "No, but if you are stubborn, I may have to use the bullhook."

Jessie approached. She scanned the grass from habit, watching for steaming piles of droppings that she would need to shovel into a bucket later.

"You are going to be riding in the parade at the beginning and end of each show, so you need to know how to climb up on an elephant." Jessie nodded. "Now watch and listen."

Samuel turned to Jo-Jo and said firmly, "Jo-Jo, foot." He also tapped her left foot with the cane.

Jo-Jo obediently lifted her foot and held it in the air.

"Now you can step up on the tub, then her foot, and pull yourself up on her back." He used the cane to point from her to the elephant, and for a moment, Jessie thought he might tap her with it.

She stepped up two feet up onto the tub. Jo-Jo's leg was another foot higher, so it was an easier step. Then she was stuck. She couldn't jump, but she couldn't find a purchase to grab onto and pull herself up.

"You can grab her ear," Samuel said. "It won't hurt her."

Jessie cocked her head to the side and raised an eyebrow. "If I pulled on your ear, it would hurt."

"Yes, but I'm not an elephant. For shows, she'll have her harness on. You'll be able to grab that and pull yourself up." Jessie hesitated. "Hurry up, she can't hold her leg up all day, especially with you standing on it."

Jessie sighed and reached up with one hand to grab the leathery ear. "Sorry, Jo-Jo." She used her other hand to reach as high as she could on Jo-Jo's back. She pushed off with her left leg and swung her right leg upward as if she was mounting a horse.

She only succeeded in feeling like she was doing a split and giving Samuel a good laugh. She was so ungraceful that she knew couldn't possibly do this for a show.

"Pull your body over first," he said. "Then swing your leg over."

She tried it again and regretted having to pull on Jo-Jo's ear again, although the elephant didn't seem to mind. Maybe Jessie weighed so little that it only felt like a tug to the elephant. She got her upper body slung over Jo-Jo's back and then swung a leg over while straightening her body so she could sit up.

Once she was upright, she felt like she was on a horse, a very tall horse that apparently had a very bony neck. She rubbed the top of Jo-Jo's head.

"Not bad," Samuel said. "Luckily, the audience doesn't have to watch you mount."

"Does it get any easier?"

Samuel nodded. "Easier and faster, but no less graceful."

"Do I get a saddle or something to sit on?"

"You're sitting on it."

"It hurts."

"You don't have to stay up too long, and the elephants won't be running so you won't get bounced up and down. Now let's see you get down."

Jessie looked at the ground below her. She was definitely higher up than a horse.

"Jo-Jo, foot," Samuel commanded.

Jo-Jo obediently raised her foot. Jessie took a deep breath and slid down the elephant's neck until she found her footing on Jo-Jo's foot. Then she stepped back onto the pedestal. She raised her hands over her head in triumph and then nearly lost her balance and fell off the pedestal.

Samuel worked with the elephants for a couple hours. Some of the work was done individually if a particular elephant needed help with a trick, but most of the time the work was done as a group. He tried to keep the attention of the elephants he wasn't working with by calling their names or tapping them with his cane.

Meanwhile, the elephants got to enjoy standing in the sun and the warmth.

During a break, while Jessie filled a trough with water for the elephants, she asked Samuel, "Why are none of the elephants boys?"

"First off, women and church groups would be up in arms if we had a bull performing. You worked for a veterinarian, right?"

Jessie nodded.

"Well, can you imagine how the audience would react if a bull mounted a female during a performance? Even if he just pissed, pardon my language, it could be disruptive. Do you know how much an elephant pisses a day?" Jessie shook her head. "Fifteen gallons. That means there's a good chance of things popping out that parents don't want their children seeing."

Jessie's eyes widened. She had seen it happen with dogs and horses. She couldn't imagine the scale of what would happen with elephants.

"On a practical level, bulls are harder to keep. They are larger, stronger, and less manageable. That's not a good combination, especially when I'm trying to use the bullhook as little as possible."

"I've seen elephant calves in the circus," Jessie said. "Where do they come from?"

"Some are captured in Africa or Asia. Some are bred in zoos, and if the zoo doesn't have room to keep them, they are sold off. Sometimes a circus may even have a bull, though he won't be a performer. He'll be kept for labor or breeding. It can be kinda risky, though."

After a couple more hours of work, Samuel took a break and had Jessie take the elephants back to menagerie and feed them.

"Why not feed them here?" she asked.

"I want them to associate the menagerie with where they eat. I don't want them getting stubborn in the ring because they get hungry and want someone to bring them food."

Jessie was starting to realize she had so many little things she needed to learn. It wasn't like caring for farm animals.

Once the elephants were fed, she headed over to the cookhouse for lunch. She walked past Mick, who was sitting on a chair tossing bread crumbs to birds that gathered at his feet.

It looked odd to see such a large man looking much like an old person in a park. He was broad shouldered like many of the roustabouts with thick arms from all the physical labor they did. He had a snake tattooed on his arm so that it appeared to curl around his arm with the head on the end of his shoulder. The snake's mouth was open and its fangs were bared and tongue flicking out.

It was excellently drawn, and Jessie paused for a moment thinking it was real. The roustabout noticed her stop and turned to look at her.

"Hi, Jessie," Mick said. "Did you want something?"

"Do you feed the birds often?"

He shrugged. "I wouldn't say often. So much attention gets paid to all the exotic animals around here that regular animals get ignored, but birds are beautiful."

"They are," Jessie agreed.

"I like that they're free. They can go wherever they want. It's why I like the circus. I still have to take orders, but other than that I get a lot of freedom."

Jessie continued on to the cookhouse. She sat down at a table on the performers' side of the tent with another show girl she knew from the train named Veronica. She was about ten years older than Jessie with platinum blonde hair. She was a quiet woman who usually kept to herself, but she was the only person Jessie knew on this side of the tent.

Veronica didn't say anything when Jessie sat down and started to eat her Salisbury steak and mashed potatoes. Jessie tried asking questions, but Veronica either didn't answer or gave short one-word replies.

Jessie was nearly finished her lunch, when Veronica said, "I saw you talking to Mick."

The sudden change surprised Jessie, but she said, "I saw him feeding the birds, and I asked him about it."

"Be careful with him. You don't want him paying attention to you."

"Why?"

Helen looked at her tray. "You just don't. That's all."

Then she stood up and walked away, carrying her tray. Jessie watched her go, wondering why she seemed upset Jessie had spoken with Mick. It had been a quick thirty-second meeting. People seemed wary of Mick, but no one was able to fully explain why.

As Samuel had said, during the afternoon, they worked the elephants through the routine they had performed last season, stopping where Samuel wanted to insert a new trick and working on that. The ground trembled whenever the elephant trainer had the elephants run into the ring to start their performance. It felt like a small earthquake.

She took the elephants back to the menagerie at the end of the day and washed them. As she looked at some of the other animal handlers feeding and cleaning their animals, she noticed that a lot of them had tattoos. Nothing elaborate like Thelma the Tattooed Lady in the freak show. These were more like identification badges. The lion handlers had lion tattoos. The horse wranglers had horse tattoos. She supposed Samuel had an elephant tattoo somewhere on his body. She would have to ask him about that.

That made her wonder why Mick had a snake tattoo. He didn't work with snakes, and there weren't any in the circus.

She also noticed that many of the men who worked with the lions, tigers, and bears could be identified in other ways.

They were missing fingers. Those who performed with the big cats also had ugly scars from bad wounds, but those were covered by sequined costumes when they performed.

Elephants seemed to have friendly faces, but Jessie had read they could be just as dangerous as a tiger or lion, although she had yet to see it. Samuel had told her that more trainers were killed by elephants than the big cats.

Looking into their amber eyes, Jessie found that hard to believe. Those eyes seemed to open up to an old soul, even in the young ones like Myrna.

16

February 1937

Jessie was walking toward the cookhouse, which had raised its blue flag, when she heard her name called.

She turned and saw a clown waving her over to him. As she got closer, she asked, "Bradley?"

"Who else?"

"Well, it could be anyone under that makeup."

She certainly didn't recognize him. His face was painted white, except for the large red mouth painted over his real one. It was also painted to look like he had two large buck teeth. He wore a wig full of frizzy red hair and two large ears that stuck out on the side. Bradley had told her that each clown had his own look. She just needed to get used to how he looked both in and out of makeup.

He wore green-and-yellow-striped pants and a blue shirt with orange polka dots, and of course, he wore the oversized red shoes that every clown wore.

Jessie laughed. "You know you look ridiculous, don't you?"

"I'm supposed to."

He stepped back into the dressing tent and pulled off his wig and ears and set them aside. Then he sat down in front of a lighted mirror and started wiping the makeup from his face with a rag.

"Do you have to put that on and take it off every day?" Jessie asked.

"Only when we have a dress rehearsal like today or an actual performance."

"It looks like it takes longer than a woman putting on makeup."

"It does, but we can pick out our clothes quicker."

She laughed again and slapped him on the shoulder. "Stop that."

"If you can wait, I'll go to dinner with you." She nodded and sat down next to him. "You know, I haven't seen you perform yet. How is work as an elephant trainer?" Bradley added.

"I think I'll like it. It's a lot of repetition, but I like working with the elephants."

He started wiping the greasepaint off of his face. "Get used to it, Jessie. The circus is all about repetition. We learn our routines backward and forward to ensure things move as smoothly as they can. Even the loading and unloading of the trains is done to a routine. Learning something that well allows for precision."

She nodded. "I understand, but it can get boring at times."

The repetition of everything was worse than at the Wilson Home with chores, meals, and school. She'd gotten used to that, and even come to enjoy it because she got to spend time with Dr. Stultz, Leanne, and the Wilsons.

With the circus, she got up, fed the elephants, ate breakfast, trained the elephants, fed the elephants, ate lunch, trained the elephants, fed and washed the elephants, ate dinner, and then usually went to bed early. She would get used to this, too, when she got to know people like Bradley, Samuel, Carl, and Gail better, but it certainly wasn't the glamorous job she had envisioned. From talking to people like Bradley, she doubted it would get any better on the road. There would be different routines, but they will still be routines. Performances would replace training. She probably wouldn't see much of the towns she visited.

"I guess getting bored depends on what you are doing," Bradley said.

"How so?"

"If an aerialist gets bored, he might mess up and that could be deadly. Same with the people who handle the big cats."

"Yea, I noticed that a lot of their trainers and handlers have injuries and scars."

Bradley took a bow. "That's the nice thing about being a clown. If I get hit on the head with a hammer, it is made with balsa wood, so I'm not hurt."

"Do you have a tattoo?" Jessie said suddenly.

"A tattoo?"

"Like a clown face."

Bradley grinned. "Oh, you mean a circus tattoo." He shook his head. "Not yet. I've been thinking about it, though. I'm not sure if I would want a tattoo of my clown face on my arm, though. Are you going to get one of an elephant?"

"Maybe. I just noticed the tattoos today. Does everyone have one?"

He shrugged. "I don't know, but a lot of people do."

When he finished removing his makeup, they walked to the cookhouse. Dinner was spaghetti and meatballs with garlic bread. Pasta was a common meal for the circus because it was inexpensive compared to some of their other meals.

"You seem to use a lot of tumbling in your routines," Jessie remarked at one point.

Bradley thought about it. "I guess I do. Maybe it's part of my aerialist blood coming through. Maybe it will help me create a signature move."

"Signature move?"

"Yes, something that only I do or something that people associate with me."

"Did you always want to be a clown? Why did you change your mind about wanting to be an aerialist?" Jessie asked him.

He paused and got a faraway look in his eyes. Finally, he shook his head. "No. I always liked the clowns, but I didn't start out wanting to be one. Growing up in a family of aerialists, I was swinging on a trapeze as soon as I could hold onto the bar."

"So how did you wind up as a clown?" She twirled the spaghetti on her fork and took a bite of the pasta.

Bradley took a deep breath, and he started telling her a story. He had loved hanging from the trapeze as a child. He had loved feeling free of gravity and seeing the big top from the platforms at the top of the tent poles.

His hopes for work as an aerialist had crashed quicker than he did the first time he swung on a trapeze to train. During that first time on the trapeze, he had swung out over the net and tried to swing his legs up over the bar. He'd wound up flipping himself over the bar, and he fell, experiencing a few moments of terror until he landed in the rope net.

People had watched his debut during a dress rehearsal and saw him make a fool of himself. They laughed. It didn't matter that he was a kid. Even his siblings had laughed at him. His brothers and sister were older, and they already knew how to swing. Trapeze work was supposed to be in his blood, but he just couldn't master more than the basics.

Tim Chapel, the head clown had been one of the people laughing at Bradley. He had said if Bradley wanted to make people laugh, he should become a clown. He had meant it as a joke at Bradley's expense, but Bradley gave it serious thought. When he mentioned the offer to his family, they mocked him.

Then one of Bradley's four uncles fell when he missed a catch. He hit the ground hard from twenty feet in the air. He had eighteen broken bones and organ damage. He died after spending two days in pain in the hospital.

That's when Bradley took Tim Chapel up on the offer. His family didn't even mind at first. They were upset over Bradley's uncle's death, and they didn't want him to risk his life and become careless because he didn't like being an aerialist. Only later, when they realized Bradley was serious about becoming a clown, did they expressed their disappointment.

"I didn't settle for this work, despite what my family thinks. I love making people laugh," Bradley said. "So much of the work of an aerialist and a clown depends on timing, just like with a trapeze, except this is comedic timing."

"You're like Charlie Chaplin in his silent films," Jessie said. "The comedy has to translate into a story that can be told through actions that the audience at the back of tent can see and enjoy."

"Wow! That's almost profound."

"I'm as smart as an elephant."

"Are elephants smart?"

"Smarter than a clown."

Bradley smiled. "Be glad I don't have my props with me. I'd spray you with a squirt gun."

By the time they finished dinner, most everyone else had

gone. Jessie realized how late it was and rushed off to feed the elephants one last time before she turned in for the evening.

The next day, Jessie was leading the elephants out of the big top after practicing their act when she noticed Alexander Dupree, the knife thrower, throwing knives at his assistant who stood against a wooden board, unmoving. How could she not flinch when he threw those knives at her? Jessie jerked when she saw him throw a knife, and it wasn't aimed at her. The sound of the knife striking the board made the goosebumps on her arms appear.

Alexander was a good-looking man with wavy black hair and dark eyes. He wore a tight top that showed off his broad shoulders.

Jessie heard the thwock of a knife hitting wood. It was a sound she was used to, hearing it often as Alexander practiced. However, this time, she heard a yelp of pain. She lifted the side of the canvas tent and crawled inside. She saw Alexander standing over Tina, looking at blood on her arm.

"What happened?" Jessie asked.

"Tina flinched," Alexander said quickly.

"I did not," Tina snapped. She held her hand on her arm as blood seeped between her fingers.

"If you hadn't, I wouldn't have hit you."

Tina pushed herself to her feet. "Of course, you never miss," she said sarcastically.

"I don't."

"I guess that means you meant to hit me." He tried to help her stand, but she pushed him away. "I'm going to the infirmary."

Tina walked away, holding her hand over his arm to staunch the bleeding.

Alexander watched her leave, and then turned to Jessie.

"I didn't mean to hit her," he said.

"I believe you," Jessie said automatically, although she wasn't sure. She didn't know Alexander except by name, but he seemed sincere and truly upset.

Alexander sat down on a nearby stool and wiped the blade off in the sawdust. She noticed his hand was shaking.

Had it been shaking when he was throwing the knives? If so, it was amazing that he hadn't hit her sooner.

"Are you all right?" Jessie asked.

His head bobbed up and down, but he didn't look at her. "Yes, yes." He paused. "It's just that I have never hit a person before. I might miss a balloon, but I have never hit someone before."

"You'll just have to be more careful."

He chuckled. "I am very careful, but I suppose you are correct." He stood up. "I need to go check on Tina and apologize. Thank you."

He left and Jessie continued on to the menagerie.

While she and Samuel were working the elephants, she asked, "How can Alexander's assistant not run away when he throws a knife at her?"

"Tina has nerves of steel, especially since she is Alexander's ex-wife."

"Really? They must get along well, so I wonder why they would divorce."

"They divorced because Alexander likes women too much," Samuel told her. "She stays with him because it's a job, and jobs aren't easy to come by nowadays."

Jessie couldn't understand how two people who had bad enough problems to divorce could still work together. Especially when Tina had to face Alexander and let him throw knives at her. No wonder she had been so upset when he had nicked her.

Jessie was still thinking about it when she left the menagerie at the end of the day. She saw Mick leaning against a light pole feeding a pair of cardinals. He straightened up when he saw her and waved. She waved back. She didn't mind being friendly. She was friendly with everyone, but Mick always seemed to be around her nowadays.

He looked like he was about to walk in her direction, so she looked away and casually veered away from him.

Then she saw Bradley coming out of the clown tent and called out to him. That gave her an excuse to hurry over to him and away from Mick.

"Hi, did you need something?" he asked.

"Yes. An excuse," she told him. She saw the confused look on his face and added, "Mick always seems to be around. I think he likes me, but he is starting to make me nervous."

They started walking toward the train. "I warned you about him."

"Yes, everyone warns me about him, but without being specific." Jessie sighed. "I don't know the whole story, but I found out that some of the girls he's been seen with have wound up leaving the circus. One was a girl for the coochie show, and people thought she had just gotten tired of the after show she was expected to do. However, the second woman was a showgirl who people liked. She just didn't get on the train after Nashville."

They walked along what midway, which was closed up. It was only set up in winter quarters, so that repairs could be done and games tested. Also, near the end of winter quarters they opened up the show for dress rehearsals. Locals would come in for a day or two and the performers could gauge from their reactions how the new acts were received.

Jessie was talking about the outfit she was going to be

wearing in the parades when Bradley stopped. Jessie walked a few steps before she realized her friend wasn't beside her.

"Why'd you stop?" she asked.

"Look at her. Isn't she gorgeous?"

He didn't point so Jessie had to follow his stare. She saw a busty woman with long legs and a narrow waist. Her bright red hair hung around her shoulders. It took Jessie a moment to recognize her because she wasn't used to seeing the woman dressed casually. On the road, she wore a very small sequined outfit with a lot of ostrich feathers on it.

"Isn't that Barbara?" Jessie asked.

Bradley nodded.

"She's one of the coochie girls," Jessie noted. That meant she was a stripper in the men-only tent behind the big top and out of sight of the townies. Circuses weren't supposed to have coochie shows, but if the circus owner paid off the right people and kept things quiet, they could get away with it. It was worth the risk because it increased the circus's profit: men paid more to get in the coochie show than they paid to watch the circus.

Jessie didn't necessarily have a problem with the shows. The girls had a make a living. She knew she couldn't do it, though. However, she knew some of the girls earned extra money after their performances by meeting up with men for sex in the smaller tents that had been set up for that purpose behind the coochie show tent.

"I know what she does, but she's so pretty," Bradley said.

Jessie rolled her eyes.

Bradley must have glimpsed her because he said, "Don't be like that. You moon over Alexander or my brother whenever you see them even though you know they won't be faithful to you."

"That different. I'm not trying to go out with him" Jessie

felt herself blush. "Anymore."

"How's that different? I haven't even talked to Barbara."

"She would probably do more than talk to you if you paid her." Jessie knew it was the wrong thing to say the moment she said it, but she had still been trying to cover her embarrassment over Alexander and hadn't thought about what she was saying.

Bradley gritted his teeth, sighed, and walked away.

She was tempted to run after him, but she knew he wouldn't talk to her right now.

17
MARCH 1937

Jessie would have known the circus season's start was drawing closer even if she hadn't known the date they were leaving winter quarters. The first sign was that the performers had daily dress rehearsals of the full performance. Then she saw Mr. Conroy, Carl, and Juan Sanchez walking around inspecting tents and equipment for rips or other damage. Carl was Mr. Brady's right man and Juan was the head roustabout. Juan was in charge of making any repairs, and Carl made sure they were completed by the next day.

The day to leave Florida arrived, and winter quarters, what was essentially a small town, disappeared into train cars. Men and elephants brought down the big top while other roustabouts lowered the smaller tents. The canvas was separated into smaller panels, loaded onto horse-drawn wagons, and hauled to the train. Performers and workers packed up costumes, equipment, and props in labeled trunks to be loaded onto the trains. Handlers led animals onto their train cars and had their cages pulled into the place on the cars. Everyone had multiple jobs to do, but they knew the jobs and did the work.

The trains, made up of dozens of brightly painted cars, stretched out for nearly a mile when they were finally packed and ready to go. The train carrying the tents and animals was the first to leave. It would arrive hours before the second train, so that the tents could be set up when the second train arrived.

The route the circus train would go from Florida through the southern states. At Texas, they would begin moving northeast. Then in Massachusetts, they would move south until they finally reached Florida and winter quarters once again. They would be on the road for ten months before returning to winter quarters.

Mr. Conroy supervised the operation, walking from location to location, calling out orders, and checking the time. Everybody knew their jobs. Since Jessie was the assistant elephant trainer, she guided the elephants as they helped in some of the heavier labors, such as lowering the big top. Samuel had shown her what needed to be done and taught her the orders to give to the elephants.

He stood nearby watching her to make sure she knew job since it was the first time she had had to help in the circus breakdown.

Samuel wasn't the only one watching her. She saw Mick a couple times, looking in her direction with a blank expression, but he couldn't stand around staring for too long because someone would shout an order at him. Set up and breakdown of the circus was when the roustabouts were the busiest.

When everything was packed and ready, Mr. Conroy inspected the train to see how it looked. After all, it had been a few months since winters quarters had been set up. New people like Jessie had to get used to the bustling confusion.

Jessie looked out over the field that had been covered with a circus. It was now just a rail siding and a few buildings to house the utilities for the area and a small home that Mr. Conroy stayed in while they were in winter quarters.

Once the chaos of packing up the circus calmed somewhat, Jessie walked to the train car where the elephants were housed. Her rail car with female workers was part of the early train. While most performers traveled on the late train so they wouldn't have to endure the smell of animals and urine filtering back through the train, the animal trainers were on the early train to care for the animals. Additionally, the elephants and horses were used to help erect the circus when it arrived at towns.

Jessie made sure the elephants had plenty of water and food. They had earned it for the work they had done, hauling wagons and lowering the big top. She also made sure they were calm since they were now staying somewhere different than they were used to.

She walked over and patted Myrna. "You probably have more experience riding on a train than I do," Jessie told her.

Myrna curled her trunk over Jessie's shoulder and under her arm. Jessie leaned her head against Myrna's forehead.

She left Myrna and the elephants after a few minutes and made her way back to her car, careful to hold onto a railing as she made the jump between cars. It was a short jump, but one misstep could leave her crushed between two rail cars if they had been moving.

She used a wet washcloth in the bathroom to clean herself. The shower house had been taken down with everything else. Then she went to the cook car, which was an odd name for it since it didn't serve anything cooked. Everyone got boxed meals. She took her meal, which consisted of a soda pop, ham and cheese sandwich, and potato chips and went back to her room to eat while leafing through a copy of *Life* magazine.

Some performers sat in the few chairs and tables in the cook car talking, but it wasn't large enough to hold everyone for a meal. Most people took their meals back to their rooms.

Even though the cook car prepared meals, some performers preferred to make their own meals in their rooms. The cook car served regular meals, but some of the performers were from foreign countries and they took the opportunity to cook some of their native meals on hot plates. The smell of exotic spices often filled the halls of different cars as Jessie passed through on her way to the elephants.

Around eight o'clock in the evening, she heard the train whistle blow. The lights flickered and then went off, but they came back on a few moments later. She heard the sound of metal whining against metal as the car connectors took on weight. It was still a couple of minutes before she felt movement, though. It began very slowly, an inch or two at a time, and gradually increased to a walk and then a running speed.

Circus trains traveled on the freight routes. Passenger trains had priority because they had schedules to keep. Circus trains did, too, but their schedules had more flexibility, so their trip might be a series of stops and starts.

When Jessie finished eating, she climbed into her bunk and attached the straps that Gail had shown her how to use when Jessie first arrived at winter quarters. This was the first time she had needed to use them. One end of each strap attached to the edge of the bunk and the other end clipped onto a metal loop on the ceiling. The result was a loose barrier that would keep her from rolling off the bunk.

It wasn't that Jessie rolled around in her sleep. She had slept on the upper bunk at the orphanage and here on the train. The train ride was not the smoothest, and it sometimes needed to stop in the middle of the night until other trains passed. The rocking and stops had been known to throw sleepers out of their bunks. The straps kept someone from being thrown on the floor and bruised or, worse, injured. Even some of the people who slept in lower bunks used them.

The train made slow progress. Every time it stopped for another train, it took minutes to slow down. Then they had to wait for the other train to pass, and it took minutes for the circus train to get moving once again.

This not only happened when the circus train stopped for other trains, but also when it stopped to water the animals. The hotter the days were, the more often the stops were made. The animals were the precious commodity. The circus did have full water wagons they used to water the animals and avoid stopping, but depending on how far it was between towns where they were performing, water stops were still needed.

The circus condensed onto two trains became a different experience than it was at winter quarters. It was louder and more cramped as people moved around. The cars had rarely been filled to capacity while they were in winter quarters. Someone had always been off doing something and not on a rail car. But now, not only was everyone with the circus on the trains, so were all the equipment, tents, and belongings. The animals were cramped in their cars with little room to move. Their tight quarters were planned so they wouldn't fight, rock the rail cars, and, maybe, cause a derailment. Jessie thought the animals might actually have more space than the people. At least if she stayed in her room, it was just her and Gail.

She visited the elephants every few hours to make sure they had water and were calm. She ran into Samuel a few times in the elephant car because he also checked on the elephants. A few times, she saw him just sitting on a hay bale and reading a book.

"Are you reading to them?" Jessie asked the first time she saw him doing this.

He dog-eared a page in the book and closed it. "No, I'm just keeping them company, although when I read something interesting, sometimes I will comment on it out loud."

"Why don't you read in your room?"

"I like it here with the elephants. It's quieter, and the elephants are good company."

The train arrived in west Texas after more than a twenty-four-hour journey. Jessie was still asleep when the rocking of the train car woke her as it came to a stop. She wanted to roll over and go back to sleep. She had discovered she did not sleep well on a moving train. She hoped it would be something she could get used to, but for now, she still felt tired and achy.

Gail stirred in her bunk. Then she stumbled to the window and looked out.

"It's still dark, although I think it's getting a little lighter on the horizon," she said.

Jessie groaned.

Gail said, "You better get moving. The elephants will be hungry after their work." Elephants and horses served dual roles in a circus, acting as both performers and beasts of burden helping with the set up and take down of the circus.

"I know. I know."

Jessie turned he head toward the wall and saw Leanne's doll she had won at this circus. Jessie had taken to keeping it in her bunk to remind her of Leanne, and to a lesser extent, the other orphans at the Wilson Home. Jessie smiled at the doll, and then gently slid it under her pillow. She didn't want

Gail to see it and think she was a child with a doll.

Jessie undid the straps on her bunk and climbed down the ladder. She slipped into her jeans and work shirt and headed back to the elephant car. She could hear some people stirring in their rooms as she passed through the passenger cars, and she envied them; they could still stay in bed for a while longer. She hoped she would have a chance to catch a nap before the matinee performance today, but she doubted it. At least they would be here three days, so she might get a decent night's sleep.

She met Samuel at the elephant car. He was supervising the unloading of the straps, costumes, and equipment the elephants used. At other cars, roustabouts loaded canvas and tent poles onto wagons pulled by horses. The horses were undoubtedly happy to be out of their rail car where they had been tightly packed during the journey.

The big top and other tents needed to be set up first because everything else went inside them.

At the chosen location, towering wooden poles, draped in rigging lines and topped with an American flag or circus flag, rose up with the help of the elephants to mark the bones of the circus.

Around the poles, men lifted heavy bundles of canvas, drop them on the ground, and slowly unfolded them while grunting and groaning. As the tent panels were laid out, another group of men came in to stitch the seams together as tightly as they could.

Finally, men and elephants pulled on ropes attached to the poles and canvas and the tents popped up like umbrellas being raised in a storm. Once in position, teams of men hammered stakes into the ground with machine-gun rapidity to anchor the tents in place. Samuel saw her and said, "The elephants should be about finished with their work and headed for the menagerie. Go get them fed and watered."

Once the animals had done their job, they could relax until the show.

Jessie ran off toward the big top, but it wasn't obvious where the menagerie tent was in the twilight. She had to run around the outside of the big top until she found it.

Inside, the animals were restless. They had just come off the train after a long ride and were in a new place. Jessie decided to lead the elephants to a clearing outside of the tent and stake them in the open. They had been cooped up too long and needed to see the sky.

The temperature was cool, but pleasant, and the fresh air would do them good. The rail car had been stuffy and confined. This change would help them relax.

She set up a canvas trough and filled it with water. While the elephants drank their fill, Jessie opened a crate of apples and carried it over to the elephants.

She walked among the elephants and stroked their sides. She spoke to them and tried to get a sense of their mood, or maybe she just wanted her contact with them to help calm her down.

She watched as the cookhouse went up and the cooks got their equipment ready. Soon the smell of biscuits baking and bacon frying filled the air as they started preparing breakfast.

More quickly than Jessie expected, the circus took shape and once again looked like winter quarters. However, it now seemed to have more life to it as everyone moved around doing their work with the anticipation of the audiences that would be filling the tent at midday.

She grabbed a quick breakfast of oatmeal with cinnamon on it and milk. Honestly, she wasn't even hungry for that, but she knew she would need her energy. Only a few people sat on the performer side of the tent. Most of them would be coming on the second train, which hadn't arrived yet.

On her way back to the train to wash up, Jessie stopped in to look at the big top. It was dark inside, but some of the lights were turned on, allowing the roustabouts to do their work. The bleachers were set up and most of the rigging was in place at the top of the tent. Seeing how much the elephants had strained to lift it, Jessie wondered how much the canvas actually weighed because the tent was immense. It probably could have held a dozen rail cars.

Back in her room on the train car, she filled the wash basin and washed off. Then she dressed in casual clothes. She had a few hours before she would need to change into her costume for the parade through town. That would bring the townies to the fairgrounds for the circus opening, and shortly after that she would make her debut as an elephant trainer.

When she looked at the clock on the wall, she realized she had time to take a nap before needing to feed the elephants.

She climbed back into her bunk to catch a two-hour nap.

18

MARCH 1937

Jessie sat nervously on Myrna's back waiting for the first show of the season in Little Rock, Arkansas. Both of them still wore their costumes from the parade through town. Jessie had on a satin red, white, and blue outfit that had a skirt so short it would have been considered scandalous if she had worn it outside of the circus. However, it was her large, feathered headpiece that kept her from dwelling too much on how exposed her legs were.

The headpiece felt like it weighed ten pounds. How could feathers weigh so much? The feathers protruded from a cone cap hidden beneath the feathers. The headpiece bore a closer resemblance to a peacock tail than a hat of any sort. She had to keep her head perfectly straight. If she bent slightly in any direction, the headpiece started to slide and choke her. However, Myrna's rhythmic walk tended to jiggle the headpiece loose at least once during the parade no matter how tight she tied it. It had made the parade a grueling affair, and now, she would have to wear it for the opening spec, which she had learned was what circus folk called the parades in the big top.

Spec was short spectacular, which the parades were. They would be less so if her headpiece fell off and crashed into Myrna's head.

Jessie had tried using hair clips during a dress rehearsal, but that had only resulted in nearly pulling her hair out. She had settled for walking around with the headpiece on as much as she could so she could learn to balance it in all instances.

The lights in the big top went off. The cacophony quieted down, but did not fall silent entirely. Mr. Conroy walked to the center of the big top and stood atop one of the elephant tubs. A spotlight turned on, focused on him.

"Ladies and gentlemen and children of all ages, welcome to the Conroy and Pepperidge Circus, a collection of wonderous talent and creatures from around the world that has thrilled royalty to the lowliest street urchin in the capital cities of Europe. We have now returned to our homeland to delight and amaze you with the wonders of the world." As far as Jessie knew, the circus had never performed outside of the United States, but Mr. Conroy's welcome message added to the mystique of the circus.

The band started playing the march, and the clowns led the way onto the avenue—the lane between the circus rings and the bleachers—around the big top. They skipped, jumped, fell, and warmed up the crowd.

The band followed. Then the horses pulled wagons filled with the performers dressed in outfits nearly elaborate as Jessie's. They waved and smiled to the cheering crowd. In between the wagons were the tumblers who walked along, occasionally somersaulting in the air, and the jugglers, who tossed Indian clubs back and forth as they walked.

Finally, it was time for the elephants.

"Forward, Myrna," Jessie said.

She was the only person on top of an elephant for the

opening parade. Samuel walked along beside them to guide the elephants with his bullhook. As Jessie waved to the cheering crowd, she could feel her motions starting the headpiece sliding. She nonchalantly rebalanced it.

Despite the cool spring temperature outside, it was already hot in the big top. Six thousand spectators plus the performers and animals created a lot of heat that was held in by the heavy canvas.

She listened to hear if Samuel called anything to her, but with the loud music and cheering crowd, it was impossible. She smelled roasted nuts and popcorn, which made her stomach rumble, and it didn't mix well with the nervousness she already felt.

By the first turn, she gave up trying to hear, balance the headpiece, and wave. Instead, she gave in to the grandeur and excitement. She started enjoying the circus just as she had when she had been a child, except now she was part of the circus and not just a spectator. That made it so much better.

About halfway around the big top, she gave up on the headpiece. She lifted it from her head as if it was part of the act and set it on Myrna's head. This way she could keep it balanced between her knees. It was literally a weight off her shoulders and head.

Samuel didn't scold her, or if he did, she couldn't hear it.

As she finished the elephants' walk around the big top, Jessie exited the tent and led them to the menagerie. She also needed to clear the way for the other acts coming behind her in of the parade. Everyone had to be able to exit the big top without pausing.

Jessie stopped the elephants, and then patted Myrna's shoulder. "Myrna, up."

The elephant obediently lifted her leg. Jessie dismounted onto Myrna's leg.

"Myrna, down."

As Myrna lowered her leg, Jessie held on to the harness and slid down the elephant's side.

She walked over and grabbed a hose to fill the trough with fresh water, so the elephants could drink. It had been pretty hot in a large canvas tent crammed with 6,000 people.

"You did some improvisation in there," Samuel said. Jessie couldn't tell if he was angry or not. His voice was flat.

"I had to. That headpiece it too tall. It's keeps sliding off."

Samuel nodded. "Fine. We're just not going to be able to make it work. I'll let the costumers know that it has to be smaller. Don't even bother with it for the grand spec."

Jessie could hear the music playing as acts filled the circus's three rings to entertain the audience. She knew they would be at their peak because having an audience responding to one performance energized all the performers.

Jessie couldn't enjoy the acts herself, though. She had to remove the cloth drape that covered the elephants like outfits and then change into her own outfit for her performance. The elephants performed in ring one, which was the one closest to the menagerie entrance into the big top. The center ring was reserved for the headliner acts like the trapeze artists and the dangerous acts like the lions. The smaller animal acts were often held in ring three.

Once the elephants were watered, Jessie ran into a small tent outside the menagerie where she and Samuel changed into their costumes. They had hung a sheet down the middle of the tent to give each of them their privacy.

Jessie stripped out of her satin outfit and draped it over a chair. Then she dressed in khaki shorts and shirt. She laced up boots and put a pith helmet on her head. She thought it looked ridiculous, but it was how people expected someone on safari to look. That was the image she and Samuel were trying to project. He was dressed the same way, but they would at least lose their helmets at the beginning of the show when they doffed their hats to each other and the elephants, and then handed them off to an assistant.

Mick was standing outside the tent when she stepped outside. She didn't have time to talk. She had to get the elephants ready to go out.

"Hi, Jessie, you looked great in there," he said as he stared at her bare legs.

Jessie wanted to step back inside the tent, but she was afraid he might follow her. Luckily, Samuel came out from his side of the tent, wearing his matching outfit.

"Next season, we'll use a different—" He stopped when he saw Mick. "What are you doing here? Don't you have duties during the show?"

Roustabouts walked under the bleachers, making sure no one dropped a cigarette butt that could start a fire. They also emptied the trash cans and made sure the midway booths had anything they needed.

Mick shrugged and turned and walked off without saying anything.

"Thanks," Jessie said.

Samuel's eyes narrowed. "He's going to be a problem."

"He hasn't done anything," Jessie said. "He's just odd."

Samuel sighed and shook his head. "That's good, but I've seen people like him before. Circuses don't always have the best people working for them. We hire people who can do the job. As long as they do it, they can stay. The roustabouts don't need to be nice. They just need to be strong. That's good for the job. Not so much for everyone else."

Jessie promised to be careful and went to the elephants. She led them to the entrance to the big top to wait until the jugglers ran out of the left ring. She and Samuel led the elephants out to the ring. Each elephant held the tail of the elephant in front in their trunk, and they walked out as if they were a small line of children holding hands.

In the ring, they had each elephant place her front legs on the back end of the elephant in front of her until they formed a ring of elephants. Then the elephants started walking in a circle.

The steel tubs were already in the center of the ring. At Samuel's command and with guidance from his walking stick, the elephants stood up on their back legs, backed onto the platforms, and sat on them. This act was harder than it looked because it was a tight formation with the elephants' backsides all touching in the center of the ring. If one of the elephants leaned back too far, it could push the opposite elephant off the tub.

Jessie had watched them practice this new trick for weeks. She felt pride at seeing how well they had mastered it.

She held her breath and watched as Samuel directed this part. Jessie just reassured the elephants they were doing great and got in position. Flo picked her up with her trunk. It wrapped around Jessie's waist and lifted her off the ground. The trunk started swinging, and Flo turned toward Patti. Patti's trunk reached out and grabbed Jessie, as Flo passed her to the next elephant.

Jessie panicked for a moment, although they had practiced this move, and she knew what to expect. The elephants continued passing her around the circle to the wild applause of the audience.

The crowd responded with loud applause, and Jessie was happy. This was the hardest part of the new tricks she and the elephants had learned during winter quarters for this season. Samuel had wanted to do the trick for a couple years, but he hadn't had an assistant willing to be passed from elephant to elephant.

Jessie then worked the elephants through some simple tricks like sitting and moving in unison. They performed well, and Jessie loved the thrill of leading them. Meanwhile, Samuel moved things into place for the final trick.

Jessie led all the elephants except Daisy out of the big top. All eyes were focused on Samuel and Daisy. He had Daisy step onto the tub. She then carefully stepped onto a large metal ball that had been painted yellow, red, and blue to look like a child's ball. There was barely enough room for Daisy to place all her feet on the ball. As soon as she did, Samuel pulled the tub away so the audience could see the precisely balanced elephant.

The audience clapped. Then Samuel set the tub in front of Daisy. Daisy stepped onto the tub and then onto the ground. As the audience clapped, Samuel had Daisy stand up on her back legs. When she finally brought all four legs on the ground, Samuel led her out of the big top.

Jessie and Samuel then led all the elephants to the menagerie. Jessie was bouncing up and down on her toes.

"That was great!" she said.

Samuel smiled. "It went very well. The audience responded well where I thought they would."

Jessie got a ladder and used it to climb up beside each of the elephants and drape them with their costume for the grand spec. She also made sure to compliment each elephant on her performance. She wanted them to know how much she appreciated them.

Once they were ready, she fed them some fresh fruit as a reward for their performance. Then she went into the changing tent to get ready. Samuel didn't have to change for the finale.

Jessie pulled on the satin outfit and checked her makeup. It looked atrocious close up, but it had to be overdone so that it looked fine from the grandstands.

When she was ready, she walked back out and made sure the water trough was filled. The elephants worked hard and they needed to be treated well.

Samuel was walking around, checking each elephant.

"Are they all right?" Jessie asked.

"They're fine," he said. "I just like to check them out when I think about it. It helps me catch any problems early, so they don't become big problems. They are all big, beautiful behemoths."

They heard the cue music that let them know to form up the parade line. Since the elephants weren't at the front, they didn't have to rush to get in line.

The grand spec was just as much a spectacular parade as the opening spec, although it had one less headpiece in it, which suited Jessie just fine. It made the performance go a lot smoother for her.

She watched at one point as Bradley walked along, exaggerating the lift of each step, so he wouldn't trip over his oversized shoes. Once he did a handstand and the tops of his shoes fell open, exposing large fake toes. He squirted water in the face of teenage girl who laughed hysterically. He pretended to trip over a prop at the edge of the center ring, did an exaggerated fall, rolled into a somersault and jumped back to his feet.

Jessie smiled at his antics because he looked like he was having a lot of fun.

He saw a little boy in the front row of bleachers and danced over to hand the boy a lollipop. The boy took one look at him, screamed, and ducked behind his father.

Bradley hurried on. He stayed in character, although he

must have wanted to try and calm the kid. However, the best thing to do was hurry away and allow the child to calm down.

Kids either liked or hated clowns. Jessie hadn't even like them until she met Bradley. Bradley had told her he could tell from the expression on their faces, but sometimes one of them fooled him.

After the performance, Jessie changed into her work clothes and washed the elephants. She also made sure they had fresh hay for the evening.

Then she took a deep breath. Her first performance in front of an audience was done. She was officially a circus performer now. She danced around, skipping and waving her hands in the air. The elephants just looked at her and snorted.

19
MARCH 1937

Jessie found Bradley still sitting in the clown's tent after she had fed and watered the elephants. She had gone to find him to have dinner with him. She thought he would have changed out of his costume and makeup, but he hadn't.

The tent had two rows of tables with mirrors in the center of the tent. The clowns could apply their makeup before a show and take it off afterward. However, Bradley was the only clown still in the tent, and he still had his makeup on. He sat staring at himself in a mirror.

Jessie gave him a reassuring hug and sat down next to him.

"Bradley, you need to change so we can get something to eat."

His shoulders sagged. "You had better go without me."

He didn't look away from the mirror. Although he had a smile painted on his face, this close Jessie could see he was actually frowning.

She laid a hand on his back. "What's wrong?"

"I terrified a child tonight. I was just goofing around, but he took one look at me and screamed."

She remembered seeing his reaction while she was riding around the big top during the grand spec. "I guess he didn't like clowns."

"Why? I was just trying to make him laugh. I love the sound of laughter, but but he was crying. I wanted to apologize, but I was afraid to get close to him because I might have upset him more."

Jessie thought about her own feelings about clowns. "It's the makeup. It makes the clowns look like a smiling ghost or a badly make porcelain doll."

He turned his head to look her in the eyes. "Is that what you see when you look at me?"

"Not anymore. I got used to seeing you in makeup. I think most people get past their fear eventually."

Bradley sighed. "Eventually, but until then, I will scare little kids."

"He was just one kid, Bradley. It happens sometimes. I've seen kids afraid of the elephants, especially when the elephants reach their trunks out to them. I think they see it as a type of snake."

"Maybe, but Jessie, I never purposely scared anyone before."

"You didn't this time. You are too nice to do that."

Bradley sighed again. "Thanks. You had better go on and eat. I'm not hungry, and I won't be such good company tonight."

"Are you sure?"

He nodded.

Jessie wasn't sure what more she could do. She left and said she would check on him later. She walked to the entrance, looked back at Bradley once more, and headed toward the cookhouse.

She grabbed a light meal of tomato soup and rolls and sat

down at an empty table. Within a minute, Alexander Dupree the knife thrower sat down beside her.

"What's wrong, my beauty?" he asked.

"Bradley had a bad experience tonight."

"Bradley, he is the one who is your friend you are always with."

Jessie nodded. "I wish I could help him, but I'm not sure how."

Alexander nodded. "He is a good man. He comes from a good family, but working as a clown, that is something different for him. He is as new to it as you are with the elephants. You learned. He will learn. We all have setbacks."

Jessie knew he was right. She had had so much to get used to when she joined the circus, and she still had a lot to learn. She hadn't considered that Bradley was new, too. Sure, he had grown up in a circus, but it had been as an aerialist, not a clown.

"How is Tina?" Jessie asked, changing the subject.

He chuckled. "She is fine. She has forgiven me, but she threatened to use one of my knives to cut off something very precious to me if it happens again."

Jessie's eyes widened. "Did she mean it?"

"Most certainly."

"Are you worried?"

He shook his head. "No, it is a reminder to me to stay focused. If I cut her, she certainly has reason to cut me, but oh, the ladies would be so disappointed."

That was when Jessie realized what Tina had threatened to cut off Alexander, and she blushed.

He patted her shoulder. "Things will get better, my beauty. Both for Bradley and for me. I have Tina to keep me focused, and Bradley has you."

After she ate dinner, Jessie walked back to her room at

the end of the train car.

The doors had been closed, and it was hot in the corridor. Her room would be hot, too. She would need to open the window in her room and turn on the fan. It might be cooler by the time Gail came in.

With everything happening on the midway, Jessie was surprised she wasn't swept up in the excitement. Instead, she was tired and felt like getting a good night's sleep. She didn't have any duties on the midway, and unlike many of the other performers, she couldn't sleep late in the morning. She would need to be up early to feed and water the elephants.

She unlocked the door, went inside, and flicked the switch to turn on the lights. She saw a bouquet of flowers sitting on the table. Someone must have been trying to impress Gail. Jessie wondered if it was a townie or someone with the circus. Whoever it was, given that Gail was off somewhere, the flowers might have worked.

Jessie opened the window and turned on the small fan mounted in a corner of the room. With the sun down, it had cooled off outside. She wanted to get some of that cooler air into the room.

Jessie took a nightgown from a drawer and her bag of toiletries. She went back to the bathroom and washed the sweat from her with a washcloth and brushed her teeth. When the trains were stopped, water lines could be run to the train cars parked on the fairground siding. She had removed her makeup earlier so she didn't have that to worry about. She just wanted to try and cool down a bit. She changed into the nightgown and went back to her room.

While she was brushing her hair, Gail walked in.

"Hi, dearie. You're turning in early," Gail said.

"I'm exhausted, and I have to get up early to feed the elephants."

"The noise from the crowds might keep you awake. It can take some getting used to."

Jessie shrugged. "Not much choice. I need to sleep. Are you going to put your flowers in a vase?"

Gail looked over at the bouquet. "Those aren't mine."

Jessie stared at her. "I thought an admirer gave them to you."

Gail chuckled. "I'm not that lucky. The guys I attract would give me a beer before they gave me flowers."

"But they were in the room when I came in."

Gail's eyes widened. "What?"

"They were just sitting on the table."

"Was the door locked?" Jessie nodded. Gail shook her head and frowned. "It's Mick."

"What?"

Gail looked around, frightened. She opened the closet doors and looked inside. Then she looked out the window.

"I told you not to encourage him," Gail said.

Jessie's face reddened, though she had done nothing wrong. "I haven't been, other than saying hello if he says hello to me."

"He did this to one of the showgirls. He left flowers in her room. He must know how to pick locks. I don't know how else he could get into the room. Carl keeps track of the room keys," Gail said, sounding slightly frantic.

"Should we report him?" Jessie felt worried. Had she done something wrong? Was she responsible in some way?

"It wouldn't do any good unless someone saw him on this car, and even then, someone would need to see him go into the room."

"What about that other woman he left flowers for? Maybe she could tell us something to help. Obviously, Mick's not bothering her anymore."

Gail sighed and sat on her bed. "She didn't even finish last season. When we left Baltimore, she wasn't on the train. She didn't say anything to anyone about leaving."

Jessie felt a knot form in her stomach. "No one saw her?"

Gail shook her head.

"And you think Mick did something to her?" Jessie asked as she climbed into her bunk.

"He left her flowers. They saw each other for a while until Eve—that was her name—started showing bruises. She stopped seeing him, but that's kind of hard to do in a circus. They worked around each other; they were going to see each other. After they broke up, she got very quiet. She wouldn't say anything. Some of us said something to Mr. Conroy. He talked to Mick and Eve, but nothing else happened. No one said anything about what was said. Eve just got more quiet and withdrawn, and two weeks after Mr. Conroy talked to her, she left."

Jessie felt a chill run down her back, and it wasn't from the cool air coming into the room.

"I just hope she left on her own."

Gail nodded, but didn't seem certain. "I do, too. It would have been the best thing that could have happened."

"Why doesn't Mr. Conroy fire him?"

"Whatever else he might be, Mick is not dumb. He behaves in public and works hard. He doesn't give anyone a reason to fire him."

Neither of them said anything for a few minutes.

Mick had come into the room to leave flowers. Did he think that would be romantic and impress her? It was creepy.

"Obviously, I'm not going to see him," Jessie said finally. "Will that be enough for him to leave me alone?"

Gail shrugged. "I don't know. I'd make sure not to be out at night alone."

"He beat Eve?"

"We thought so. We think that is why she had bruises. I can't say he attacked her while she was by herself. He probably did it when they saw each other, but if you turn him down, you need to be careful."

Jessie sat up. "Turn him down?"

Gail waved at the flowers. "If he left you flowers, he is going to ask you out."

Jessie shook her head. She had just started with the circus. She was getting to work with the elephants. Things were going great. She didn't want someone to drive her away from here.

"Can we shove the chair under the door handle tonight?" Jessie asked.

Gail nodded. "If you don't, I will. I'm not in for the night, though. I just came to fix my hair. Peter asked me to go into town for drinks."

Peter Sizemore was the dog handler along with his sister, Cecile. They had a dozen different dogs they used in their act. Women swooned over the dogs, wanting to pet them, which brought the women to him and gave him his choice of dates. He also had thick, blond hair that the women liked.

"You're not worried about him?" Jessie asked.

Gail chuckled. "Peter? I've known him for years. We go out from time to time, but he doesn't get serious with anyone. He is nice, though."

She stood up and walked over to the mirror hanging on the wall. She touched up her hair and slid a barrette with a red silk rose on it into her black hair. She wore her hair short so that it wouldn't get stuck in her outfits she wore as a showgirl, but she also liked to wear wigs. Gail was a woman who liked to change up her appearance.

She changed out of the summer blouse she had been

wearing, although she kept the pleated skirt. It was something she had made herself since she also worked as a seamstress for the circus.

"It looks like it might be more than casual," Jessie said.

Gail shrugged. "You never know, besides even if nothing happens, I want the man to wish something would."

Jessie grinned. "Oh, he will."

Gail stared at her in the mirror. She sighed and turned around. "I can stay with you if you don't want to be alone. Peter will understand."

Jessie was tempted to take her up on the offer. She wasn't sure she wanted to be alone in the room even with the door locked. Mick had shown he could get inside the locked room. She didn't want to be a burden to anyone, though. The circus had taught her she needed to pull her weight.

"I'll be fine," Jessie replied.

Gail raised an eyebrow.

"I'll be fine," Jessie repeated more firmly.

Gail nodded. "Okay. I won't be out too late. Peter's like you. He has to get up early to take care of his dogs."

She came over and gave Jessie a quick hug. Then she headed out of the room. Jessie locked it behind her. It wouldn't stop Mick if he tried to get inside, but at least it would delay him.

Jessie didn't connect the straps since the train wouldn't be moving tonight. The room was still warm, but it was cooling down.

She could hear the noise of the crowd in the distance. It was a constant rumble of voices, occasionally punctuated by a cheer or shout. The railroad wasn't close to the crowds. It was still a lot of people though, and they made a lot of noise.

Jessie lay on her back, thinking she wouldn't be able to fall asleep. Her mind raced, and every little noise made her look at the door.

As she tried to calm herself, she thought about the performance and how well the elephants had done. Then she started thinking about other tricks the elephants might be able to do. She wasn't sure how much the elephants could do—dancing was out of the question—but there were other things Jessie was sure they were capable of. She even thought about trying to incorporate Peter's dogs in the act. Could dogs and elephants work together?

At some point she fell asleep, and she didn't even stir when Gail came home. Jessie didn't wake until her alarm went off next to her head. She kept the alarm clock in the corner of her bunk so she could reach it and turn it off without waking Gail.

She turned the alarm off and lay in bed surprised, first that she had fallen asleep and second that she hadn't awakened when Gail came in without waking her. What if it had been Mick instead?

She climbed down from her bunk and saw Gail under her blanket in her bunk. She also noticed that Gail had shoved a chair under the doorknob.

Jessie tied her hair back in a ponytail and dressed in her work clothes. Then she headed out to the menagerie. Luckily, Samuel was also there with Dr. Portman, the circus veterinarian.

"Is something wrong with the elephants?" Jessie asked, slightly panicked.

Samuel shook his head. "No, it's a routine check-up. Sometimes, traveling on the train will upset them or make them stressed."

Jessie filled the water trough. She was glad the two men were there. It was unlikely Mick would try to approach her with the other men around.

She greeted each elephant, speaking to them and touching

them. Myrna seemed to sense something was bothering Jessie. She wrapped her trunk around Jessie's shoulders and patted her on the head as if Jessie were a puppy.

"Thank you," Jessie whispered to her.

Jessie brought out a bushel of peaches and let the elephants eat. While they did, she changed the straw to give them fresh bedding.

Once she finished, she hurried back to the train car to get ready for breakfast. She washed herself in the bathroom, and when she came back into the room, Gail was awake.

"You're up early," Jessie said. "Did you have fun last night?"

Gail laughed. "A lot, but I need to do laundry."

"Already? We've only been away from winter quarters for a couple days."

Gail shrugged. "I go through a lot of clothes. Besides, our next couple stops are just one-day stops. I won't have time for laundry for another week."

Most everyone did laundry when they had a multiday stop because they had extra time and space to hang their laundry and let it dry outside.

Jessie met Bradley at breakfast. He still seemed depressed, which was not a good state for a clown to be in.

"I'll get over it," he explained. "As long as I don't scare another kid."

"Do you think you will? You're so funny as a clown."

"The other clowns say it will happen again, probably a few times each season. They've been doing this for year, and they still scare kids. Tim told me that sometimes our acts make people laugh. Sometimes they don't. We don't get upset about the people who don't laugh. We just try to make more people laugh. The answer to both scared children and people who don't laugh is that we need to be funnier." Tim

Chapel was the head clown with the circus.

"There are worse things to be," Jessie said.

Bradley reached over and gave her hand a light squeeze. "What are you afraid of?"

She hesitated. This wasn't something she had ever talked about except with Leanne. "Fire and being alone."

She expected him to make light of it, but instead Bradley asked, "Do you know why?"

Jessie looked away unable to look him in the eyes. "I think so."

"Is it something you can change or deal with?"

"I try when it comes up. Usually, I just don't worry about, but when something happens that makes me think about it, I try to be calm. I tell myself how to be careful around fire or that I shouldn't worry about being alone."

"Does it work or help?" Bradley asked.

"Sometimes. I'm better than I used to be, though. Fire used to make me cry."

He reached out and rested his hand on her arm. She resisted flinching as his hand rested on her scars. He hadn't seen her scars because she still wore long-sleeved blouses and avoided some of the revealing clothing that other women with the circus wore.

"Sometimes I wonder if it will get easier for me."

"I'm sure it will, but it will take time."

After breakfast, they decided to take a walk and headed into the city. They walked along the streets, enjoying the morning. It was like a different world. This was what most people considered normal, working in one place at a job like so many other people.

Jessie saw sights that reminded her of Harrisburg from time to time. She supposed it was just because she was in a city again, but she was surprised at how few memories she still had from her hometown. She should have remembered more, especially about her family.

Bradley saw her frowning and asked, "What's wrong?"

"Nothing. I was just a bit sad that I can't remember more of when I lived in Harrisburg."

"How long did you live there?"

"Until I was thirteen."

"And you had to leave Harrisburg because of the fire?" he asked.

Jessie nodded. "I didn't have any say in it, but yes."

"I'm so sorry, but at least you're alive."

Tears ran down her eyes. "But I shouldn't be. I caused it. Sparks jumped out of the fire and caught my book on fire. I threw it off me, and it caught the carpet on fire and it spread quickly. Too quickly. My dad and I rushed out of the house, but he ran back inside when he heard my mother yelling. No one ever came out."

Bradley put an arm across her shoulders as they walked. He saw a bench under a tree and walked her over to sit down. He didn't say anything. He just let her cry.

"It wasn't your fault," he said finally. "You have to know that."

"I can tell myself that, but I just don't feel that way. They're gone because of me."

"Fires happen, and sometimes, there's nothing you can do about it. That belief is hurting you to the point where you are forgetting those memories of them, some of them which are very happy, because you don't want to let go of your guilt."

Jessie heard the words, and they pricked at her like little needles. She wasn't sure whether she was hurt because what he was saying was right or because it was wrong.

She stood up. "You don't know that!" she snapped.

Bradley stayed calm. "You're right. I don't know, but I

can see what this is doing to you. Do you really want to forget about your family?"

"I won't. People just forget things when they get older."

Bradley nodded. "Sure, but they can remember plenty of things from when they were little kids. I can remember things from when I was five. Not many things, but when I told my parents about them, they told me how old I was when it happened."

"You have good memories, though."

Bradley looked away. "I told you about my uncle falling from the trapeze." Jessie nodded. "I was only eight. I told you that was when I decided to become a clown, but really, I think it was decided for me. It wasn't just what Tim said. After I had such a bad debut, I realized I was suddenly afraid of heights. I couldn't be up there, but I was too afraid of falling. I couldn't climb down the pole because I was afraid of falling. I was up there for half an hour before my family realized I hadn't come down. My dad had to climb up and carry me down.

"I've never gone up again. I'm terrified of heights now. It's why I became a clown. An aerialist who is afraid of heights is no aerialist."

"But you're still afraid of heights."

"Yes, and you're afraid of fire. I found my way forward like you have done. The difference is I can still admire what my family does up there. I can still remember how my uncle used to carry me on his shoulders, and he and my father would toss me back and forth. I can smile at those memories. The fact that he's dead makes those memories even more precious to me because I know I won't have any more memories of him."

Jessie started crying again.

"If you want to remember your family, you have to work

to keep those memories and think about them. If you start to forget, that's when you remember the fire. It's your reason to keep the good memories."

He reached out and took her hand. He gently pulled her back to the bench. She was sobbing harder now. Some passersby on the sidewalk stared at her.

"Tell me about your family," Bradley said finally.

Jessie looked at him in disbelief. Then she nodded. "My father always seemed to be wearing a suit"

She kept talking. The more she did, the more other memories appeared in her mind. Occasionally, if she faltered, Bradley would prod her with a question. After a while, he got up silently and they walked back to the fairgrounds. She kept talking about her family the whole time.

20

APRIL 1937

Jessie had mulled over what trick she could teach the elephants to impress Samuel and show him that she deserved her position. Not that he complained about her work, but she still wanted to prove herself—maybe to herself and not Samuel. She had been thinking about what Bradley had said about wanting to prove to himself and others that he deserved to be a clown. Was that what she wanted to do? Prove that she deserved her position as an elephant trainer?

The unbalanced headpiece was what gave Jessie her idea. She taught a trick to Myrna and worked on it in private for a few weeks until she thought it was good enough to show Samuel.

One afternoon, she asked Samuel to meet her at the menagerie. When he walked into the tent, Jessie was wearing her safari outfit.

Samuel looked her up and down. "You got dressed early, and in the wrong outfit."

Jessie smiled. "No, this is the right outfit."

She walked over to stand in front of Myrna. "I have been

working on a trick with Myrna."

Samuel smiled. "Why didn't you say anything?"

"I wanted to surprise you. I'm hoping if it's good enough, we can work it into the act."

He looked skeptical, but he nodded. "So what's the trick?"

"Myrna, hat."

Myrna's trunk reached out and grabbed the helmet by the brim. The elephant took the helmet off Jessie's head, lifted it up, and set it on her own head. Then she gave a slight trumpet, lifted the hat and took a slight bow by bending one leg and moving it behind her other front leg.

Samuel's eyes widened. Then he laughed and clapped. Jessie couldn't remember ever hearing him laugh before.

"That's delightful!" he said.

Jessie smiled at the praise.

"It's very clever. I would say Myrna is a pig because she acts like a ham. We can easily work this into the act right at the beginning as we get rid of the helmets."

Jessie nodded, excited that she and Samuel were thinking the same thing. "That's what I was thinking."

"The next town where have an extra day is Des Moines. We'll do a run through during the morning there to smooth out any rough edges it takes to work it in."

"That would be great."

Samuel nodded and walked off.

She turned and patted Myrna's head. "You did great, girl."

Jessie nearly ran to the cookhouse. She was walking on clouds until she noticed Mick heading in her direction from the far end of the midway. He waved, but she acted like she didn't see him and quickened her pace.

She had been avoiding him since their stop at Little Rock.

He had seen her there and asked if she liked the flowers. She thanked him, but told him going into her room to leave them was wrong. He had looked angry at the rebuke. Jessie had switched to some light-hearted comments to diffuse the situation and left as soon as she could.

She got to the cookhouse ahead of Mick. There were plenty of people there eating breakfast. She wouldn't have to worry about Mick causing a scene. She grabbed a tray and started down the food line.

She saw Mick enter the tent. He got a tray and walked over next to her.

"Good morning, Jessie."

"Hi, Mick. How are you?"

She put some bacon and toast on her plate. She avoided the eggs. They were powdered and didn't taste good. Her typical breakfast was oatmeal, bacon, toast, and jam, with coffee to drink.

"Fine," Mick said. "I haven't seen you much lately."

"Well, we both have our jobs to do."

"There's still time off we could get together."

Jessie shook her head. "Mick, you're nice, but I'm seeing Bradley."

His eyes narrowed. "The clown?"

"Yes."

He reached out and grabbed her forearm. He squeezed it too tight. Jessie tried not to wince.

"I saw you first."

Jessie could feel her heart race. She said nothing at first. She calmed herself and reminded herself she was in a very public place. Mick would have to be careful because she could call for help.

She didn't try to pull her arm free because she doubted she could break his grip.

"Let go of my arm, Mick," Jessie said firmly.

"What if I don't? Are you going to yell?"

He didn't seem to be afraid of that. What was he thinking?

She grabbed her fork and held it above his hand.

"A fork?"

"Better than a knife. A knife will stab you once. This will stab you four times at once."

She sounded more confident than she felt. It was something she had learned from working with the elephants. You had to sound as if you were in charge. The elephants were more likely to obey a command than a request.

Mick glanced around and then let go her arm.

"You're mine," he said.

"I'm no one's unless I say I am. I used to think you were nice, Mick, but I think a lot of people are nice. It doesn't mean there was anything between us."

She turned and walked away with her food. Luckily, she saw Bradley sitting at a table. He wasn't eating. He was just watching her, looking like he was ready to jump up if she needed help. He might perform as a clown, but beneath his baggy costumes, Bradley was surprisingly lean and hard muscled. Yet, she had never seen him exercise.

She walked over and sat down next to him.

"Good morning," she said with a smile.

"Trouble?"

Jessie glanced up. Mick was staring at her. He left his tray on the food line and stomped out of the cookhouse.

"Not this time," she said.

"Will there be a next time?"

"I hope not. Why hasn't anyone done anything about him? Everyone says he is a problem."

"Saying he's a problem is one thing. Proving he's a problem is something else. The roustabouts side with Mick.

They're their own group. If he gets fired, and they don't think it's right, the circus could find itself short some roustabouts, or worse, find itself plagued with problems."

It didn't sound like Jessie would be lucky enough for Mick to quit. She wasn't going to run off, though. She had found her calling, and she was going to stay.

"I showed Samuel Myrna's trick this morning," she said.

He rolled his hand forward, urging her to continue. "And?"

Jessie waited, letting the tension build. "He loved it."

"I told you he would. It's cute. People will love it."

"I hope so."

Samuel and Jessie worked on the trick at Des Moines, and it easily fit into their act. The only change they made to it was that they reordered the elephants in line as they entered the big top. Myrna was placed at the rear. Jessie led the elephants in and turned them in a circle. Then she turned to face the audience. As Myrna entered the ring, she reached over to grab the helmet with her trunk and place it on her own head.

Jessie made a big show of discovering the helmet was missing and looking around for it. Then, finding it on Myrna's head, she made the elephant place it back on her head. After which, Myrna took her bow.

The audience loved it and laughed as hard as they did for some of the clowns' antics.

21
MAY 1937

Jessie looked into the big top. Most of the crowd from the matinee performance had left to enjoy the midway games. Inside, roustabouts were setting up tables and benches. The assistant cooks rolled out carts filled with hot dogs, potato salad, and pitchers of lemonade. Meanwhile, dozens of orphans waited in the bleachers growing more excited.

Jessie saw Mick helping with the set up. He smiled and looked happy, but she knew how he could really be behind that smile. She didn't want to see that side of him again. He wasn't the reason she stayed outside the big top, though.

She looked around for Bradley and saw him shambling toward her. He was still dressed in his costume.

"There you are," she said, reaching out to take his hand in hers.

"I don't want to do this. I can barely stand being in the big top during a performance."

"That's why you need to do this. I think it will help."

Bradley peeked in between the canvas panels. "There are

so many kids."

"But not as many as during the show."

"But these kids will be closer to me."

"That's the whole idea, Bradley. Sure, some kids don't like clowns. Some don't like elephants or large men or cars. We've all got fears. These kids will enjoy meeting you."

"And what if one of them is afraid of clowns?"

"Then this is a learning experience. You'll be close enough to see how they react. You can learn those reactions and know when to back off. It's part of the way we train elephants. You have to learn their personalities and what to watch out for if they are getting upset or stubborn because they can't tell you what's wrong."

Bradley hugged her. She relaxed against his chest. She heard his heart racing, and she knew it wasn't from excitement. He was afraid of facing these children. She might have kissed him if he hadn't been wearing more makeup than she was.

"Don't get any of your makeup on me," she warned him.

"I won't."

When he let go, Jessie looked inside again, remembering the Orphans Days she had attended while living in the Wilson Home. Those days had helped her fall in love with the circus, and that love had reunited her with Myrna.

"This brings back memories," she said.

"Me holding you like this?"

She shook her head. "No, I went to Orphans Day every year. It was great fun, and I got to see Myrna." She paused and added, "I may have even seen you and not realized it."

"You would have remembered if you had. I was the best-looking kid on the midway. I helped with games and sales."

Jessie elbowed him in the stomach.

"Why don't we do this at every stop?" Jessie asked.

"I don't know. It's Mr. Conroy's decision."

Jessie thought about it. It seemed like the circus only did Orphans Day at their stops in eastern Pennsylvania and northern Maryland. That meant they had Orphans Day at a dozen stops in a row, but nothing before or after. Odd.

The only Orphans Day Jessie had skipped watching so far was in York. She hadn't wanted to risk being seen by the Wilsons or any of the orphans they took care of. While she wanted to see them, she was worried about what their reaction might be. Would they try to take her back to the home? Would they tell her she had made they ashamed? She wasn't willing to risk her life with the circus now that she was getting used to it.

She had retreated to the menagerie after the show, then snuck around behind the tents to get back to the train unseen by anyone other than circus folk. She had stayed there until it was time to get ready for the evening show, and even then, she snuck back to the menagerie.

"You had better go in," Jessie said. She watched the children swarm off the bleachers toward the tables.

Bradley straightened up. She could see that under his makeup he still wasn't smiling. He walked into the big top with his oversize feet slapping the ground and waving his hands at the excited orphans.

Jessie watched him draw closer to the children. As they saw him, they started shouting. He waved to them. Then one little boy ran toward him. He froze. The little boy grabbed him around the legs and hugged him. Bradley patted the boy's head, but the boy still held on. Jessie couldn't hear what Bradley said, but he lifted the boy up and carried him to the tables.

When he set the boy down, Bradley took off the tiny party hat he wore as part of his costume and fastened it on the boy's head.

Then he started dancing and skipping, and occasionally falling. The children loved it. They laughed and cheered, and some of them followed Bradley around, dancing with him.

The children slowly settled down to eat. Bradley sat down next to the little boy with his hat.

Jessie watched Mr. Conroy walk around talking to the children. He would be asking them how old they were and if they remembered anything from before they were orphaned. As she watched, though, she noticed that he didn't speak to all the children. She had always thought he asked the same question of all the orphans, but it appeared that he was only speaking to the older teenage orphans.

When the group started to separate to go the midway, Mr. Conroy was quick to leave the big top.

"Hello, Jessie," he said when saw her standing outside the big top. "What are you doing out here?"

"Just lending some support to Bradley."

He looked over his shoulder at the activity in the ring. The orphans loved him. None of them seemed the least bit scared of him.

Mr. Conroy started to walk away.

"Mr. Conroy?" she asked.

He stopped and turned back.

"Why don't you do Orphans Day at all our stops?"

He shrugged. "I can only afford to do it at a few places."

"But it's just in eastern Pennsylvania and northern Maryland. Why not alternate places? It's a wonderful experience for orphans. I loved it when I was younger."

He smiled. "I'll think about it."

Something suddenly clicked in her mind when she thought about the questions he asked her compared to the questions he asked now.

"Are you looking for someone?"

Anger flashed over his expression for a moment, then fear.

"Why would you say that?" he asked, his circus persona back in place.

"I just remembered when you asked me questions, you asked all the kids who looked my age the same questions. When I watched you in there, it was also the older orphans, maybe a little older that you talked to. It seems like you are only interested in orphans who are fourteen or fifteen. When I was in the Wilson Home, it was twelve or thirteen. It's like you're trying to find an orphan who is near my age."

Mr. Conroy took a deep breath. "Where we stop and who I speak with is my choice, Jessie. You're doing well here, but don't pry into people's business. We all have things we don't choose to talk about. Respect that."

His flat, emotionless voice scared her nearly as much as Mick grabbing her arm had scared her. What had she said that was so wrong?

He started to turn away, but Jessie couldn't help but ask, "What happens when the person you are looking for is an adult? Will you stop Orphans Day then?"

Mr. Conroy's back stiffened, but he continued to walk away without answering.

22
MAY 1937

Jessie was excited for the three days the circus performed at Hampton Roads, Virginia. Yes, it was nice to be in one place for three days, but she was excited to see the ocean. She had never seen the ocean. Even in Florida, she hadn't made it to the shore, even though it was only ninety minutes away. She had seen pictures in magazines of the waves and sand and wanted to see if the real thing matched what she imagined they would be like.

When the circus arrived and set up, she could tell the difference immediately. The air smelled salty. She thought she could hear the waves crashing on the shore. She doubted it, though, because Bradley told her they weren't close enough to the shore.

The morning of their second day in the city, she and Bradley boarded a bus that had a stop near the ocean. He arranged for the animal handlers to feed the elephants in the morning.

As soon as Jessie spotted the green water in the distance, she started bouncing in her seat. Bradley chuckled. When the bus let them off, they needed to walk four blocks until the buildings ended and she saw the beach and the ocean.

Jessie took off her sandals and walked into the sand.

"Oh, it's so soft!" she exclaimed.

"Not when it gets wet. Then it feels very gritty. It will also get really hot once the sun has been up for a while."

"How hot?"

"You won't be standing there with your toes buried in the sand."

Jessie smiled. "Can we go down to the water?"

"That's why we're here."

She took his hand, and they walked toward the water. She paused a couple times to stare at the waves as they rolled toward the shore, broke into white foam, and rushed up onto the beach.

"I wish I had a bathing suit."

"There are places nearby where you can buy one if you want."

The walked across the sand and stopped where the sand changed color because it was wet. She reached out her foot and sunk her toes into the sand. When she pulled her foot back, the impression of her toes remained. Bradley was right. It felt grittier and colder than the powdery sand.

She noticed it was windier here at the water than it had been at the fairgrounds. The salt smell was stronger, too.

She walked closer to the water as a wave washed up on the beach and foam swirled around her feet. The water was cool, but not cold. She laughed as it tickled her feet.

Then she started running along the beach, dashing in and out of the water. She kicked and splashed, but she went no deeper than her ankles so she wouldn't get her skirt wet.

Bradley followed behind, stopping occasionally and bending over, picking up things. When Jessie walked over to him, he held out three seashells for her. One resembled a fan. The second was circular like a snail shell, and the third one looked like a cone. She picked each one up and examined it.

"They're lovely," she said.

She slipped them into her pockets. Then she hiked her skirt up to her knees and tied the loose fabric in a knot.

She walked back into the water and was able to go as deep as mid-calf without getting her skirt wet. Bradley rolled his pants legs up to his knees and followed her into the water. Jessie ventured out a little further and the water started lapping at the edge of the skirt. She didn't mind, though. She was having too much fun.

She looked back at the shore and was surprised there weren't more people. They were supposed to enjoy the beach and the water.

She saw Bradley grinning and ran over to him. She flung her arms around his neck and hugged him tight. He hugged her back.

"I guess this means you like it," he said.

She kissed him as the ocean water swirled around her feet. It felt natural and right. She felt Bradley's lips against hers, she inhaled quickly. Their lips met softly at first, a hesitant brush that quickly turned into a deeper, more passionate kiss. The world faded. They were left with a perfect, fleeting moment. Jessi didn't even hear the waves any longer. The sound of her heart pounding in her ears drowned it out.

She pulled her head back and stared at him. His blue eyes sparkled with a reflection off the water. He stared into her eyes and smiled.

"That was… nice," he whispered.

She lifted a hand to his cheek. "Yes."

She felt Bradley's hands slide onto her back. A shiver raced along her spine. She leaned in and kissed him again.

The water around her feet sucked away some of the sand. She felt her foot rock backwards and took it as a sign. They fell back into the soft sand and kissed. As the kiss deepened, a wave rolled onto the beach and around her body. The warm rush of water around her did nothing to cool the heat she felt building inside her.

The water soaked their clothes, and the sand clung to their skin, gritty and uncomfortable, but they didn't care. They were lost in each other, oblivious to everything else. Then a larger wave splashed over them, spraying saltwater on their faces.

Bradley jerked his head back, sputtering a bit. "I guess the ocean wanted to kiss you as much as I did," he said, smiling.

She could taste a bit of saltwater in her mouth, but when she ran her tongue across her lips, they seemed to taste sweet and warm, a lingering effect of Bradley's kiss.

Then she began itching from sand that had made its way into her clothing. "Well, this won't be fun for the ride home," Jessie said.

Bradley pulled back and stood up. He reached down and helped Jessie get to her feet. He brushed some sand from her face. His touch made her skin tingle.

"We can use the showerhouse to take our clothes off and shake out most of the sand." He pointed to a building near the edge of the beach.

They walked over to it. It was two rooms. One for men and one for women.

"You can go inside and pass your clothing out, piece by piece, and I will shake them out for you," Bradley offered.

She went inside and took off her blouse. She opened the door a few inches and stuck her hand out, holding the blouse. Bradley took it and shook it like a small rug. While he was doing that, she took off her bra and shook it free of sand. He passed the blouse back to her. She peered around the edge of the door and grinned at him.

"You know I'm nearly nude."

Bradley. "I can imagine."

She chuckled. "I bet you can."

She slipped off her skirt and bloomers. She passed them out the door. Bradley took them and shook them off. However, he didn't pass them back.

"My clothing, please," Jessie said.

Bradley looked at the skirt and bloomers. "Now I suppose you are really nude."

"And I'd like not to be."

"So what happens if I don't give them back? I don't suppose you will come out and get them."

"I will not," she said indignantly.

"I could come inside and give them to you."

"Or you could just hand them to me."

Bradley rubbed his chin.

"Bradley, you're being mean."

He shook his head. "No, I'm just thinking about how much I enjoyed kissing you."

Jessie had to admit she was thinking about it a lot, too. She made a decision and opened the door wider.

"Why don't you bring my clothes inside?"

He did. He locked the door behind him. Then he just stared at her.

"Something wrong?" she asked.

"You're beautiful."

She kissed him. Then she fumbled with the buttons on his shirt and slipped it off his shoulders. He undid his belt and pushed his pants down and quickly stepped out of them.

Jessie looked around and saw a bench in a changing booth. She pushed him back into the changing area, and he sat down. Then she was kissing him again as they fumbled their way into exploring each other.

The sun was high in the sky when they left the changing room in a blissful daze and dressed in sand-free clothing. They held hands as they walked back to the bus stop. They still needed to get back to the circus in time for the matinee performance. She rested her head on his shoulder on the ride back and wrapped her fingers in his.

"This is a perfect day," she whispered.

"Don't jinx it."

"Jinx?"

"You have to know by now circus folk are superstitious."

Jessie nodded. "So I can never be thankful for the good stuff?"

"Great stuff."

"Great stuff in my life?"

"Fine. I just want to I don't know shout for joy," Bradley said.

"I would have wanted to stay on the beach all day."

Bradley asked, "With or without clothes?"

She slapped his arm. "What happens now, though? With us?"

"We've been headed in this direction for a while now. If we keep going, I imagine we'll be married."

"Are you asking?"

"Not right now. There are things we'll have to figure out, like where we'd live. And I'd need to get a ring first."

She sighed theatrically and leaned her head against his chest. "Mr. Romance."

"And I also have to figure out how I want to propose."

Jessie sat up straight. "You're serious?"

"Aren't you?"

"What do you think?"

When they arrived back at the circus, they could see the midway was already open and crowded. Jessie needed to check on the elephants. Bradley needed to put his makeup and costume on.

"Want company later?" he asked.

"If it's you. Where do you want to go?"

He lived with his family. Jessie had Gail as a roommate, and Bradley couldn't come aboard the female car.

"I'll come get you about one o'clock. Leave your window open. I'll call up to you."

She nodded, and they parted with a quick kiss.

Jessie skipped and danced her way to the menagerie, humming along the way. Some of the animals had already been taken out to get in their positions for the start of the performance. She carried out a bushel of apples to let the elephants snack on while she got them into their opening parade costumes.

"Where have you been?"

Jessie spun around and saw Mick. The joy of the day ebbed away.

"I don't think it is any of your business," she said.

He rushed up to her before she could react. He pulled a long knife from behind his back. It must have been tucked into his waistband.

"I'm making it my business. I'm tired of you teasing me, you whore. It's time for you to give me what I want."

She was shocked at the sudden change and realized that all the rumors had been true. Knowing that, she had an idea of what he was about to do. Would Jessie be the next woman leaving the circus just to get away from him?

He leaned in to kiss her. When she pulled back, he brought the knife up just below her chin.

"Would you rather this kiss you?" he asked.

Jessie whimpered and froze in place.

Mick smiled. He lowered the knife and put his other hand behind her head to pull her closer.

Then he suddenly yelled.

An elephant trunk wrapped around his hand with the knife and jerked his arm away from Jessie. Mick let go of Jessie and raised his fist to punch Myrna.

Another trunk wrapped around that arm. Jo-Jo had joined the fight. The two elephants stepped back so Mick's arms were stretched out between them.

Jessie watched Mick struggle between the two elephants. He kicked out and jerked his arms, trying to free himself. Nothing worked. The elephants held him tight. She picked up the knife that he had dropped when Myrna grabbed him.

She took a deep breath to calm her racing heart. "You should stop struggling, or the animals might start pulling. They could pull you apart like a wishbone."

"They wouldn't do that," he said. Jessie noticed he had stopped struggling, though.

"You wouldn't be the first person killed by elephants." She wanted him afraid like she had been. "All I would need to do would be to say the elephant's name and say back. You would be in a lot of pain, but just until you died."

Mick's eyes widened. "Don't."

Jessie moved closer to him. "Why shouldn't I? You were about to do something very violent to me."

Mick shook his head. "I wasn't. You wanted it. You would have like it."

"Is that what you think?" She turned to Myrna. "Myrna"

"No, don't! What do you want me to do?"

Jessie hesitated. What would be an appropriate way to punish him? "You are going to quit today—now—and leave.

If I see you again, I won't stop the elephants."

"I need this job."

"I need to feel safe. While the elephants help with that, having you gone will also help. Maybe now you'll understand how some of the other women you chased away felt."

"You wouldn't talk to me like that if the elephants weren't here." He tried to sound intimidating, but he kept his volume low as if he was afraid he would scare the elephants into pulling him apart.

"So?"

"When they let me go—"

"You don't get it, do you?" Jessie said. "The only way I am telling them to release you is if you agree to quit or we wait until someone comes by and I send for Mr. Conroy and the police."

She waited while he struggled again and quickly gave up.

He sighed and said, "I'll quit."

Jessie nodded sharply. "Good. If you change your mind, though, I will tell Mr. Conroy. I'm sure he can find plenty of people who will tell him about you and other women. Do you understand?"

He looked away. "Yes."

She hesitated. He could be lying. She knew that, but she couldn't keep him suspended. She held out the knife.

"Jo-Jo, release. Myrna, release."

The two elephants let go of Mick. He pulled his arms in to his sides and rubbed his wrists. He glared at her and the knife.

Jessie saw him tense and thought he still might attack her. "I wouldn't try it," she said. "Alexander taught me how to handle a knife."

Mick relaxed. She was lying about the knife thrower teaching her about knives, but Mick didn't know that. He scowled at her and then turned and stomped away.

Jessie lowered the knife and walked over to hug Jo-Jo and Myrna. "Thank you," she told them as she patted their foreheads.

She filled a bushel with watermelons and brought them out as a reward for the elephants.

Samuel showed up a few minutes later, and Jessie told him what had happened. He was furious. "Forget the elephants. I'll throw him in the cage with the tigers." His face grew red.

Jessie put a hand on his arm. "Hopefully that won't be needed, although I appreciate the thought."

"I'll make sure he's left. Are you all right to perform?"

Jessie nodded. "I'll feel safer around the elephants."

"I'll bet you will." He stroked Jo-Jo's side. "These ladies are certainly the heroines today."

23

JUNE 1937

When the circus reached York for a two-day stay, Jessie started searching the crowds for Leanne. It was almost reflexive. She paid a lot more attention to the faces of the young women she passed when the circus was in Pennsylvania. Every raven-haired girl Jessie saw made her heart race until she could verify whether or not it was Leanne.

As Jessie waited to enter the big top, she scanned the faces of the people sitting on the bleachers, hoping to see Leanne's bright smile. Seeing Leanne didn't worry her like seeing anyone else from Abbottstown did. Jessie knew Leanne would keep her secrets just like Jessie had kept Leanne's. Besides, Jessie wanted to see her friend so badly and talk to her, it was worth the risk.

Jessie knew that York wasn't the only place where she might see Leanne. Once she had been adopted, she might have moved anywhere. She might not even attend the circus any longer.

Jessie walked to the menagerie to feed the elephants before the evening show. As she walked into the tent, she saw a man standing in front of the tiger cage, staring at Luna.

"You can't be back here, sir," Jessie said. "We will have some of the animals outside to look at after the show, but only circus workers are allowed in here."

"It's all right," the man said. "I have permission from Dr. Portman to be here."

He turned around. It was Dr. Stultz. His hair was still bushy, and he had more gray hair in his beard. He still resembled an aged lion.

Jessie wanted to run off, but she knew it wouldn't do any good. She'd been seen.

He jumped slightly. "Jessie."

"Hello."

Dr. Stultz cocked his head to the side. "Hello? That's all you have to say?"

"I thought you didn't like the circus."

The veterinarian chuckled. "Yes, but I do like animals, and I like to check on the ones in circuses that come through York. Circuses like this one with a good veterinarian on staff have no problem with extra eyes examining the animals in case someone should complain."

"Well, how do you find the animals?" Jessie asked.

"They are well cared for. They have plenty of water, and this tent is well ventilated."

Jessie smiled. She knew she did her part to make sure the elephants were well cared for. However, she couldn't look Dr. Stultz in the eyes because she knew what he wanted to hear.

"You should go talk to the Wilsons," he said after a few moments. "They will be here for Orphans Day."

Jessie stared at her feet. "I can't."

The doctor snorted. "Of course, you can. You won't.

There's a difference."

Jessie said nothing.

"So, why won't you go talk to them?" Dr. Stultz continued. "They can't make you leave here. You're too old."

"I know that."

"Then why? Are you ashamed? Embarrassed?"

Honestly, Jessie wasn't sure. It might be both of those things or something else. She just knew she didn't want to have to face the Wilsons and explain herself.

"They deserve to know," Dr. Stultz said. "When you ran away, they were beside themselves. They were sad and worried, and they just didn't understand what they did wrong."

Jessie looked up. "They didn't do anything wrong."

"How were they to know? They were questioning how they cared for children. Frank said they even talked about closing the home."

Not because of her, certainly. They did too much good for the children they cared for. Whether Jessie left or not shouldn't have mattered.

"Please tell me they didn't."

Dr. Stultz shook his head. "No, they didn't, but it shows you how deeply you running away affected them. They need to know what happened, and if you are happy here, they need to know that, too."

Jessie nodded.

The veterinarian patted her shoulder. "I am happy you seem to have found a place here. As long as you are here caring for these animals, then I am somewhat at ease about them. I know how you feel about animals."

"I care for the elephants."

The veterinarian nodded. "Then I have no doubt that they are the best-cared-for animals in this circus."

Jessie smiled.

Jessie stood off to the side and looked into the big top. The tables had been set for the orphans, and they were excited to meet with the performers and to just be in the middle of a circus ring, even if they weren't performing.

Jessie remembered the feeling well, and it brought a smile to her lips.

Then she saw the Wilsons guiding the orphans to the tables for lunch. She thought they looked older, but it had only been a year since she had seen them last. They couldn't have changed that much.

She recognized some of the orphans in the group. Jeremy and Paul weren't with the boys. Hopefully, that meant they had been adopted. Although it had only been a year, Jeffrey looked like he had grown half a foot. Mary wasn't among the girls, but she would have been old enough to have gone out on her own.

Jessie took a deep breath to try to calm herself. Her heart was beating so fast she could feel it pounding in her chest. She wasn't sure she could go through with this.

Dr. Stultz walked up behind her and looked into the big top. Then he nudged her forward. He didn't have to say anything. He had said it all in the menagerie, but his touch reassured her. He had accepted this change in her.

She took a deep breath and stepped into the big top and headed toward the crowd in the ring. Nobody noticed her. Everyone was too focused on the orphans and confusion in the ring.

Jessie found it harder to move forward the closer she got to the Wilsons. She wanted to look behind her to see if Dr. Stultz was there, but she felt if she turned, she would continue to walk in that direction away from the Wilsons.

As she drew closer, Miss Erin looked up and saw her. It

must not have registered that she was seeing Jessie because she just went right on gathering the orphans and getting them seated.

Then she paused and looked back at Jessie. Her eyes went wide, and she raised both her hands to her mouth.

Mr. Frank saw his wife's reaction, and he turned to see what she was staring at. He stared at Jessie slack jawed.

Jessie continued walking forward, but Miss Erin ran over to her and grabbed her in a tight hug.

"Is it you? Is it really you?" she said through her sobs.

"Yes, ma'am."

"Oh, Jessie. You're all right. We were so worried about you."

Mr. Frank joined them in the hug. He didn't say anything, but she saw tears on his cheeks.

"I'm sorry. I didn't mean to worry you." She had been selfish. She hadn't thought about anyone else other than herself when she ran away.

Miss Erin drew back and ran her hands over Jessie's face. Then she took another step back and stared at Jessie. Jessie noticed that Miss Erin didn't let go of her hands.

"You're taller now," Miss Erin said.

"She's filled out a little, too," Mr. Frank said. "She's not so skinny now."

Miss Erin nodded vigorously. "So, you're healthy. That's good."

Jessie nodded. "The food here isn't bad."

"Here? You work for the circus?"

"Yes, ma'am. I'm the assistant elephant trainer."

Mr. Frank grinned. "Elephants?"

"We have six."

Erin squeezed her hands. "Jessie, why did you leave? I thought you were happy with us."

"I was." Jessie started feeling tears well up in his eyes.

"Then why? It has upset me so much not knowing why and not knowing what happened to you."

Jessie wiped a tear away. "It was more than one thing. Leanne got adopted, and it was like I lost my sister. I was so sad, and I felt so alone. Then Mary stole my money."

"Mary?"

"I had been saving money so I could come here and join the circus. I've known I've wanted to do this since I started working with animals."

"Don't you think it was before that?" Mr. Frank asked.

Jessie thought for a moment. He was referring to when Jessie had tried to care for Myrna in the cornfield. "Maybe, but I don't think I realized it until I started working with Dr. Stultz."

"But why did Mary taking your money make you want to run away?" Erin asked.

Jessie thought hard about how to put what she had been feeling into words. It seemed so complicated because she had been dealing with so much at the time.

"That money was mine. I had earned it, and it was supposed to help me get started when I had to leave the home. When she took it, I felt trapped, especially sharing a room with her."

Erin put her hand on Jessie's cheek. "I'm so sorry."

Jessie leaned into Miss Erin's touch. "Feeling that way along with still being sad about Leanne was too much, and I just left." She paused. She saw the tears running down Miss Erin's cheeks. "I am sorry I hurt you."

Miss Erin sighed. "I feel better now. I am glad to know you are all right. Are you happy?"

Jessie nodded. "It is a lot different than I expected. It took some time to get used to living on a train car and learning how things work in a circus. I love working with the elephants, though, and I have made friends with other performers."

Miss Erin smiled. "I am glad to hear it."

Jessie hesitated, not sure whether what she wanted to say would make Miss Erin happy or sad. "Miss Erin, have you heard anything from Leanne? Is she happy?"

Miss Erin sighed and stroked Jessie's hair. "Sadly, we haven't heard from her. We always wait for an adopted child to contact us. Some do, but sadly, we never hear from most of them after they leave us."

Jessie frowned and lowered her head. "I miss her."

"We do, too. We miss all of our children who leave, whether they are adopted or just grow up and go out on their own.Don't give up hope, Jessie. You never know what life will bring. We never thought we've see you again, and now, look what's happened."

Jessie looked up, her eyes bright. Something Mr. Frank had said a moment ago gave her an idea. "Would you like to see the elephants? We can take your children to the menagerie to see them up close."

Miss Erin looked at her husband.

"I know I wouldn't mind seeing them up close," he said with a smile.

Jessie bounced up and down on her toes. "We can go after they finish eating before they go and spend their tickets on the midway."

Miss Erin hugged her and took her by the hand to lead her to tables where the orphans were eating hot dogs and potato salad.

Some of the orphans recognized her and ran over to hug her and pepper her with questions. Again, Jessie was surprised at how tall some of them had grown.

Then she saw Bradley sitting at the table. He was still in

makeup and helping serve the food to the orphans. She took Miss Erin and Mr. Frank by the hands and led them over to Bradley. He saw them approaching and met them halfway.

"Bradley, this is Miss Erin and Mr. Frank," Jessie said.

His smile broadened, although he had a large red smile painted on his face. "The ones you told me about?" Jessie nodded. "Wonderful! It's great to meet you." He shook their hands.

Then Jessie said, "This is Bradley Starr. He works here, too, as you can see. He's my boyfriend."

After lunch, the free tickets for the midway were passed out. The orphans headed outside, but Miss Erin and Mr. Frank gathered their children and Jessie led them to the menagerie. Some of the children's noses wrinkled at the smell of animal musk and urine, but they were excited to see the animals up close.

Jessie led them to where the elephants were tethered. Daisy was lying on her side sleeping. Jessie and Flo looked like they were playing a game with their trunks. It looked like one of them would reach out to touch the other one while the other one blocked. Their trunks kept getting tangled together. The other elephants were eating or drinking.

Myrna saw Jessie and walked over. Jessie stroked her forehead and then turned to the group.

"This is Myrna. I love all the elephants, but she is my favorite and the youngest," Jessie said. "You might be interested to know that she is also an orphan. She was taken away from her mother at a young age and has been with the circus since then. The other elephants acted as her adopted mothers."

She allowed the orphans to start to move forward to pet Myrna. Some of the other elephants saw and walked over to get attention, too. Some children laughed when a trunk reached out to touch them. Others flinched away at first.

"There is something else you should know about Myrna," Jessie said. "When she was just a little calf, she stayed at the Wilson Home for a few days."

Jessie glanced over at Mr. Frank. His eyes had grown wider.

"This is that calf?" he asked. Jessie nodded. "She's gotten a lot bigger since then."

"Did she stay in the house?" one small girl whom Jessie didn't recognize asked.

"Of course not, Sally," Douglas said. "She would have stayed in the barn."

"Actually, I hid her in the cornfield."

"Really?" Douglas asked.

Jessie nodded. "Really."

"Awww, I wish I could find something fun like an elephant and hide it. All I have is the garter snake I caught."

"And where are you hiding that?" Miss Erin asked.

Douglas blushed. "Well… I'm… It's…"

"Uh huh," Miss Erin said with her hands on her hips. "We'll talk about this later."

Jessie bent down in front of one of the youngest orphans. He was a little boy who reminded her of Jeremy with his chubby body and bright smile. Of course, Jeremy was now six years old and had apparently been adopted.

"What's your name?" Jessie asked.

"Harold."

"You weren't at the home when I was." The boy shook his head. "How would you like to help me with a trick?"

"Sure."

Jessie reached out her hand and took Harold's small hand in hers. She had him stand beside her and Myrna.

Jessie patted Myrna's leathery leg. "Myrna, foot."

The elephant raised her foot in the air. Jessie lifted Harold up and set him on the foot. She continued holding his hand and told him to hold onto the collar with his other hand. Harold looked nervous, but he obeyed her.

Jessie tapped the foot again. "Myrna, up."

Myrna obediently raised her foot higher. Harold squealed in delight. Miss Erin looked nervous, but Mr. Frank smiled as did most of the other children.

"Myrna, down," Jessie said.

The elephant slowly lowered her foot and Jessie caught Harold as he slid off the leg. She lowered him to the ground. Jessie passed him a peach.

"Now hold that out in front of her mouth," Jessie said. "It's her treat for doing what I asked of her."

Harold held out the peach. Myrna caught the scent and reached out with her trunk. She grabbed the peach and stuffed it into her mouth.

Harold clapped.

"You did a great job," Jessie said. "Maybe you'll be an elephant handler when you get bigger."

Jessie passed out peaches to the other children and allowed them to feed fruit to the elephants.

"They will definitely remember this visit to the circus," Mr. Frank said as he gave a peach to Myrna. "So this is the little one who was in our cornfield."

Jessie nodded.

"Not so little anymore. Nor are you."

Jessie smiled. She had nothing to say to that.

Once the elephants were fed, the Wilsons took the orphans to the midway. Jessie walked along with them and introduced them to some of her friends as the children threw balls at milk cans or tried to catch a metal fish with a magnet.

As it grew closer to the evening show, Jessie knew she needed to leave to eat and get ready for the performance. She hugged the Wilsons tightly and cried again.

Miss Erin held her by shoulders and looked into her eyes. "Promise you will write to us, and let us know how you are doing."

Jessie nodded vigorously. "I will."

She waved to the children and told them to have fun.

Throughout the performance, Jessie watched to see how the orphans reacted. She also looked to the Wilsons for their reaction. She felt a weight lift off her back she hadn't realized she was carrying when she saw the delight and pride on their faces.

During the elephant act, she hoped to see Dr. Stultz in the crowd, but he wasn't sitting with the orphans if he was watching the performance at all. She hoped he was. Jessie wanted him to see that the elephants weren't mistreated during their act.

That evening, when Jessie collapsed into her bunk after helping the elephants lower the big top, she pulled Annie out from under her pillow and propped Maria the doll against the wall.

Jessie smiled at the doll and whispered, "We'll see her again someday, Maria, and boy, will we have a lot to talk about!

24

SEPTEMBER 1937

After the performance in Pittsburgh, Pennsylvania, ended, Jessie walked back to the big top to watch Mr. Conroy and orphans for Orphans Day. Pittsburgh was on of several stops where the Conroy and Pepperidge Circus would host Orphans Day.

She still wondered why only the twelve stops in Pennsylvania and Maryland, out of the dozens of places they performed each season, were the ones Mr. Conroy decided to host Orphans Day. She was scared to ask him after the way he had reacted the last time, but it didn't mean she was any less curious.

She talked and joked with the children, but she kept watching Mr. Conroy and trying to listen for the questions he asked the children. She knew what they would be. *How old are you? Do you remember your real parents?*

She watched him stagger a bit as he walked around, and when he passed near her, she thought she smelled alcohol.

Jessie was surprised not to hear him ask any questions. He just walked around, patting the children on the head, and she thought she saw tears in his eyes.

He had never acted like this during an Orphans Day. Something was very wrong. Her biggest surprise was when she saw him sneak a drink from a flask. She had never seen him drink before. Although he probably did, he would never do it when there was work that needed to be done, and there was always work when you ran a circus.

After one of the cooks set a platter of hot dogs on the table, Jessie grabbed him by the arm.

"Find Carl, and tell him I need to see him here. It's important."

The cook nodded and hurried off.

She hoped he would come. Despite working for a circus, Carl avoided children. They pointed and stared and made him feel self-conscious because of his height. He had worked his way out of the sideshow before Jessie had joined the circus, and didn't want to be considered part of it.

Mr. Conroy's walk became more unsteady. Jessie could see from the expressions on some of the adults that they were starting to notice it as well.

She saw Carl walk into the big top. He paused, and Jessie thought he might turn around and walk away. She caught his eye and waved him over.

"This had better be good," he said as he walked up to her.

He was wearing jeans and a button-up shirt, either of which could have been worn by an eight-year-old boy.

Sure enough, the children started staring and pointing at him. Some of them laughed, but Jessie wasn't sure whether it was because of Carl or just that they were having fun.

"Look around, and you tell me."

Carl rolled his eyes. "I don't have time for games, Jessie."

"No games. I just need you to see it to make sure I'm not imagining it."

Carl sighed. "Fine."

He stood beside her and looked around the big top and the orphans. She could tell from his movements that he was getting impatient. She wondered if she was imagining things. Then Carl froze.

"Damn!" Carl muttered. "Is he drunk?"

"I think so. I saw him take a drink earlier, but only the one."

Carl cocked his head to the side. "He's had more than one drink. We need to get him out of here before he does something he shouldn't in front of the kids."

"That's why I wanted you here. He won't listen to me."

Carl looked at her without saying anything. Finally, he shrugged. He walked over to Mr. Conroy.

"Jeremy, I need you to come see something in the office," Carl said.

"What?"

"Bennie wants you to check the attendance counts." Besides managing payroll, Bennie McNabb also kept track of show attendance at every city where the circus stopped. He even compared it to other circuses when he could get their numbers.

"That can wait." Mr. Conroy slurred his words.

Carl tugged gently at Mr. Conroy's arm. "That's what I told him, but he said you needed to sign off on it for some reason."

Mr. Conroy's hands flailed around as he pulled free from Carl. "Fine. Fine. Let's go."

Jessie tried to take him by the arm to lead him out of the big top, but Mr. Conroy shook her off. "I know where I'm going," he said sharply.

Jessie didn't want to create a scene around the children, so she settled for walking behind Mr. Conroy and Carl as they slowly left the big top.

Once they were outside, Carl asked, "What now?"

Jessie looked around. "Let's take him to his rail car. He needs to sleep this off before this the evening show."

Mr. Conroy turned around and nearly fell. "What are you talking about?"

"You're drunk, Jeremy," Carl said.

"I am not."

"You nearly fell over just turning around."

Mr. Conroy snorted. "Fine."

He stomped off toward his rail car, although he was leaning to the side and couldn't walk straight.

Carl shook his head. "I've never seen him like this. Something is wrong."

Carl and Jessie helped Mr. Conroy up onto the platform of his rail car. He had half a rail car to himself. The other half was used for the circus office. Carl shoved his hand into Mr. Conroy's pocket and fished out his keys. He unlocked the door and opened it.

They were standing in a large sitting room with a sofa and plush armchair. A bar ran along one wall and a desk sat against the other. Mr. Conroy sighed and dropped into his armchair.

"Do I really come across as creepy? I don't want to scare the kids," he said. "Not that it matters anymore. It's too late for answers to those questions." Jessie remembered what she had told him when the talked about Orphans Day before.

"Then why ask them?"

Mr. Conroy shook his head lazily back and forth. "I won't be asking them anymore."

She wondered why that was? Had he finally gotten his answer? If so, it didn't appear that he had liked it.

"The children try to answer your questions truthfully,"

Jessie said.

Mr. Conroy shook his head. "That's not it."

He stood up and walked over to his small bar. He poured himself a drink and then looked over at Jessie.

"Do you want something to drink?"

She remembered how sick she had felt after drinking on New Year's Eve. She didn't want to feel that way again ever.

"No, thank you."

He poured his drink, sipped it, and then walked over and looked out his window.

"Years ago, one of the showgirls with the circus was a woman named Natasha Lambda. It wasn't her real name, which was not surprising with circus folk. She was a beautiful woman, and I fell for her hard, and we became close."

"Close?" Jessie asked, suspecting she knew the answer.

"Intimate. It was frowned on because I'm management, and she was a performer. She became pregnant, but she never admitted I was the father, although pretty much everyone in the circus knew it. You know how that goes."

Jessie nodded. People she barely talked to knew about her and Bradley dating. A few of them even knew they were sleeping together.

"She decided to leave the circus, especially since we couldn't have a pregnant showgirl. I paid for her to stay in York since she said she had family in the area. I wrote to her and visited if we had a nearby show. She had the baby, but Natasha died in childbirth. The circus was still on the road, so I didn't realize what had happened until my letters started being returned undeliverable in winter quarters."

He walked over and sat down on the armchair and took another sip of his drink.

"I wasn't able to get back to York until the season ended. By then, the baby had been sent to an orphanage, but no one could tell me which one. They couldn't even tell me if the baby had been a boy or a girl."

"Didn't they have records?"

Mr. Conroy nodded. "They did, but apparently Natasha was admitted to the hospital under her own name, which I didn't know."

Tears ran down his cheeks. He grabbed Jessie's forearm.

"I have a child out there somewhere, Jessie. I am just trying to find him or her."

Jessie could figure out the rest. Mr. Conroy sponsored Orphans Day for the circus in the hopes that the orphanage where his child was staying would bring him to the circus. Mr. Conroy might look into eyes of a child and recognize Natasha or himself in the child's appearance.

"What would you do if you found your child?" Jessie asked.

"Adopt him, of course."

"What if he was already adopted?"

Mr. Conroy frowned. "I don't know. I don't know how likely it is I will ever find the child. I haven't found him yet, and he has probably left any orphanage he was in by now. I would like to know if he is happy, though. I want him to be. His mother made me very happy. I think I would have married her." He sipped at his drink. "Before the show today, I was thinking that he is an adult now, eighteen years old. He may even be married. I'll never meet him. If he has children, I'll never meet them." He sighed and teared up, although no tears rolled down his cheeks.

Jessie realized that his child's birthday must be this month, but Mr. Conroy didn't even know the birthday of his child, and he would probably never know. It was too late now for the questions. The orphans wouldn't have the answers.

Mr. Conroy started sobbing finally. Jessie shifted uncomfortably. What should she do? Mr. Conroy was a private man. If he realized what he was doing, he would be embarrassed, but she couldn't leave him alone.

Then the circus owner made the decision for her when he fell over unconscious.

Jessie sighed. She took off his boots to give him a little comfort. Then she left him alone to sleep.

Everyone in the circus had a secret, and nobody in the circus had a secret. Both were true. People came here often to hide from something, but even if they weren't hiding, everyone had things about themselves they didn't want other people to know about. The circus was the wrong place to come for that. People here spent too much time together too close together. It was hard to hide anything.

The odd thing was that circus folk were good at keeping secrets. They might know others' secrets, but they rarely talked about them. It gave people in the circus an illusion of privacy.

25

DECEMBER 1937

Jessie finished feeding the elephants and packing up the costumes and equipment after the evening show. She walked over to the clown tent and found Bradley packing the last of his costumes and props in trunks so they could be loaded on the train. She gave him a hug, surprised at how tired she felt. She was feeling the hectic pace of the long season lifting. He smiled and locked the trunk.

"I'm just finishing up," he said.

He stood up and kissed her. She could still smell the makeup on him. It would linger until he was able to take a shower.

"Good. I'm tired. I'll sleep like a log tonight. I'm actually getting used to sleeping on a train."

"Yes, but that is hours away."

She shook her head. "No. I am going to catch a couple hours' nap. I'll set my alarm and get up when the midway closes."

She didn't have much that needed packing, so she and Samuel helped guide the elephants as they assisted with lowering the big top and pulling some of the heavier wagons. Then she got the elephants settled on the train car with food and water.

Jesse didn't bother changing when she got back to the train. She set her alarm and climbed into her bunk. The alarm startled her when it went off. She woke up feeling like she had just climbed into her bunk.

She went back outside. The sounds of children laughing had been replaced by men calling out commands as the tents slowly came down, were folded, and lifted onto wagons to be taken to the train.

Jesse hurried to the menagerie tent. It was virtually empty. Most of the animals were either loaded or in the process of being loaded onto the trains. Only the horses and elephants were still inside because they needed to help with the takedown of the circus.

Jessie pulled the stakes holding Jo-Jo and Myrna and led them outside to the big top. Ropes from the top of the massive tent were tied onto their harnesses. Then the command was given and the big top started shrinking like a deflating balloon. The elephants slowly walked toward the tent poles as Jessie kept them calm under the sudden pulling. They were doing what would usually take a couple dozen men.

Once the tent was down, the parts had to be separated, folded, and lifted onto wagons. The horses could pull the lighter wagons, but with thousands of pounds of canvas on a wagon, it wouldn't budge without a tractor or an elephant to pull it.

With the big top loaded, Samuel and Jessie led the elephants up the ramp and into their rail car. It was lined with troughs they had filled with food and water. This wouldn't be enough to last the entire trip, but it would have to last until the train made a stop.

She made her rounds to tell the elephants goodnight and pet them before heading back to her room. With the shower house taken down, she had to use the water in one of the two buckets of water she was given for each train trip to wash the smell of elephant off of her so Gail wouldn't complain.

Gail was already in bed when Jessie came into the room. The whistle blew a warning that the train was about to start. Then the lights flickered and went out briefly. A few moments later, she felt the train lurch as the connectors took on the weight of each car.

Jessie smiled and climbed into her bunk. They were heading back to Florida and winter quarters to rest up until next season.

The train was still moving when she woke in the morning. Unlike when they were traveling from town to town, it would be early afternoon until they stopped to water and feed the animals. Mr. Conroy wanted to get as many miles between stops as he could.

Jessie dressed and made her way to the cook car where she picked up a box meal. It was bread and jam, an apple, and a pint of milk. Then she made her way to the clown car, so she could eat breakfast with Bradley.

She had been surprised the first time she visited the clown car. She had expected them to be, well, clowning around. She found them relaxing. Quite a few of them lay on their bunks with the doors open reading books. Usually, the clowns spent their travel time repairing their costumes and props.

She and Bradley shared their breakfast sitting on the outside platform, watching the countryside pass by as they ate.

"It will feel weird being in one place for more than a night or two," Jessie said.

"You grew up that way."

"Yes, but for the last ten months, I've been on this train more than I have been on the ground. I'm used to it."

"I dream about winter quarters sometimes," Bradley admitted. "Sometimes, I just want to take a break from performing and stay in one place with nothing to do for a while. Winter quarters is as close as I come to that."

Jessie took a bite from her apple and then asked, "Can we get time off while we're in winter quarters? I mean like a few days or a week?"

"Probably. You have to make sure your work is covered for the time you're away."

"I can talk to Samuel about that. I was thinking of visiting the Wilsons. I was glad to see them again in York, but we didn't have a long time to talk."

"Well, I can also help take care of the elephants so you can go."

"I was hoping you'd go with me. They're like my parents. I want them to know you."

He reached out and took her hand. "I'd love that."

It was around two-thirty in the afternoon when the train stopped at a siding where trucks of meat and produce were waiting. The animal handlers fed the animals they were in charge of while others filled the water wagons and refilled the buckets of water everyone had in their rooms.

Jessie visited the elephants and reassured them everything was fine and that they would get to enjoy some sunlight shortly.

They reached Florida the next day, and winter quarters took shape just as quickly as the show went up at any town. It even went a little quicker since things didn't need to be made ready for a crowd, such as assembling the bleachers in the big top or opening the midway booths.

Once the circus was set up, things settled down somewhat and performers, workers, and animals relaxed. Although not too much. Performers still practiced and planned new routines. Costumers sketched new outfits and repaired old ones. The grounds crew inspected the tents and patched any holes. However, things weren't operating under a tight schedule like they did on the road.

Jessie talked to Samuel and wrote the Wilsons about her idea of visiting. They decided that she would spend Christmas week with them.

Then one day while Jessie was visiting Winter Garden, shopping for Christmas gifts, she saw a tattoo shop. She went inside and asked for a tattoo of an elephant on her wrist.

The tattoo artist looked at her, and his brow furrowed. "Are you sure? Tattoos are permanent, ma'am."

Jessie nodded. "I've thought about it for a while."

"What are you considering? A picture of Dumbo?"

"No. I'm with the circus. I want a real-looking elephant."

"Ahh, I see," the tattoo artist said as he nodded. "I've done a lot of the performers' tattoos. So how do you want the trunk?"

Now it was Jessie's turn to be confused. "What do you mean?"

The man smiled. "I've had to study circus animals to draw them correctly. I found out that there's a lot of beliefs with elephant statues and the kind of luck you get based on their trunks."

"Really? So what are the differences?"

"Well, if the trunk is raised, it is supposed to bring good luck. If the trunk is down, it brings wisdom and knowledge. If two elephants have their trunks crossed, it is supposed to strengthen the ties of with your friends and family. And three elephants are supposed to bring harmony."

Jessie barely had to think about her choice. "I want two elephants with their trunks crossed."

The tattoo artist sat her down and sketched out a picture of two elephants in profile with their trunks entwined over their heads and forming a heart. Once Jessie approved it, he moved her to a chair on one side of a small table. She laid her arm on the table, and the man swabbed it with alcohol.

"Have you ever had a tattoo?" he asked.

"No."

"It will hurt somewhat."

"Really?" He nodded. "How much?"

"It depends how sensitive to pain you are."

Jessie's eyes widened a bit. She thought about it. So many people in the circus had tattoos. It couldn't hurt that much. No one ever talked about the pain or warned her that getting a tattoo was painful.

Jessie took a deep breath and nodded. "I want it."

The tattoo artist set the picture beside her arm. He used a pen to redraw the design onto her forearm that didn't have burn scars. It was smaller than the original drawing, probably three inches square. When that was finished, he picked up something that resembled a screwdriver, except that it had an electrical cord coming off the end.

He turned it on. It whirred.

"Now it could start to hurt, but you either need to bear whatever pain you feel or tell me to stop. You can't jerk your arm away." Jessie nodded. "Whatever happens now will be permanent, so if you can't handle the pain, stop early before too much is drawn."

He pressed the tattoo needle against her arm. She yelped but stayed still.

"You okay?" the tattoo artist asked.

"Yes, I didn't know what to expect. It hurts some, like

someone pinching my skin a lot or a cat clawing at me to get away."

The man smiled and went back to work. He outlined the design. Then he cleaned it and started again. This time he gradually filled in the outline with shading and color. Jessie watched in amazement as her arm became a canvas for a piece of artwork.

Once the work was done, the man cleaned her arm once again. Jessie panicked when she saw blood.

"Did something go wrong?" she asked.

"No, there's always a little blood. It will stop soon enough."

He bandaged her arm with gauze. Jessie couldn't help but glace at her other arm, which was covered by the sleeve of her shirt. It still carried the scars from the fire and so did the arm with the tattoo. Now that she thought about it, getting a tattoo hadn't been nearly as painful as being burned.

When she returned to winter quarters, she showed the tattoo to Bradley. He chuckled when he saw it.

"What's so funny?" Jessie asked.

"Now people can definitely call you the elephant girl." Then he raised an arm in front of his face and raised it up and down like a trunk as he took heavy steps to walk in a circle.

"You make me sound like Lily." Lily was the 600-pound fat lady in the sideshow. She actually only weighed 300 pounds, but she wore padded clothing, and Jack Nash, the sideshow barker exaggerated when he announced her weight. He even used a rigged scale, so that it showed a much heavier weight when Lily stepped on it to be weighed.

"What do the elephants think of it?"

Jessie raised an eyebrow. "What?"

"You're one of them now. You and the elephants are family. Did you show them?"

"They won't know the difference."

Bradley held out his hand. "You should show them."

"You're being weird."

He shrugged. "Maybe I'm just happy."

"You are usually happy."

"But I'm happier around you."

Jessie rolled her eyes and took his hands. "Fine, let's go see the elephants. It's about time to feed them anyway."

Samuel had staked them outside so they could enjoy the warmth of the Florida sun. They were on twenty-foot-long chains, so they had room to wander around and interact with each other.

When Jessie and Bradley approached, two of the elephants were batting a ball back and forth between them using their trunks. Daisy was munching on hay. Two of them were standing around watching everything going on in winter quarters. Myrna had her face raised to the sun.

Jessie walked over to an elephant and patted her side. "Hello, Daisy."

The elephant turned and reached her trunk out to Jessie. She held her wrist out to the elephant.

"Bradley wants me to show you this." Jessie peeled back the gauze on her wrist. Daisy's trunk sniffed at the gauze but ignored the tattoo.

"See, I told you they wouldn't notice," Jessie said to Bradley, but when she looked over her shoulder to him, he wasn't there.

She turned away from Daisy and saw Bradley standing by Myrna feeding her by hand.

"You're not supposed to feed them treats."

"I'm not."

She walked over to him. "Why is your hand under her mouth then?"'

"I taught her a trick."

"*You* taught Myrna a trick. When did you become an animal trainer?"

"Samuel helped me."

"Samuel?" She realized that he wasn't teasing her. "Why didn't you let me help you?"

"I wanted to surprise you." Bradley held out his arm. "Myrna, trunk."

Myrna rolled out her trunk to Jessie. Jessie held out her hand, expecting to feel Myrna's breath on it. Instead, she felt something hard in the trunk. Myrna dropped a small box into her hand.

Jessie opened the box and found a ring inside. She gasped.

Bradley reached over and took the ring out of the box and held it up.

"Jessie Parsons, will you marry me?"

Her eyes widened and she felt like her racing heart would explode from her chest. Her lower lip quivered a bit. She knew what she wanted to say, but the words just wouldn't seem to come out of her mouth. She was suddenly mute.

So she nodded fiercely.

Bradley smiled and slid the ring onto her finger. She threw her arms around his neck and kissed him deeply.

Once the reality of what had happened settled on her, Jessie felt a bit of panic over the reality of planning a wedding. The women on her rail car were quick to jump in to help. Gail insisted on sewing her a wedding dress.

Amid all this, Jessie received a letter from the Wilsons. Bradley had written them, saying he was going to ask Jessie to marry him. They congratulated Jessie on her engagement. Miss Erin was excited to have her come back to Pennsylvania for Christmas and insisted that she also bring Bradley.

She also wrote that Mr. Powers, her father's lawyer, had stopped by looking for Jessie. Miss Erin had given her address to him.

That explained another letter she received a week later from the lawyer. It contained paperwork he wanted her to sign and have notarized. She read through the documents; she was going to receive her inheritance from her father. The letter also said that her father's broker could continue managing the money or she could transfer it wherever she might want.

Jessie showed the letter to Bradley. He read it and looked over the documents.

"That's a lot of money," he said when he finished.

It wasn't a fortune, but it was enough that she could do a lot with it.

"What are you going to do with all that money?" Bradley asked.

"I don't know. What do you think I should do?"

Bradley shook his head. "It's your money."

She thought about traveling, buying a big house, fancy clothes, and so much more. Then she thought about how quickly all that money could disappear. She could quickly be left with nothing.

"I think I will leave it alone for now. I might use a little bit to help with the wedding, but I don't really need a lot. I get food and a room from the circus, and I get enough money to pay for extras."

He patted her on the hands and kissed her on the cheek. "My little heiress."

26

MARCH 1938

Amid the planning for her wedding, Jessie also had to continue working with the elephants, taking care of them, and planning for the next season. She and Samuel brainstormed new ideas for the act and narrowed it down to a couple new ones. The one Jessie was most interested in working on was trying to teach the elephants to play catch with a large rubber ball.

When the train pulled out of winter quarters in March, Jessie felt excited to start performing. She had felt that way last year, too, but this time, she knew what to expect and even how things would unfold at the different stops.

At least she thought she did.

When she was leading the elephants off the train in Memphis, Tennessee, she noticed that Myrna was limping. She had never seen an elephant limp. She didn't even know that they could.

While Samuel took the other elephants to help raise the big top, Jessie took Myrna off to the side and examined the foot and leg she was favoring. She didn't see anything wrong, except for what might have been a slight swelling at her hip. Jessie had thought Myrna might have stepped on something, but the bottom of her foot was clean and her nails were trimmed.

"What's the problem, Myrna?" Jessie asked. She patted Myrna on the side, but the usually friendly elephant side-stepped away.

When Samuel came back with the other elephants, Jessie led Myrna around and showed Samuel her limp.

"Damn!" he muttered.

"What?" Jessie asked.

He ignored her and walked over and put his hands on the elephant's hip. He ran his hands over the hip and leg, pressing occasionally. Myrna sidestepped away whenever he did it.

"I think she's got arthritis," Samuel said. "Either that, or she might have a greenstick fracture."

Jessie had heard about arthritis, but only in people and old people at that. Myrna was only not even ten years old. That wasn't even middle age for an elephant.

"What's that mean?" Jessie asked with a slight panic in her voice. "What do we do to help her?"

Samuel ran his hand over the back of his neck. Then he closed his eyes and sighed.

"It doesn't matter. She can't perform. Right now, she needs rest. I'll need to rework the act without her."

"What about Myrna, though?" Jessie didn't want to think about Myrna being in pain or unable to perform ever again. The thought brought tears to her eyes.

"I'll see about getting a town vet in here this afternoon, but a visit might not happen until somewhere in Texas." Dr. Portman had left the circus to open his own practice in Kentucky. He said he had gotten tired of traveling all the time and living on a train.

"Not all vets are comfortable with circus animals," Samuel continued. "For now, get her to lay down and apply cold compresses to her hip. There's a lot of inflammation there. If we can get rid of that, it should be easier to figure out what the problem is."

None of the elephants had been sick since Jessie had been working with them. Myrna had to get better. Jessie couldn't imagine Myrna not being a part of the act.

She hurried off to get a bucket and fill it with cold water.

"Check with Jeremy about getting some ice that we can use," Samuel called after her. "Those compresses need to be cold enough to get through her thick skin."

Jessie nodded.

The veterinarian came in a few hours later. He seemed in awe of the tigers, bears, llamas, and all the other animals. Jessie wondered if he even knew anything about exotic animals. She wished Dr. Stultz was here.

This veterinarian examined Myrna and diagnosed the problem as arthritis. He said that elephants were too heavy to perform some of the tricks they were called on to do.

He had Samuel recite the act to him and advised that he remove walking and standing on hind legs.

"It concentrates too much weight on their hindquarters and can cause problems," the veterinarian advised.

"Take it out for all the elephants?" Samuel asked.

The veterinarian nodded. "I would. Elephants aren't designed to be walking around on two legs. While the other elephants might not show any signs of arthritis, if they keep doing those types of tricks, they might start having problems. Other things like their age, weight, work hours, and diet can also play a part."

"We take good care of our elephants," Samuel snapped.

The veterinarian held up his hands. "I'm not saying you

don't. I'm just telling you everything that can influence whether they get arthritis or not. Some of the things you have control over. If you want to give them the best chance to be healthy, you need to deal with the things you can."

Samuel sighed and nodded.

It was odd only working with five elephants for the show that evening, but Samuel had been able to keep most of the act the same. The only thing missing was Myrna.

As the days went on, Myrna's condition did not improve. Rest and the compresses helped, but she still walked with a limp and certainly could not perform.

The other elephants seemed to try to comfort her, standing near and touching her with their trunks.

Samuel took the veterinarian's advice and removed walking on hind legs from the act.

Mr. Conroy came to the menagerie tent one afternoon about two weeks after Myrna had stopped performing. He had Jessie walk the elephant in a circle. He frowned as he watched her limp.

"She's no better?" he asked.

Jessie wanted to lie and say she had seen some improvement, but it was obvious Myrna was still unfit to perform. "No, sir," she answered.

Mr. Conroy looked over at Samuel. "We'll have to get rid of her."

Rid? What did that mean?

"We need a replacement," Samuel said.

"I'll ask around. Maybe one of the other circuses will be closing up. Maybe someone has a baby elephant."

Samuel shook his head. "I don't want to have to train a calf. Myrna's a good elephant now, but do you remember the problems she gave us when she was young? I need an elephant I can work right into the act."

Jessie watched as Mr. Conroy and Samuel continued to debate about what to do with Myrna. Myrna was part of the herd that the six elephants had formed. If she left, it would affect them and maybe the act. They would miss her.

"I have an idea," Jessie spoke up, surprising both Mr. Conroy and Samuel. "What if we create a new act for Myrna? One that doesn't require her to perform any tricks that could aggravate her arthritis."

Both men looked at Jessie skeptically, but she continued. "We could teach her to paint. I've heard of elephants being able to do it. People would pay to see a painting elephant." She would pay to see one, since she wasn't sure it could be done. She had lied about hearing about an elephant that could paint.

"What would she paint?" Samuel asked, tugging at his beard.

"Does it matter? If she can hold the brush and make marks on paper, people will love it. You could even sell her paintings to the attendees."

Mr. Conroy rubbed his chin thoughtfully. "Painting, huh? It's not a bad idea. It's something different, and we wouldn't have to worry about her health getting worse."

Samuel looked apprehensive. Jessie suspected he knew that she was making up a story to save Myrna. "We can't have people see her limping into the big top."

"Then have her do it in the menagerie," Mr. Conroy said. "It will increase ticket sales for the walk-throughs."

Jessie's mind was filling with ideas. "I can have the costumers make her a beret, so she looks like an artist."

"And do you think you could teach her?" Samuel asked Jessie.

"I want to try. It sounds like it will take a while to find a replacement anyway."

Mr. Conroy nodded sharply. "Let's do it." Then he turned

and walked out of the menagerie.

Samuel turned to Jessie. "Do you know what you've gotten yourself into?"

"I trained her to take the hat off my head."

"This will be harder. I saw the look in Jeremy's eyes. He's going to be expecting Rembrandt, and you'll be lucky to get paint by numbers."

"I think he'll be happy with anything."

"If you can get her to paint something, it will be a miracle—and a draw. Good luck."

Jessie hesitated and then asked. "What happens if we have to get rid of her? What does that mean?"

Samuel's eyebrows raised. "Ah, so that's why you're so worried." He paused. "You probably should be."

"Why?"

"No other circus will want an elephant that can't perform. They cost too much to maintain. Mr. Conroy would probably sell her to a zoo. She wouldn't like it. She be in a cement cage that wouldn't give her near enough room, but it would be her best option."

"What are the others?"

"She might be sold to a laboratory. Some rich man might want an exotic pet. Worst cases I've heard of are someone buying an old elephant to hunt and one circus that was near bankruptcy, couldn't find a buyer for its elephants, and decided to kill them and feed them to the meat eaters."

Jessie gasped. "No, that's cruel!"

"The bears and big cats have to get meat from somewhere Jessie. An elephant can feed a lot of tigers, but they are more valuable alive."

Jessie shuddered. This had to work. She couldn't let Myrna be sold or worse.

27
JUNE 1938

Jessie spent her days watching Myrna intently, eagerly flicking her wrist to demonstrate the brush strokes she wanted the elephant to imitate. With each failed attempt, Jessie grew more frustrated and worried whether Mr. Conroy would find a replacement for Myrna before the elephant mastered the skill.

Bradley watched Jessie's anguish, patiently offering any help he could provide while trying to attend to their wedding preparations on the side.

It wasn't until early June that an unexpected breakthrough occurred. With one graceful motion, Myrna swept her trunk over the paint palette, delicately placed the brush on the canvas, and produced a sketchy stroke that she repeated across the paper until she had crafted an abstract masterpiece.

Jessie was thrilled by Myrna's sudden artistic talent. She jumped up and down, clapping her hands in excitement, and hugged the elephant's trunk.

The "painting" was a mix of vibrant colors slashing across the paper and crisscrossing each other.

"Myrna, you're a genius!" Jessie exclaimed, still hugging the elephant's trunk. "We should show this to Mr. Conroy.

He'll be so impressed!"

Bradley nodded in agreement as he eyed the painting. "I think you're right, Jessie. This is amazing."

They brought the circus owner and Samuel into the menagerie, and Jessie had Myrna repeat her painting. Mr. Conroy laughed—actually laughed—with delight.

"We will have her debut after the show this evening," Mr. Conroy said. "Let's see how the crowd reacts, but I think they will love it."

He lifted up the first painting Jessie and Bradley had showed him.

"Meanwhile, I am going to get this framed and hang it in my rail car. I will have some canvases purchased and we will have Myrna paint on them to sell."

He walked over and patted the elephant on her side. "You did a good job, Myrna."

Jessie and Bradley spent the rest of the afternoon creating an area where Myrna could paint and a crowd could gather to watch.

They set up a giant easel that held a board with a large sheet of paper attached to it. This would serve as Myrna's canvas until actual canvases were brought in. Beside the easel, Jessie set up a table that held bottles of paint. She could prepare the palette while standing next to Myrna and hold it for her.

Myrna quickly became a star. As word got out that the Conroy and Pepperidge Circus had an elephant that painted, people flocked to the menagerie and happily paid a dime to watch Myrna. Many of them also paid five dollars to have one of Myrna's original paintings.

With Myrna's place in the circus secure, Jessie turned her attention back to planning her wedding. Bradley had been thinking about it for weeks while Jessie had concentrated on saving Myrna, and with the help of some of the women in the circus, he came up with what Jessie considered a perfect plan.

When they arrived in York, Bradley put his plans into motion. After the parade to lead the townspeople to the fairgrounds, Mr. Conroy closed the big top.

The performers and workers who knew Jessie and Bradley and weren't needed out on the midway came in and sat on a section of bleachers. They wore their best outfits, which for most of them were their performing costumes. The bleachers in front of the center ring were awash in every color of the rainbow. What wasn't seen among them was a formal suit.

They laughed and joked as much as any audience would have as they waited for a performance to start.

The Wilsons and Dr. Stultz drove in from Abbottstown with the orphans. They wore their Visiting Day clothes, and Mr. Frank looked uncomfortable, as usual.

Bradley's mother and sister had draped long lines of white linen from the trapeze bars above the center ring so that it formed a white canopy within the larger big top. They had also wrapped the tent poles nearest the center ring with garland intertwined with linen. However, it was still a circus so the scent of popcorn and cotton candy mingled with the faint hint of sawdust, creating an intoxicating blend that was uniquely circus.

The local justice of the peace stood in ring one on a tub, looking like Mr. Conroy at the start of a performance. He looked around slightly wide-eyed, as if wondering why he was there and what he had agreed to.

Bradley entered the tent. He wore a brown suit he had purchased just for this occasion. While his tie was traditional, his tie had been sewn from the fabric of a worn clown costume. It was a loud mix of green, yellow, and blue. He had joked about wearing his oversized clown shoes to the wedding until Jessie threatened to have Myrna lift him up by his ankles and remove them if he did.

Bradley's father joined him, and they walked to the center ring and stood in front of the justice of the peace and next to a red carpet that ran from the menagerie entrance to the tub.

The circus band started playing the wedding march. Perhaps because it was brass- and drum-heavy band playing it, even the song felt like it belonged with a circus. The ethereal sound of violins was replaced with drawn-out notes from trumpets. Jessie didn't know if the band had already known how to play the song or if Bradley had had them learn it for this occasion.

Samuel, standing on the ground, urged Myrna forward from their place outside of the menagerie entrance to the big top. They didn't rush because they didn't want Myrna to be in pain, but Jessie had insisted that Myrna be the elephant she rode into the big top on.

Jessie wore her white wedding gown with a wide shirt and no train so she could mount and dismount Myrna. Although it wasn't elaborate, the satin shimmered, drawing eyes toward Jessie. She hadn't wanted anything elaborate. Just the fact that Gail Westinghouse had sewn it just for her was enough.

Although not a bride, Myrna was draped in a white cloth trimmed with yellow. She also wore a beaded headpiece Gail had made for her.

The circus performers gathered in the bleachers with the Wilsons and the orphans in the front row along with Bradley's family. Everyone cheered wildly when Jessie and Myrna entered the big top. It wasn't often they got to be the audience for a show, and this was a unique performance. The cheers startled the justice of the peace who almost fell off the metal tub he was standing on. Jessie waved to her audience.

Myrna stopped next to Bradley.

"Myrna, foot," Samuel said.

The elephant raised her foot. Jessie dismounted gracefully and rode the foot down as Myrna lowered it. She kissed Myrna on the face.

"Thank you, Myrna."

Jessie walked over to stand next to Bradley who suddenly looked nervous. He had been so casual and unconcerned about things leading up to the wedding, but now he looked nearly as uncomfortable as Mr. Frank.

Getting into the spirit of the occasion, the justice of the peace said, "Welcome, one and all, to the wedding of Jessie Parsons and Bradley Starr! Let us give them a round of applause for their dedication to commit their lives to each other."

Everyone cheered for the happy couple, and the justice of the peace continued. He said a simple ceremony without elaborating much. He seemed too stunned by his surroundings to want to continue standing on the tub.

Jessie and Bradley joined hands as the justice of the peace had them repeat the matrimonial vows. When the justice of the peace pronounced them man and wife, the crowd erupted into cheers again and started throwing popcorn at the couple.

Bradley swept Jessie into his arms, and they kissed for the first time as man and wife.

28

AUGUST 1938

Married life took a little getting used to. It's not that things changed all that much. Jessie and Bradley still traveled with the circus. Jessie was still an elephant trainer, and Bradley, a clown. They ate in the cookhouse and slept on the train.

But the things that did change highlighted the biggest changes in Jessie's life. When she woke in the mornings, it wasn't in an upper bunk. It was in a bed with Bradley beside her. She could feel the warmth of his body nestled against hers. When she returned to her room at the end of the day, Bradley was there to greet her, not Gail.

True, she had spent much of her free time with Bradley, but it was never on the train. That little difference—being together on the train—was enough to show her that her life had changed and changed for the better.

Myrna continued drawing a crowd. More people came to see her than snuck off to see the coochie show or the sideshow. And painting was less stressful on her than performing under the big top.

The elephant seemed to enjoy her new work. Jessie thought she had developed a bit of a flourish to her strokes, and she often trumpeted when she finished a painting.

At a show in Richmond, Mr. Conroy had an art expert come out to appraise Myrna's paintings. He called them "raw, primal masterpieces." This shocked Jessie. As much as she loved Myrna and what the elephant could do, her paintings were not much more than strokes of color across a canvas.

When Jessie told Bradley about the appraisal, he laughed.

"What's so funny?" Jessie asked.

"That art expert could probably barely paint better than Myrna. He was someone Mr. Conroy hired to drum up even more interest in Myrna."

That made sense. Jessie should have realized that on her own. This was the circus after all.

At a stop in Frederick, Maryland, Jessie finished the grand spec and rode Jo-Jo out of the big top to the menagerie. She dismounted quickly and changed back into the khaki safari outfit she wore for the act. Then she was back at Myrna's side in the menagerie to assist with her painting.

Jessie set up the poster-size canvas on a weighted easel so it wouldn't be easy for Myrna to knock over. She brought out her cart of paints and brushes and added small mounds of paint to the palette.

By now, a crowd from the big top had started gathering. Jessie led Myrna out and fastened a leg bracelet around her foot. The elephant had plenty of room to move around, but she couldn't reach the crowd standing on the other side of rope barrier.

"Welcome, ladies, gentlemen, and children," Jessie announced. She pointed at Myrna. "This lovely lady is our resident artist, Myrna, who likes to express her creative side by painting."

Jessie walked over to her cart and picked up an eighteen-inch-long paintbrush and held it up to Myrna. Myrna reached out her trunk and took it.

Then Jessie stood to Myrna's side with the palette in front of her. "Myrna, paint."

Myrna moved the brush around in the air as if getting the feel for it. Then she stabbed the yellow mound of paint on the palette. Jessie had noticed that yellow and orange seemed to be the elephant's favorite colors.

Myrna swiped the brush across the canvas, leaving a trail of color. She repeated it twice more. The crowd oohed and ahhed and clapped with delight.

Jessie held up a clean brush. Myrna dropped the used brush on the cart and took the new brush from Jessie's hand.

From inside the big top, she heard the band start playing *The Stars and Stripes Forever*. Jessie wondered if there was a special performance, or if the band was practicing.

Then Samuel rushed over. "I'm sorry, everyone. You need to leave. We have an emergency. You need to head out beyond the ticket booth."

"What's wrong?" Jessie asked.

"That's the Disaster March."

"It's Stars and Stripes Forever."

"Not today it's not. Something bad happened in the big top."

Then Jessie smelled smoke. Samuel did, too. His eyes widened, and his face paled.

"Damn, it's a fire," he said.

"Get the animals back to the train."

Jessie's heart raced. She ran outside of the menagerie and saw smoke rising from the big top. She thought she saw yellow flames, but it was high up, and she hoped she was mistaken.

She clenched her eyes shut and saw the flames devouring the curtains and furniture in her home when she was thirteen. She heard the crackling flames and smelled smoke.

"Jessie! The animals!" Samuel called. He grabbed her by the arm, and she snapped out of the flashback.

Townies were filing toward the entrance. It was slow going because so many of them kept looking back, wanting to see if the big top was on fire. For them, it was just a continuation of the show.

Jessie ran back inside the menagerie wanting to get Myrna out. Then she saw Samuel had already hooked the chimpanzee cage to Daisy's harness.

"Lead her back to the train," he said. "There should be people there to load it. Leave the cages there and bring Daisy back here for another set of cages."

"What about Myrna?"

"We'll get her out, but we need the elephants to haul cages right now. We need to get all the animals out of danger."

Jessie grabbed a hold of Daisy's reins and yanked her toward the train. The elephant lumbered behind her, but Jessie knew that time was of the essence. They had to get everyone out before it was too late.

"Come on, girl. We gotta go now," she said, patting her trunk. Daisy let out a loud trumpet, as if she knew the urgency of the situation.

Panic bubbled in her chest as she thought about all the other animals that needed to be saved. The circus was efficient in breaking down its equipment, but it still took time. Time wasn't something they had. Fire traveled quickly if it caught on the canvas. Some of the workers would also be busy fighting the fire.

As they neared the train, Jessie could see the confusion spreading around them. The animals were confused and frightened, and the handlers were struggling to get them all to safety. Jessie could hear roars and growls over the commotion. She.dismounted Daisy and ran toward the lions' cage where she also heard men shouting

The sight that greeted her was chaos. Roustabouts and even some performers were helping to move things away from the big top. The animals were scared and making loud noises while the rest of the crew rushed to load them onto the train. Emergencies brought all hands on deck.

Where was Bradley? Was he safe?

She turned back toward the big top, and she noticed the smoke getting thicker and thicker. Something had definitely caught on fire. Panic set in as she thought of all the people still inside the big top trying to remove rigging and the bleachers. If the fire reached places the roustabouts couldn't get to, it would burn through the rigging and bring down heavy sheets of burning canvas on everyone still inside.

She hurried back to the menagerie for more animals. She panicked when she saw smoke where the menagerie tent should be.

Jessie froze. She was overwhelmed with another flashback. She saw her home in Harrisburg in flames. Her arm throbbed painfully. She grabbed it, expecting it to be on fire. Tears filled her eyes.

Then she heard a worried trumpeting from one of the elephants. She blinked and took a deep breath. Then she ran inside, yelling, "Samuel, the menagerie is on fire!"

"I know!" He shouted, but it turned into a cough as he breathed in smoke. He pointed to Jo-Jo and Patti who were harnessed to the bear cages. "Get them out of here!"

Jessie hurried over to the elephants. She grabbed Patti's harness and urged her forward, knowing that Patti would follow. The animals didn't like the smoke. She worked to calm them. Jo-Jo hesitated at first, flapping her ears and letting out a low rumble, but Jessie urged her on with a steady hand. Together, they stepped out of the menagerie tent, the bear cages dragging behind.

Jessie could feel the heat from the fire on her back. She knew they had to move quickly before the flames spread too far.

As they made their way toward the train, Jessie spotted Bradley running toward them. Relief flooded through her as he approached.

"Jessie, are you okay?" he asked, panting heavily.

"I'm fine. We need to get the animals out of here," she replied.

Bradley quickly assessed the situation and started moving the other animals toward the train. Jessie helped as best she could, making sure each animal was secured on the train before moving to the next one.

The smoke was getting thicker, making it difficult to see. Jessie could feel her throat getting scratchy from inhaling the smoke. But she couldn't stop now. They had to get everyone out.

When she went back inside the tent, she saw Samuel throwing open the cages and releasing the animals.

"We don't have enough time!" Samuel called. "Just let them out. Better to have to catch them later than have them burn in the fire."

Jessie ran over to the llamas. She unbuckled their harnesses and shooed them out of the menagerie. When she turned back, she saw a tiger, pacing back and forth quickly. It growled and looked afraid of the fire but unsure of where to go.

It spotted her and moved toward her. Jessie moved away, and the tiger started to run toward her. Suddenly, Myrna was in front of her and rammed the tiger in his side with her head.

"Myrna, let's go!" Jessie called. She grabbed Myrna's harness and pulled.

Jessie moved away, but part of the canvas fell. She dodged out of the way of the canvas but got tangled in the rigging. The burning canvas fell on Myrna's back and she trumpeted in pain. The elephant swung her head back and forth. Then she raised up on her back legs trying to get the burning canvas off.

Jessie grabbed at the canvas and struggled against the tangled rigging to pull it off the elephant's back. It was too heavy and it just seemed to bring her more pain. Suddenly, Bradley was there pulling the canvas off Myrna.

The tiger saw Jessie and started heading toward her again. Something else moved off to the side, and Alexander ran up next to her, waving his arms. He pulled one of his knives from his belt.

"Don't hurt him," Jessie called as she twisted frantically, becoming even more tangled in the rigging. "We're trying to keep them safe."

"Tell him I would appreciate the same consideration," Alexander shouted.

He continued waving his arms and shouting, but the tiger was more afraid of the flames. It faced in their direction and crouched. Alexander threw his knife.

Jessie screamed, but the knife hit the tiger with the haft. The tiger finally gave up and ran off in another direction.

"Jessie! Jessie!" she heard Bradley yelling.

"Over here!" Alexander called.

Bradley appeared out of the smoke and rushed over to her. Alexander cut away the rigging, and they pulled Jessie free.

"There's nothing more we can do here now," Bradley

said. "The fire department's here. We need to get out of the way."

Jessie, Bradley, and Alexander staggered out of the tent. She was grateful to breath in clear air once again.

She heard shouts and sirens and looked around. Where was Myrna?

Through the cacophony, Jessie heard the trumpet of an elephant in pain. It had to be Myrna. The burning canvas had fallen on her back and burned her.

Jessie ran toward the menagerie. This was what had happened with her family. She had been too afraid to go back into the house after them, and they had died. She couldn't let that happen to Myrna.

Bradley grabbed her by the arm and pulled her back. "You can't go in there!" he shouted.

"I heard Myrna!"

"It doesn't mean she's in the tent. We released the animals we couldn't haul out."

"Then where is she?" Myrna wouldn't leave Jessie.

"I don't know, but you can't go back in there."

A fire truck pulled up near them and firefighters jumped from the truck. The started shouting orders and unraveling hoses.

Bradley kept his arm around Jessie and half pulled her away from the burning tent as she sobbed into his chest.

PART III

HOME FOR WAYWARD ELEPHANTS

29
AUGUST 1938

Myrna chuffed and whined as Dr. Lyons, the new circus veterinarian, stood on a ladder, examining the ugly red marks across her back where the pieces of burning canvas had fallen on the elephant. They gave her the appearance of a red-striped tiger, if tigers stood ten-feet tall and had a five-foot-long trunk.

The veterinarian was careful how he touched the wounds. Although Myrna's hide was tough, it couldn't stand up to fire. The flesh was still raw and appeared to glow red when Myrna moved around a lot. Any kind of contact with the wounds made Myrna start to shuffle around.

Jessie stood at Myrna's head, hugging her trunk and resting her head on it.

"Dr. Lyons is trying to help you, Myrna. Don't worry. He'll get you better in no time," Jessie said quietly.

"Don't make promises I can't keep, little lady," the doctor said.

"I have faith in you."

Honestly, she would have preferred Dr. Stultz to care for

Myrna, but he was in another state. Dr. Lyons had been with the circus for two weeks, and the most serious ailment he'd had to deal with was singed fur on one of the tigers. Jessie had called Dr. Stultz, and he had assured her that Dr. Lyons was a good veterinarian who knew how to care for elephants better than Dr. Stultz.

"I'm just a country doctor," Dr. Stultz had told her. "If Myrna was a cow or a horse, I would help, but I can only give you a general assessment of an elephant. Yes, I can take care of burns, but Dr. Lyons knows the circus animals better than me. I met him when he worked for the Cole Brothers Circus. He's a good doctor from what I've seen. He'll do his best for you."

From atop the ladder, Dr. Lyons said, "It's not a matter of faith. It physiology. The canvas burned her badly. I have no doubt that she'll get healthy, but she'll have bad scars all over her back. Now hold her steady. I'm getting ready to spread more salve."

Jessie tightened her grip on Myrna's trunk. "Stay still, girl. Don't knock Dr. Lyons off the ladder. He's only trying to help you."

Myrna snorted and Jessie knew the doctor must have started spreading the green slime over the elephant's back. Myrna shuddered as her muscles twitched involuntarily, which must have made her hurt even more.

Mr. Conroy walked into the makeshift menagerie tent. He looked over the animals and shook his head. A lion, three horses, and a black bear had died in the fire. The roustabouts had burned the bodies last night while some of the tent pieces and equipment had been smoldering still.

Myrna was lucky. It could have been worse for both her and Jessie. Seven people had died in the fire, including an eight-year-old boy who was at the circus with his family.

Luckily, it was nowhere near as bad as the Hagenbeck-Wallace train crash in 1918. A military train engineer fell asleep and missed signals about the stalled circus train. The trains collided and the wooden cars on the circus train caught fire, killing eighty-six people and leaving 187 injured.

Even though this fire had proven far less deadly, it had been more public, and anytime a townie died, there'd be hell to pay. And this time, a boy had been killed.

Mr. Conroy saw Jessie and headed in her direction.

"How is Myrna?" he asked.

"She'll recover," Jessie told him.

The circus owner looked up to where Dr. Lyons worked. He saw the salve and frowned.

"How does she look, Doc?" Conroy asked.

"She's lucky. Her tough skin helped minimize the worst of the burns."

Conroy wiped his sleeve against his sweaty forehead. "Minimize? Will she be scarred?"

"Afraid so."

"Damn!"

"What's wrong?" Jessie asked. "She'll be okay."

"Don't get me wrong. I'm glad we didn't lose another animal, but I can't have a scarred elephant performing. People will complain."

"About what?"

"The scars will remind them of the fire, or it will make them think we are abusing the animals," Mr. Conroy said. "We don't want either."

"You won't be able to see the scars when she has her outfit on."

"That would work for parades, but not for her painting. The people are too close. Someone would notice."

"Then what will you do with her?"

Conroy scratched the back of his head. "Normally, I would sell off an elephant I couldn't use, but no other circus will want her for the same reasons I can't use her. I'll have to try and see if a zoo is interested in her."

Jessie grabbed his arm. "No! She would be miserable in a cage."

"I don't want to get rid of her, Jessie, but it costs a lot to keep an elephant, and if that elephant isn't pulling her weight helping the circus make money, I can't keep her."

"It's not fair."

He swung his arm around the tent. "Look around, Jessie. None of this is fair, but it is life."

No one knew how the fire had started. It could have been a stray cigarette butt a townie threw on the ground. The roustabouts kept an eye out for smoldering butts because so much was flammable at the circus, but most of the crew believed this fire must have been Conroy and Pepperidge Circus's bad luck.

The menagerie tent was in tatters, but it was still better than the big top, which had nearly all burned. The midway stands fared the best. They had been barely damaged.

"What if I can come up with something better?" She had saved Myrna once. She would find a way to do it again.

Mr. Conroy shrugged. "I'm willing to listen. You have until I get an acceptable offer for her. I'll let her work helping raise and lower the big top once we get another one, and she can walk in the parade, but she can't perform."

The circus was in a shambles and had already missed its next show in Richmond. They were still in Frederick waiting for the police to complete their investigation. With the big top mostly destroyed, they might be forced to perform in the open air or perhaps raise just the side panels to keep unpaying spectators away. That is, if anyone would want to venture into a big top even without its top. The public would be skittish about fires for a while. Open air performances also meant rain would cause them to cancel shows, and they couldn't afford that.

Just when the circus needed money the most, they wouldn't have it. And now, Jessie was asking Mr. Conroy to keep a non-performing elephant. She understood his position, but Jessie loved Myrna and couldn't stand to think of her in a zoo.

After Dr. Lyons finished taking care of Myrna, Jessie walked the elephant back to the menagerie. She brought Myrna a bucket of apples to eat before heading off to eat lunch herself.

Jessie sat next to Bradley in the cookhouse. She didn't have much of an appetite and was only nibbling at the carrots on her plate.

The tent was unusually quiet. The season was over for the circus. It might even be the end of the circus. They were missing performance dates, and expenses were piling up.

Bradley walked over and sat down next to her. He gave her a kiss on the cheek. "Is Myrna all right?"

Jessie sighed. "I guess it depends on how you look at it." She explained Myrna's condition and what Mr. Conroy had told her.

"I would hate to see Myrna sold to a zoo," Bradley said.

Jessie nodded, "She likes performing, and even though she's not free, she would be even more confined in a zoo."

"Mr. Conroy is right, though. People would be upset to see a scarred elephant. They would think we are harming the elephants. Remember how mad you were when you saw the scars around her ankle from the restraint when you first met her."

Jessie nodded. "I know. I was pretty upset."

"Then imagine how people will react if they see those large scars on her back. Mr. Conroy has enough trouble already. If he is going to keep the circus open, he won't need more problems."

Jessie stabbed at a carrot. "Myrna is scarred because she helped us."

"I know, and I wish I knew a way to thank her for that."

"Putting her in a zoo isn't it."

Bradley nodded. "Too bad she's not a bull or a horse. Mr. Conroy could just put her out to pasture."

Jessie stopped what she doing. Bradley had a point. Some farm animals were simply retired once their useful life was done on a farm. Some could be used for breeding, but often the animals were kept around because of the owners' bonds with them.

Myna had made friends with people here, like Jessie, Bradley, and Samuel. She just hadn't made friends with the right people like Mr. Conroy who made the decisions about what to do with animals.

Bradley was right. Too bad Myrna wasn't on a farm. Then she could be put out to pasture.

Ideas flashed in her mind as she imagined a possible future for Myrna. She needed to talk to Mr. Frank about running a farm.

"What if we could put her out to pasture?" Jessie asked.

"You mean take her to a farm?"

Jessie nodded. "Not just any farm. I don't think cows and chickens would care much for her, although they might get used to her and keep her company."

Bradley put his fork down. "What kind of crazy idea are you cooking up?"

Jessie grinning. "It's not a crazy idea."

"What's not?"

"An elephant farm."

Bradley's eyes widened. "Say again?"

"A farm with an elephant on it."

"What are you going to do? Hitch Myrna to a plow?"

"No, she could be put out to pasture like an old horse."

Bradley scratched his cheek. "Okay, if you could find a farm willing to take her, how would that farmer support her?"

"Maybe I could pay to house her like people pay to stable horses. I have that inheritance coming."

"You would probably use it up pretty quickly paying to stable an elephant. Then there's the problem of how a farm would stable an elephant. She could fit into a barn at night, but she'd be too big for a stall. The fences around a farm are too low for an elephant."

Jessie was nodding as he spoke, but her mind was elsewhere. She was envisioning possibilities. This could work. She would need to talk to some people like Samuel and the Wilsons. Let them bring up questions and possible problems, but Jessie thought this idea had a chance of working.

30

NOVEMBER 1939

Jessie spun the small diamond ring on her finger. It was something she had started doing when she became nervous. She wasn't nervous about her wedding to Bradley. That had felt natural, almost destined to be. She was happier than she had ever been.

No, what was making her nervous was the pile of papers in front her that she needed to sign. Once she did, she would own 150 acres of West Virginia mountain woods and fields. She and Bradley had been able to purchase it for a very low price. Sadly, the previous owners had lost it when they went bankrupt because of the depression. The bank that took it had wanted to sell it as quickly as they could, preferring to have cash at this time of uncertainty for banks rather than own property.

She and Bradley were sitting in a lawyer's office, which also made her nervous. It had been months since she was inside an office or a home. She lived in tents and rail cars.

Bradley sat beside her, saying nothing. He had told her it was her money, part of her inheritance that she was about to spend. It was her decision.

"Can we do this, Bradley?" she whispered, pleadingly. "Tell me we can."

Instead of saying anything, he reached into his shirt pocket and removed a picture of Jessie washing Myrna, and the elephant raising her trunk into the air and almost seeming to smile while Jessie laughed. He slid it across the table so that she could see it.

Jessie smiled fondly at the photo before returning to her task, signing the documents where indicated with an X.

As she signed the last paper, Bradley placed a reassuring hand on her shoulder. "We can do this," he said. "Together."

Jessie leaned into his touch, grateful for his support. She trusted Bradley with her life, and she knew he would always be there for her.

With the papers signed, they stood up and walked out of the lawyer's office, into the warm afternoon sunshine. The crisp air filled their lungs as they made their way to Bradley's truck, eager to start their new adventure. It had also been a long time since she had felt a true winter day, probably since she lived with the Wilsons. She was very much beyond what felt comfortable and familiar to her. It was the same way she had felt during her first days and weeks with the circus or the Wilson's Home for Children. Everything was different and new.

As they drove, Jessie couldn't help but feel a sense of unease creeping up on her. What if they were making a mistake? What if they couldn't handle the responsibilities of owning a large piece of land?

But Bradley sensed her hesitation and reached over to take her hand. "We'll make it work," he said firmly. "We'll do whatever it takes. I promise."

Jessie looked over at him and saw the determination in his eyes. She nodded. They had to make it work. They had finished with the circus to put all their efforts toward creating a place for Myrna.

What they would do with an elephant, she didn't know. They had considered how they could earn money to keep Myrna fed. Sadly, the first thing that came to mind was to have her perform.

She might be able to have Myrna paint. That could draw in some money. It wouldn't be enough to keep things going, but it would help.

Not only would that be painful for Myrna, but the goal of buying the property was to give her a place where she could be an elephant. That wouldn't happen if she was having to perform.

Then Mr. Frank had suggested she talk to foundations and rich people about making donations to create a fund that would help support the farm. It made sense, although people weren't as wealthy as they once were. But someone should want to help a brave elephant.

It seemed like Jessie would be living outside of her comfort zone for quite some time yet.

The property was located in the foothills of the Appalachian Mountains. It was too hilly for farmland, but it was just right for what Jessie and Bradley wanted.

"It's beautiful here," Jessie said, taking in the view of the sprawling acres before them. "I can't believe it's all ours."

Bradley wrapped his arms around her waist and pulled her closer. "We're going to build a life here, Jessie. You, me, and Myrna."

Jessie smiled, feeling the warmth of his embrace. "I can't wait," she whispered, before turning to face him. "But first, let's celebrate."

Bradley grinned mischievously. "I know just the way to

do that."

He took her hand and led her toward the farmhouse. It wasn't nearly as large as the Wilson home, but that had been built to hold more than a dozen people. Bradley and Jessie would be the only ones living here. It had two floors and six rooms. It didn't have indoor plumbing yet. All the water had to be pumped from the well, and they would have to use an outhouse for a bathroom. They could eventually add onto the house. They had wanted to focus their money on getting a large piece of land. Besides, they were used to living in little rooms from their time with the circus.

With determination blazing in their eyes and sweat pouring down their brows, Bradley and Jessie set to work on realizing their dream. The old farm had overgrown fields and out buildings that needed repairs. They tackled them with fervor, clearing the land day after day. They made repairs to the house and barn. They used salvaged materials as much as possible to try and manage the costs.

They also took time to create a six-foot-tall wire fence around a field where Myrna would wander. In the barn, Bradley created an extra-large stall where Myrna would stay at night. They also had regular stalls for cows that would provide milk.

They did as much of the work they could themselves. For more complicated work, they hired local men to help. They worked under the sun, hammering, sawing, and nailing until the structure stood tall and proud.

Meanwhile, Bradley made the journey to Keyser, West Virginia, in search of employment to support their growing project. As construction progressed, Jessie made countless calls to businesses, veterinarians, and zoos, pleading for donations to help bring her vision to life. Though many rejected her bold idea, some compassionate souls were touched by her passion and offered their support in any way they could.

31
MARCH 1939

As the Baltimore and Ohio train rolled into Keyser, Jessie stood anxiously at the station, her eyes scanning each passing car as the train slowly rolled to a stop with a squeal of brakes and a burst of steam.

She found the number of the car she wanted and walked over to wait for the door to slide open.

Finally, as the doors opened, Jessie's gaze fell upon an elephant, standing tall and proud inside the train. The workers who usually offloaded cargo were taken aback; they had offloaded animals before, but never an elephant. Even when the circus came to town, circus workers handled the transportation of their animals.

"What do we do with it?" one man said as he scratched his chin in confusion while staring at Myrna.

Jessie stepped forward confidently, "I'll take care of her."

They were surprised at seeing a young woman take control of the situation, but they didn't know what to do.

She walked up the ramp and into the box car, greeted by the familiar scent of hay and animal feed. Inside, a spacious stall had been set up to keep Myrna comfortable during her journey. There was plenty of food and water for her, carefully arranged by Samuel who had made sure Myrna would be well taken care of during her trip from Florida. Myrna had already been fed and watered at a few stops along the way.

As Jessie approached the elephant, she couldn't help but wonder if this gentle giant had ever traveled alone before. When she traveled on the train with the circus, the other elephants had always been with her, keeping her company.

"Hello there, Myrna," Jessie greeted her with a warm smile, "Did you miss me?"

As soon as Myrna recognized Jessie's voice, she trumpeted excitedly and playfully swung her trunk in greeting. In that moment, Jessie knew that no matter what challenges may come on this journey, she and Myrna would face them together as loyal companions.

"We've still got some traveling to do, but it's worth it. I promise." Jessie's words were filled with excitement and determination as she gazed out of the old wooden boxcar.

"Is the circus coming to town?" a worker outside of the box asked.

"No, I'm just bringing my friend to her new home," Jessie replied with a smile.

"New home?"

"My husband and I bought the old McAllister Farm outside of town."

The worker rolled his eyes. "That's not much of a farm."

"But it's a perfect home for an elephant," Jessie said.

She carefully opened the stall door and led Myrna out into the open air. As Jessie guided Myrna down the ramp, she couldn't help but notice the smooth pink scars that marred Myrna's back, smooth and slightly puffy compared to the rough skin around them. They had healed since the fire, but they were a reminder of why Myrna had to leave the circus.

After a short walk, they arrived at a large semi-truck with its trailer open and ready. The interior was spacious and inviting, lined with soft hay and filled with familiar scents.

You're doing great, girl. We'll be home shortly," Jessie whispered soothingly as she guided Myrna into the trailer.

Jessie patted Myrna's side one last time before backing out of the trailer and closing the doors behind her. She could feel Myrna's eyes following her as she made her way back to the front of the truck.

"I'll be up front. This is the last trip you need to make. You'll be home soon," Jessie promised, eager to see Myrna finally find comfort and safety at the farm.

The old truck rumbled along the winding mountain road, struggling under its heavy cargo. Curious onlookers gazed at the unusual sight as it passed by. They couldn't see the massive elephant inside, but they were taken aback by the large vehicle navigating through the narrow back roads.

An hour later, it pulled into the yard and rolled to a stop. Bradley emerged from the nearby barn, wiping sweat from his forehead with his sleeve.

The driver stepped out of the truck and took in his surroundings. "This is a nice place," he said. "But are you really going to keep an elephant here? Doesn't she belong in a jungle or something like that?"

"Myrna's never seen a jungle. She was born in a circus and has been part of one all her life."

"Will she like a farm then?"

That was the lingering question. Jessie hoped Myrna would adjust well to her new home, but there weren't many options left for them. Mr. Conroy made it clear that he could no longer keep Myrna with the circus, and no other circus would take her in. It was either this or sending her off to a zoo, which seemed even worse. There she would be confined to a small space, most likely with a cement floor. The farm would at least give her some area to roam and a softer surface for her to walk on, which would probably be good for her arthritis.

"That's our plan," Jessie replied firmly.

Bradley walked over and helped her down from the truck.

"How does she look?" he asked.

"She seemed a bit confused after the train trip, but she's handling it surprisingly well." She squeezed his arm gently. "This is the right choice, isn't it?"

"It was your idea," Bradley reminded her with a smile.

"I know, but I'm nervous it will all fall apart."

"Then we'll deal with it if it does. For now, we'll give it our all. This is a beautiful place for her to live. She'll be able to wander within the enclosure and eat what she wants and play in the water."

"She's got decades left to live. Don't you think she'll get lonely?"

"I'm not thinking about decades right now. I'm thinking about the next week, month, and year. Once we know this will work, then we can start planning what's next. Besides, she's got you."

They walked to the back of the truck where the driver was setting up a metal ramp, Jessie felt a twinge of worry about how Myrna would adjust to this new home. But she quickly pushed those thoughts aside, focusing instead on making sure the transition was smooth.

"We're here, Myrna. I sure hope you like it." She took a deep breath and said, "Myrna, back."

The elephant slowly backed up, hesitant at first but trusting in Jessie's guidance. After safely guiding Myrna down the ramp and onto solid ground, Jessie watched with bated breath as the majestic creature took in the lush, green landscape of trees in the yard and distant forest. Jessie guided her away from the truck. She led the elephant through the barn and out the other side into the enclosure. It was filled with endless possibilities for her to explore. She could wander freely and graze on whichever plants caught her fancy, or frolic in the sparkling water of the nearby pond within the fenced fifty acres.

A lone cow in the field caught Myrna's attention, and Jessie wondered if Myrna had ever seen one before during her time with the circus. Cows weren't exotic enough for a circus.

"Welcome home, Myrna," Jessie said softly, giving her a reassuring pat. "Take your time and explore your new home."

Myrna watched Jessie move off and then turned in a slow circle, taking in every detail. No one was telling Myrna what to do or where to go. She had no chain around her leg, limiting how far she could walk. The choices were hers to make, and for Myrna, that was a feeling she had never experienced before. Finally, she let out a low rumble of contentment and began to explore her new home with childlike wonder and joy.

With graceful, deliberate steps, Myrna approached the cow and reached out her trunk. The cow, startled by the movement, quickly moved away. Myrna hesitated for a moment before following, her trunk still extended in a gentle gesture.

Suddenly, a stray dog that Jessie and Bradley had adopted came bounding out of the barn. It skidded to a stop when it saw Myrna, its tail wagging in excitement. It let out a single bark. Myrna turned her attention away from the cow and toward the dog. The animal cautiously crept closer, its body language showing both wariness and curiosity. Myrna turned fully to face the dog, extending her trunk once again. The dog jumped back at first but then slowly approached, sniffing tentatively at Myrna's trunk.

In turn, Myrna sniffed the dog with interest. It darted around her legs playfully before finally settling on the ground in front of her.

Letting out a low snort in response to the dog's playful antics, Myrna watched as it barked once more before standing up and starting to walk away. Without hesitation, Myrna followed behind.

Jessie smiled.

32

MAY 1939

From sunrise to sunset, Jessie and Bradley toiled on the farm, their days filled with backbreaking work and their nights illuminated by the glow of oil lamps. It was a daunting task, learning how to run a farm while simultaneously restoring it to its former glory. But they persevered, driven by their love for the land and their deep desire to make it thrive once again.

They planned out elephant-friendly crops and fruit trees. They hoped that these would provide the bulk of the food that Myrna needed. They also plotted out a smaller garden that provide for their needs.

They hadn't been able to get any businesses or foundations to help fund them. Businesses were being much tighter with their cash nowadays. However, Bradley had found some markets in the area that were willing to give him fruits and vegetables that they were going to throw out. It was food on the verge of going bad, but it stayed good long enough for Myrna to eat it.

Meanwhile, Myrna adapted effortlessly to her new home.

She spent her days leisurely strolling around the enclosure with Thatcher, her faithful canine companion. The dog darted in between her legs as she walked, and Myrna was careful not to accidentally step on him.

Whenever Myrna grew restless or agitated, she gently used her powerful trunk to push Thatcher out of her way. They even went for a swim together in the cool waters of the nearby pond, their bond growing stronger with each passing day.

During her rare moments of free time, Jessie found herself captivated by Myrna's graceful movements in the enclosure. In contrast to her slow and laborious gait in the circus, she now moved with a newfound agility and joy. Her arthritis seemed to have miraculously disappeared, no longer hindering her from experiencing all that life had to offer. Watching Myrna, Jessie felt a sense of fulfillment knowing that she had made the right decision in rescuing her.

One winter's day in 1939, Samuel Atwell boarded a train from Florida to visit Jessie and Bradley at their farm. The circus had survived the fire, although it had scaled back to a single ring. However, it would continue, and it would grow. Right now, the circus was in winter quarters, so Samuel had time off.

Jessie and Bradley eagerly showed him around the property, proudly displaying their hard work and dedication that had transformed it into a thriving homestead. But most importantly, they introduced him to Myrna. Walking through the barn and into the spacious enclosure on the other side, Samuel couldn't help but marvel at the sight before him.

"How much space do you have fenced?" he asked in amazement.

"Fifty acres," Jessie replied with a hint of pride in her voice. "But we hope to expand it once we have a better understanding of what running this farm will take."

"Well, that's certainly more space than she's ever had in the circus," Samuel remarked.

Jessie could feel her cheeks burning with embarrassment, knowing that she and Samuel had helped keep Myrna in the confined space.

With a thoughtful expression, Samuel walked over to the fence and examined it. It was a regular wooden fence that Bradley had topped with another three feet of chicken wire. Beyond the original wooden fence, the continuing fence was nothing but a thin barrier of tall barbed wire. He reached out and pressed his hand against the wire.

"She can go right through this, you know," Samuel remarked. "I'm not even sure the barbs would bother her."

Jessie nodded, her eyes following his gaze. "We had to be mindful of our budget, but we also hope that she will come to see this fence as a reminder of her home and not a boundary to stop her."

"Has she damaged it?"

"Not yet."

"In that case, I'd say you and Bradley are doing a good job at making her feel at home," Samuel complimented.

A small smile graced Jessie's lips, pleased with their progress. That was their goal all along—to create a safe and welcoming space for their newest member. It was reassuring to have Samuel acknowledge their efforts.

During dinner later that evening, Samuel surprised them with some news.

"You two have done a lot in short amount of time," he said. "Do you feel more comfortable with the situation now?"

Bradley shrugged. "I wouldn't say I'm comfortable, but I am getting used to what needs to be done."

"I just wish we had money coming in so that we would

know we could get by," Jessie chimed in. "We've been cutting back on our expenses, but we still have them."

Samuel nodded understandingly. "That's exactly what happened with the circus after the fire. We made it through, though. It was tough for a while. Jeremy even missed payroll a couple of times. People weren't happy, but he still kept them fed and in a room and that was something."

"Yes, but at least you still had money coming in even if it wasn't enough."

"True, but when you can't pay your bills, you can't pay your bills," Samuel replied gravely. "What are you thinking about doing to change that?"

Bradley said, "We don't have enough land to farm it for sales and feed Myrna. I'm going to try and find work in town while Jessie works the farm and takes care of Myrna. She has more experience farming and caring for elephants than I do, anyway."

Samuel pursed his lips and then let out a heavy sigh. "I heard from an elephant trainer with Tetranno Brothers. He heard about your farm and wanted to know if it was working out."

"Why would he be interested?" Jessie asked, her mind racing to figure out how word had spread about their struggling farm.

"He has an elephant that is showing signs of arthritis. He is considering what to do with her."

"And he wants us to buy her? We can barely afford to keep our own farm running, let alone buy an elephant."

"That's just it. He doesn't want to sell her. He would be willing to give her to you," Samuel explained. "She's the oldest of the three elephants his circus has, and he's been working with her for fifteen years. He doesn't want to put her in a cage in a zoo."

Jessie wanted to say yes. If for nothing more than to give Myrna an elephant companion. She couldn't, though. She and Bradley knew they couldn't take on such a responsibility without first figuring out how to make ends meet.

"We don't know if we can take care of Myrna yet," she said hesitantly. "We can't take on another elephant until we know how this will go."

Samuel nodded understandingly. "You definitely have the capability to take care of more than one elephant. You've already proven that by caring for Myrna. The real issue is whether you can financially afford to take on more than one elephant."

Jessie sighed, feeling the weight of the situation. "Either way, we can't help your friend and his elephant."

"But if you can solve the affordability problem, it could open up the possibility of helping even more elephants in need," Samuel proposed.

"Of course it would, but do you have any ideas?" Bradley asked.

Samuel shook his head. "Not at the moment, but at least we now know what the main obstacles are."

Bradley's fingers curled around Jessie's arm. She turned to look at him with a questioning gaze. He met her eyes and gave a subtle nod.

"There's something else we need to consider when it comes to caring for more elephants," Jessie said, her tone serious.

"What's that?" Samuel asked, his eyebrows knitting together in concern.

Jessie hesitated before speaking again, glancing over at Bradley for support. "Besides Myrna, we'll also have to care for our own baby."

Samuel's expression shifted from worry to surprise, then quickly transformed into a wide grin. "That's wonderful news! Can I share it with the others when I return? They will be thrilled for you both," he exclaimed.

Jessie nodded, smiling at the thought of their circus family being happy for them too. "We're definitely excited," she replied.

"I should think so! Congratulations! When are you expecting your new assistant elephant trainer?"

"Or junior clown," Bradley added.

Samuel shook his head. "You need a trainer more than a clown here."

"Good point."

"She should be here in the middle of January," Jessie said.

"That's wonderful. It's even during winter. Some of us should be able to come up from Florida if you are up for company," Samuel suggested.

Jessie felt a surge of warmth in her chest at Samuel's enthusiasm. Their circus family truly meant everything to her and Bradley. And she couldn't wait to introduce their newest addition to all of them—especially Myrna. She had no doubt they would become fast friends, just like how they had all become such a close-knit group in the circus family.

33

JANUARY 1940

Jessie bundled herself up as best she could, bracing against the biting cold that nipped at her exposed fingers and cheeks. She struggled to zip up her winter coat over her growing belly, the heavy weight of pregnancy making it nearly impossible. To ward off the chill, she wrapped a thick comforter from the bed around her shoulders, feeling its soft embrace against her skin. She pulled on her hat and gloves, their cozy warmth providing some relief from the harsh winter weather. With a lantern in hand, she ventured out into the blizzard.

The snow was already calf-deep and showed no signs of slowing down. Jessie trudged through the thick flakes, her lantern casting eerie shadows on the surrounding landscape. She knew she needed to close the barn door on the far side to keep the heat inside. Myrna would surely want to stay inside until the storm passed.

The snow was a surprise. The storm had rolled in unexpectedly fast, obscuring everything in a hazy blur of white. Jessie could barely see more than a few feet in front of her.

Their life on the farm had finally settled into a comfortable routine, but now this snowstorm threatened to disrupt it for a few days.

She hoped Bradley would get home soon. After he finished work each day, he visited the restaurants in Keyser to collect any of the food they couldn't use for Myrna. He was usually home by now, but the snow must have slowed him down.

Despite the challenges they faced every day, Jessie and Bradley managed to keep the farm going. They relied on local businesses to provide them with excess food for Myrna and had even started hosting educational visits for school groups to come and learn about elephants and circus life. Most times, Myrna willingly greeted their guests, but Jessie always made sure to never force her.

In addition to caring for Myrna, they had also expanded their fence line to include ten more acres. She and Bradley had talked over Samuel's proposal and decided that, yes, they would adopt a second elephant. Her name was Sarah. She would be a companion to Myrna, and she needed help. This was the right thing to do. She would be arriving before the circus started its season, but the details still needed to be worked out.

Samuel had been right about that. Elephants were herd elephants. They needed the company of other elephants. So she had let him know that they were ready to bring on one more elephant. She wished she could take on more because she feared for retired elephants. The larger circuses sold their elephants to zoos or smaller circuses. And while zoos would take decent care of them, some of the smaller circuses wouldn't. Samuel had told her about a small circus that curiously didn't need to order meat from the butcher for a week after the disappearance of an older elephant who could no longer perform.

Meanwhile, they had eagerly prepared a nursery for their own little one, who was due to arrive any day now. Despite the discomforts of pregnancy while still working hard on the farm, Jessie couldn't wait to hold her precious baby in her arms.

She had hoped things would remain quiet until the birth, but she knew that was unlikely.

As she walked into the barn, Jessie realized something was amiss. The familiar form of Myrna was not in her stall as usual. Jessie's heart quickened with worry. The elephant usually came in at dusk to eat and drink before settling down for the night. This presented a problem. Jessie needed to close up the barn to protect against the biting wind and snow, but first she had to find Myrna.

Her breath misted in front of her face as she walked to the far side of the barn and peered out into the darkening snow. The heavy snowfall had turned the world into a hazy blur.

"Myrna!" she called out, her voice swallowed up by the wind.

Sometimes Myrna would respond with a trumpet, but tonight there was only eerie silence.

Undeterred, Jessie pulled her coat tighter around her body and set off to search for Myrna. She trudged through the deepening snow, pausing every few minutes to call out for her elephant companion.

With each unanswered call, Jessie's worry grew. She wasn't sure if Myrna could handle the frigid temperatures that were expected tonight. After all, elephants were not used to snow.

After what felt like hours of walking, Jessie thought she heard a faint response to her call. She repeated it again and this time, she heard a distinct trumpet coming from her right.

With renewed determination, she made her way toward the sound. It took several more minutes and a few more calls for Myrna to come into view—a dark shadow blending into the snowy landscape. But as Jessie got closer, Myrna came into focus and relief flooded through her.

The elephant didn't seem upset or confused. Instead, she was utterly mesmerized by the delicate snowflakes falling from the sky. She twirled in slow circles, her trunk gracefully swaying through the air as she attempted to catch and blow away the flurries.

Jessie couldn't help but laugh at her curious friend and walked over to her, bracing herself against the biting cold.

"Myrna, come, now. We need to get you inside where it's warm," Jessie called out to the elephant.

The elephant lowered her trunk and followed Jessie's lead. As they walked through the snowy landscape, Jessie searched for any familiar landmarks to guide them back to the barn. But in the darkness of night and fog of snow, everything looked different. Even their footprints had disappeared. Without being able to see the sky, she had no sense of direction and couldn't tell how far they were from the safety of the barn.

She could try following the fence back, but she wasn't sure how far Myrna was from it.

With each step, Jessie felt the cold seeping into her body, draining her energy and turning her toes into numb ice cubes. She was grateful that the wood stove was already burning in the barn, providing a source of warmth for both herself and Myrna.

"Come on, girl. Let's pick up the pace," Jessie urged as she quickened her steps.

They continued walking straight ahead, or at least what Jessie believed was straight ahead. But after some time, she started to question if they were actually making progress. It felt like it was taking longer to get back to the barn than it had taken to reach Myrna.

Suddenly, Jessie tripped on a hidden branch buried beneath the fresh snow and went tumbling forward. She managed to twist onto her side before hitting the ground, but it still left her shaken. She instinctively reached for her stomach, hoping that her unborn baby was unharmed from the fall.

With a determined push, she hoisted herself up onto her feet and resumed walking. Every step was slow and methodical, as if she were navigating through a maze. She couldn't afford to trip again. Her pace may have been sluggish, but she was alert and focused, scanning the horizon for any sign of the barn or fence.

Her toes were numb from the biting cold, and every now and then she would wiggle them just to make sure they were still attached. She feared another fall, but she knew she had to keep moving. The barn or fence had to be close by. She could feel it in her bones.

As she shuffled forward, her eyes grew heavy and eventually closed. In that momentary lapse of consciousness, she lost all sense of time.

But then she snapped back to reality. She couldn't stop. Her baby was depending on her. With renewed determination, she stumbled onward, refusing to give up.

But her body had other plans. She fell to her knees once again, the icy ground sending shockwaves up her spine. Desperately, she clawed at Myrna's leg, trying to pull herself back up. But it was no use. Her legs were too numb to support her weight.

Tears streamed down her face, freezing upon contact with the frigid air. They threatened to seal her eyelashes together, but Jessie refused to let that happen. She needed to find the barn.

Panic set in as she realized how dire her situation was becoming.

Where was the barn?

She closed her eyes just wanting to rest. Myrna prodded Jessie with her trunk and trumpeting loudly, the elephant tried to rouse her companion back into consciousness.

When that didn't work, Myrna made a split-second decision and lowered herself onto the snowy ground, curling around Jessie like a protective shield against the cold.

Snowflakes began covering them both as they huddled together against the storm.

As Bradley pulled up to the house, the warm glow of lights greeted him. He let out a sigh of relief as he turned off the engine. The drive up the mountain had been treacherous and his truck had skidded on the icy roads, but somehow he managed to keep it on track.

He stepped out of the car and was immediately hit with a gust of wind and snow. Despite his heavy coat, the cold seeped into his bones. He hurried inside, eager to escape the harsh weather.

"Jessie!" he called out as he entered their home. No response. He assumed she must have already gone to bed, exhausted from carrying around their new baby all day.

Shrugging off his coat and hanging it on the rack, he made his way upstairs to check on Jessie. But her side of the bed was empty.

"Jessie?" he called again, growing slightly concerned.

Maybe she was out in the barn, still settling Myrna down for the night. Bradley put his coat back on. He made his way back outside and trudged through the snow toward the barn where they kept Myrna. As he entered, the wind howled and darkness consumed him. He called out for Jessie but still heard nothing in return.

Where could she be? He wondered frantically as he searched every corner of the barn. The sound of the wind drowned out any possible response from Jessie or Myrna. His heart raced as he realized they were both missing in this dangerous weather.

The wind howled through the deserted farm, drowning out all sounds except for Bradley's desperate calls for his wife. He strained to hear her voice over the relentless gusts, but there was only eerie silence in response. He knew he couldn't wander aimlessly in this treacherous weather. Sixty acres may as well be sixty thousand with visibility this poor.

He squinted against the driving rain and snow as he trudged further out into the storm. He needed to find Jessie, but it felt like an impossible task. The barn was already barely visible from thirty feet away, and the encroaching blizzard made it even harder to make out its framework.

With determination, he pressed on, reaching out to grasp onto the fence for guidance and stability. Every few minutes, he called out Jessie's name, straining to hear any sign of her in the roaring winds.

Where could she be? The fenced-off area wasn't that large, but in this weather, it felt like a maze. Bradley walked and called and prayed for his wife's safety. The frigid biting wind seemed to seep through every layer of clothing, but he refused to give up.

It was then that he thought he heard a faint scream carried by the wind.

"Jessie!"

He waited anxiously for a response, but there was none. Maybe it had just been a trick of the wind rustling through the trees. But then he heard it again—a definite scream piercing through the storm.

"Jessie!"

What could be happening to her? Had she fallen or gotten trapped somewhere in the enclosure?

Bradley quickened his pace along the fence line, calling out her name with increasing urgency. "Jess—"

"Bradley!"

Her voice sounded panicked and distant.

"Keep calling my name!"

"The baby's coming!" she shouted.

Panic coursed through Bradley's veins at her words. She couldn't have the baby out here in this brutal storm. He had to find her and get her to safety, but how? The truck wouldn't stand a chance navigating down the mountain in these conditions. But he had to do something before it was too late.

With renewed determination, Bradley pushed forward, his grip on the fence tightening as he called out for his beloved wife. The race against time had begun.

He let go of the fence and counted ten steps in what he hoped was a perpendicular direction. Above the howling wind and Jessie's cries of pain, he strained his ears to hear where she might be. He couldn't afford to get lost in this blizzard; every second counted when it came to saving her and the baby. Concentrating hard, he marked the degree of his turn from the original direction before taking more careful and deliberate steps.

As he got closer, he could make out Jessie's voice more clearly. She was definitely in distress. "Hurry, Bradley," she called out, her voice strangled with agony.

He wanted to rush to her side, but that would mean risking getting lost or separated from her in the thick snow. As he continued toward her voice, he saw a large mound looming ahead. It seemed to be where Jessie was calling from. Bradley cautiously reached out and touched the mound, only to realize it was Myrna lying on the ground in front of him.

The elephant remained motionless on the ground.

Quickly scanning the area, he spotted Jessie cradled between Myrna's belly and legs. Her face was contorted in pain as she struggled through another contraction. Bradley squatted down beside her, feeling helpless and scared for both of them.

"We've got to get you back to the house," he said urgently.

"The baby's coming," Jessie gasped out.

"I know, but you can't have it here. It won't survive in this cold."

"I got lost in the snow," she cried.

Bradley's heart twisted at the fear and desperation in her voice. He couldn't let anything happen to her or their child. "I know the way back," he reassured her, even though his own confidence wavered.

With determination, he grabbed Jessie under the arms and helped her stand. She winced in pain but nodded, ready to do whatever it took to save their baby.

But when he tried to move Myrna, the elephant didn't budge. Panic started to rise within him. "Myrna, up!" he urged, trying to stay calm.

The elephant remained motionless on the ground.

"Myrna, please get up," Jessie pleaded. When there was no response, she turned to Bradley. "Bring me around to her head, I need to see if she's alright."

They cautiously made their way to Myrna's head, and when Bradley caught sight of her eye, he froze. It was open but unseeing, covered in a layer of snow.

"Jessie, we have to go," he said urgently, turning her back toward the direction they came from.

With a heavy heart, Bradley turned Jessie around and began guiding her away from the tragic scene in the snow.

"Myrna, up," she pleaded desperately.

But Bradley's words were final. "She's gone, Jessie."

The words hit like a ton of bricks, shattering any hope Jessie had held onto. "No! I saw her playing in the snow just moments ago."

"I don't know what happened, but she's dead. We need to get you back to the house," Bradley said firmly, trying to keep his own emotions in check.

As they walked through the wintry landscape, Jessie sobbed uncontrollably while Bradley counted each step and retraced their path slowly back to the fence.

"She can't be gone. She can't," Jessie repeated like a mantra.

"I promise I will come back and check on her once the snow stops, but right now we need to get you to safety," Bradley reassured her.

With Jessie struggling to walk through the deep snow, Bradley rushed into the barn and grabbed the wheelbarrow. He helped her sit in it before pushing her toward the warmth and comfort of their home.

Once inside, he quickly led her to their bedroom where he carefully undressed her and covered her with layers of quilts and blankets. But as soon as she was settled, Jessie's screams filled the quiet room.

"The baby—" she cried out in pain.

Bradley took a deep breath, trying not to let his own panic show. There was no way they could make it to town for a doctor, and he had only delivered animals on the circus grounds before. But he knew what needed to be done.

Gently moving aside the warm coverings, he could see that Jessie was already in labor. It was clear that the child was ready to enter the world.

"I can see the baby's head," Bradley announced, trying to keep his voice steady. He stood up straight and paced back and forth, trying to fight down his panic. He had to stay calm for Jessie.

He glanced at his wife who was in pain. "You just need to push," he said.

Jessie's face contorted. She strained as she pushed with all her might, determined to bring their child into the world despite the odds stacked against them.

"That's what I've been doing!"

Jessie's labor intensified as Jessie gripped the edge of the bed, her breaths coming in shallow gasps as waves of pain wash over her. Bradley took a deep breath and knelt down at the end of the bed between Jessie's legs.

Hours pass, each one feeling like an eternity. Every few minutes, Jessie screamed from the pain of a contraction. With each one, Bradley tensed and prepared to do something anything. He could see the top of the baby's head crowning.

"You're doing great, Jessie," Bradley encouraged her, his voice filled with admiration and pride. "The baby's coming out. Just keep pushing."

His hands hovered uncertainly in the air, unsure of how to guide the baby out. He didn't want to harm the by grabbing it too roughly. Jessie's screams echoed through the room as more and more of the baby slowly emerged from her body. Bradley could see the shoulders beginning to emerge and he carefully reached down to grasp them, gently pulling the baby out. Finally, with one last gut-wrenching push, Jessie yelled and pushed as the baby entered the world.

He reached into his pocket and pulled out his knife. He cut the umbilical cord and tied it off. That would have to do until he could talk to a doctor or at least a mother.

Exhausted but elated, Jessie collapsed back onto the bed, tears of joy streaming down her face.

Bradley laid the baby on a clean blanket and wiped the blood and fluids off with a warm washcloth. He wrapped the baby in the blanket and handled the bundle to Jessie.

"It's a girl," Bradley announced with a sense of wonder and awe.

34

JANUARY 1940

With trembling hands, Bradley carefully lifted his newborn daughter from the bassinette in the quaint, cozy bedroom of their small house. Her head was no bigger than a grapefruit, adorned with a thick tuft of jet black hair and twinkling blue eyes that seemed to hold all the secrets of the world. He couldn't believe how much he already loved her.

He had spent the entire night watching over her while Jessie slept peacefully. Bradley had made sure to keep them both warm and comfortable, never wanting to let either of them out of his sight.

As he cradled his daughter in his arms, he couldn't help but feel a sense of overwhelming protectiveness and vulnerability. She was so small and fragile, yet had already proven herself to be a survivor. First, by making it through the treacherous blizzard that brought her into this world, and second, by enduring her father's amateur delivery skills.

Bradley shook his head in disbelief. He had delivered a baby his own daughter. Looking down at her cherubic face, he couldn't deny the truth any longer.

But amidst the joy and wonder of this new life, there was also sorrow. Myrna, the gentle elephant who had been with them through it all, had not survived. Bradley had gone out to check on her this morning and found her buried under a thick layer of snow. She could have lived if she had returned to the safety of the barn, but she had stayed with Jessie until the very end, shielding her from the biting winds and keeping her warm with her own body heat.

Bradley wasn't sure how to properly bury an elephant, but he knew it was something he would do for Myrna. She deserved a proper grave and a marker to be remembered by.

Turning back to the bed where Jessie lay with her eyes closed, Bradley was met with a heartwarming sight as she opened her eyes and smiled at him.

"My two favorite people," she whispered. "How is she?"

"Perfect and beautiful, just like her mother," Bradley replied with a smile.

Jessie held her hands up, and Bradley reluctantly passed his daughter to her mother. She held the baby in one arm and brought up Maria and held it so the baby could see it.

"When did you get that?" Bradley asked.

"I've had it for a while. It was a gift from a friend." Then she looked at the baby. "Leanne gave me this. I hope you get to meet her someday. She told me she and I would always be friends. Now I'm giving Maria to you and promising you I will always love you."

The baby gurgled and shifted in her arm. Jessie set the doll down. She gently cradled the baby against her chest, her hands trembling slightly as she opened her blouse and allowed the infant to start breastfeeding. A rush of love and exhaustion flooded through her as she looked down at her precious little girl.

"How do you feel?" Bradley's concerned voice broke through Jessie's thoughts.

"Tired. Sore. Happy. Sad. Confused." Bradley sympathized, reaching out to rub Jessie's back in a comforting gesture.

Bradley sighed. "It's been one of those days."

"I still can't believe she's gone." Jessie's voice cracked with sadness. Bradley knew she was talking about the elephant.

"I'm so sorry. I did check on her this morning, just to make sure," Bradley reassured her.

Jessie nodded, tears brimming in her eyes. "She was my friend."

"I know, but you have to focus on the baby now," Bradley's hand found hers and gave it a gentle squeeze.

With a deep breath, Jessie composed herself and turned to face her husband. "We have to pick a name for her. I didn't want to do it without you."

He reached over and took her hand in his, a small smile playing on his lips. "You know, there's only one name I think we should pick."

Jessie nodded, tears now streaming down her cheeks. "Myrna."

"Of course, if anyone asks, we should say that she's named after Myrna Loy and not an elephant. It might make her self-conscious when she's older."

"I think we should tell her who she's named after," Jessie insisted. "Myrna saved her life, and she saved mine more than once."

"That is something I will be eternally grateful for," Bradley said sincerely.

Bradley reached out a hand to take his daughter's tiny hand in his. Her little fist could barely reach around one of his fingers.

"Hello, Myrna Starr. You have a big name to live up to."

ABOUT THE AUTHOR

James Rada, Jr., is an Amazon.com bestselling author of historical fiction and non-fiction history. They include the popular books *Strike the Fuse, Canawlers,* and *Battlefield Angels: The Daughters of Charity Work as Civil War Nurses.*

He lives in Gettysburg, Pa., where he works as a freelance writer. James has received numerous awards from the Maryland-Delaware-DC Press Association, Associated Press, Maryland State Teachers Association, Society of Professional Journalists, and Community Newspapers Holdings, Inc. for his newspaper writing.

If you would like to be kept up to date on new books being published by James or ask him questions, he can be reached by e-mail at *jimrada@yahoo.com.*

To see James' other books or to order copies online, go to *www.jamesrada.com.*

PLEASE LEAVE A REVIEW

If you enjoyed this book, please help other readers find it. Reviews help the author get more exposure for his books.

Continue your adventure in history with three FREE historical novels from James Rada, Jr.

Visit *jamesrada.com / newsletter-email*
and enter your email
to receive your FREE novels.